Praise for the work of
LOUIS L'AMOUR

MONUMENT ROCK

"[A] compelling blend of explosive action, period detail, humor, and insights about human nature."
—*USA Today*

END OF THE DRIVE

"Awesome immediacy, biting as creosote slapped on a fence post." —*Kirkus Reviews*

BEYOND THE GREAT SNOW MOUNTAINS

"L'Amour's brassy women and dusty men keep the action of these cinematic stories hot. . . . These adventure tales offer their share of the high drama L'Amour is famous for." —*Publishers Weekly*

OFF THE MANGROVE COAST

"L'Amour was a man who lived life to the fullest. Fortunately for the rest of us, he remembered the details and possessed the talent to bring those experiences to life on paper." —*Booklist*

Bantam Books by Louis L'Amour

OFF *the* MANGROVE COAST

STORIES

Louis L'Amour

Postscript by Beau L'Amour

BANTAM BOOKS

NEW YORK

2018 Bantam Books Mass Market Edition

Copyright © 2000 by Louis & Katherine L'Amour Trust

Postscript by Beau L'Amour copyright © 2018 by Beau L'Amour

Published in the United States by Bantam Books, an imprint of
Random House, a division of Penguin Random House LLC, New York.

BANTAM and the HOUSE colophon are registered trademarks of
Penguin Random House LLC.

Originally published in hardcover in the United States by
Bantam Books, an imprint of Random House, a division of
Penguin Random House LLC, in 2000.

The July 6, 1939, *Tulsa Tribune* column "The Rambler"
by Roger Devlin, is reprinted by permission of BH Media Group Inc.

ISBN 978-0-525-48630-5
Ebook ISBN 978-0-525-48638-1

Cover art: Gregory Manchess

Printed in the United States of America

randomhousebooks.com

2 4 6 8 9 7 5 3 1

Bantam Books mass market edition: October 2018

CONTENTS

OFF *the* MANGROVE COAST

FIGHTERS SHOULD BE HUNGRY

I

A BRUTAL BLOW IN the ribs jerked Tandy Moore from a sound sleep. Gasping, he rolled into a fetal position and looked up to see a brakeman standing over him with his foot drawn back for another kick. With a lunge Tandy was on his feet, his dark eyes blazing. Fists cocked, he started for the brakeman, who backed suddenly away. "Unload!" he said harshly. "Get off! An' be quick about it!"

Tandy was a big young man with wide shoulders and a sun-darkened face, darkened still further by a stubble of black beard. He chucked with cold humor.

"Nope," Tandy said grimly, and with relish. "If you want me off, you put me off! Come on, I'm going to like this!"

Instead of a meek and frightened tramp, the brakeman had uncovered a wolf with bared teeth. The brakeman backed away still farther.

"You get off!" he insisted. "If that bull down to the

yards finds you here, he'll report it an' I'll get chewed out!"

Tandy Moore relaxed a bit. "You watch yourself, mister! You can lose teeth walkin' up an' kickin' a guy that way!" He grabbed the edge of the gondola and lifted himself to the top, then swung his feet over to the ladder. "Say, Jack? What town is this anyway? Not that it makes much difference."

"Astoria, Oregon. End of the line."

"Thanks." Tandy climbed down the ladder, gauged the speed of the train, and dropped off, hitting the cinders on the run.

As though it had been planned for him, a path slanted down off the grade and into a dense jungle of brush that lined the sides and bottom of a shallow ditch. He slowed and started down the path.

Astoria was almost home, but he wasn't going home. There was nothing there for him anymore. He trotted along near the foot of a steeply slanting hill. He could smell the sea and the gray sky was spitting a thin mist of rain.

At the bottom of the muddy path lay a mossy gray plank bridging a trickle of water, and beyond it the trail slanted up and finally entered a patch of woods surrounded by a wasteland of logged-off stumps.

Almost as soon as Moore entered the thicket, he smelled the smoke of a campfire. He stopped for a moment, brushing at his baggy, gray tweed trousers with his hand. He wore a wool shirt open at the neck, and a worn leather jacket. His razor, comb, and toothbrush lay in one pocket of the jacket. He had no other possessions. He wore no hat, and his black hair was a coarse mass of unruly curls. As presentable as a hobo could be, he started forward.

Of the four men who sat around the fire, only two commanded his attention. A short, square-shouldered, square-faced man with intelligent eyes reclined on the ground, leaning on an elbow. Nearby a big man with black hair freely sprinkled with gray stood over the fire.

There was something familiar about the big man's face, but Tandy was sure he had never seen him before. His once-powerful build was apparently now overlaid with a layer of softness, and his eyes were blue and pleasant, almost mild.

The other two were typical of the road, a gray-faced man, old and leathery, and a younger man with dirty skin, white under the grime, and a weak chin and mouth.

"How's for some coffee?" Tandy asked, his eyes shifting from one to the other.

"Ain't ready yet, chum. Don't know that we have enough, anyway." The white-faced young man looked up at him. "They booted you off that drag, huh?"

Tensing, Tandy turned his head and looked down at the fellow, his eyes turning cold. It was an old song and this was how it always started.

"I got off on my own," he said harshly. "Nobody makes me do nothin'!"

"Tough guy?" The fellow looked away. "Well, somebody'll take all that out of you."

Tandy reached down and collared him, jerking him to his tiptoes. They were of the same age, but there the resemblance ceased, for where there was bleak power in Tandy's hard young face, there was only weakness in the tramp's.

"It ain't gonna be you, is it, sucker? You crack wise

again and I'll slap some sense into you!" Tandy said coolly.

"Put him down," the big man said quietly. "You've scared the wits out of him now. No use to hit him."

Tandy had no intention of hitting him unless he had to, but the remark irritated him more. He dropped the other man and turned.

"Maybe *you* want to start something?" he demanded aggressively.

The big man only smiled and shook his head. "No, kid, I don't give a damn what you do. Just don't make a fool of yourself."

"Fool, huh?" Tandy could feel them backing him up, cornering him. "You listen to me, you yellow . . . " He reached for the big man.

A fist smashed into his mouth, and then another crossed to his jaw and he hit the dirt flat on his back.

Tandy Moore lay on the ground for an instant, more amazed at the power of that blow than hurt. The big man stood by the fire, calm and unruffled. Rage overcame Tandy, he came off the ground with a lunge and threw everything he had into a wicked right hand.

It caught only empty air, but a big, hard-knuckled fist slammed into his chest and stopped his rush, then a right crossed on his jaw and lights exploded in his brain. He went down again but threw himself over and up in one continuous movement. His head buzzing, he spat blood from broken lips and began to circle warily. This big fellow could punch.

Tandy lunged suddenly and swung, but the big man sidestepped smoothly and Tandy fell past him. He cringed, half expecting a blow before he could turn, but none came.

He whirled, his fists ready, and the big man stood there calmly, his hands on his hips.

"Cut it out, kid," he said quietly. "I don't want to beat your skull in. You can't fight a lick on earth!"

"Who says I can't!" Tandy lunged and swung, only this time he was thinking and as he swung with his right, he shifted suddenly and brought up a short, wicked left into the big man's liver.

The fellow's face went gray, and the square-faced man on the ground sat up suddenly.

"Watch it, Gus!" he warned.

Gus backed away hastily, and seeing his advantage, Tandy moved in, more cautious but poised and ready. But he ran into something different, for the big man was moving now, strangely graceful. A left stiffened his mouth, a right smashed him on the chin, and another left dropped him to his knees.

Tandy got to his feet and licked his cut lips. The old guy was fast.

"You can punch, darn you!" he growled. "But this scrap ain't over. I'll fight until you drop!"

"Kid," the man warned, "we're fightin' for no good reason. You're carrying a chip but it's not for us. If I put you down again, I'll not let you get up. You know I'm not yellow, and I know you've got nerve enough to tackle all of us. What do you say we cut this out?"

Tandy hesitated, backing up. The man on the ground spoke, "Come on, son, have some coffee."

Tandy dropped his hands with a shrug.

"Mister," he said with a shamefaced grin, "I shouldn't have gone off like I did. I asked for it." He eyed Gus with respect. "You can sure use your dukes, though!"

"Don't take it hard, kid." The square-faced man smiled at him. "He used to be a prizefighter."

Across the fire the white-faced kid kept his mouth shut, not looking at either of them.

Tandy Moore shrugged. "Well he got me, but that fancy stuff ain't no good in a real scrap! Why, there's plenty of men in the lumber camps and mines could beat Joe Louis's head in if they had the chance."

"Don't kid yourself," Gus said quietly. "Fightin' is like anything else. A professional fighter does his job better than a greenhorn because he knows how.

"That fancy stuff, as you call it, is nothin' but a lot of things a lot of fighters learned over a thousand years or more. That's how scientific boxing was born. You were using it when you feinted and hit me with the left."

Tandy stared at him, then shrugged. "Ahhh, I figure you can either fight or you can't!"

Gus smiled at Tandy. "How many times have you been licked, kid?"

"Me?" Tandy bristled. "Nobody never licked me!"

"That's what I figured," Gus said. "You are big enough, tough enough, and aggressive enough so you could fight every night around hobo jungles like this one and never lose. In the ring, almost any half-baked preliminary boy would cut you to ribbons.

"I was through as a fighter ten years ago. I haven't trained since but right now I could chop you into pieces and never catch a punch. I was careless, or you wouldn't have clipped me as you did."

Tandy scoffed. "Maybe, but if I had a chance at one of those prelim boys you talk about, I'd show you!"

"Gus"—the square-faced man had seated himself on a log—"maybe this is the guy? What do you think?"

Gus stared at Tandy with a new expression in his eyes. He looked him over thoughtfully, nodded slowly. "Maybe . . . Kid, did you mean what you said? Would you want to try it?"

Tandy grinned. "I sure would! If there was a shot at some dough!"

THE GYMNASIUM IN Astoria was no polished and airy retreat for overstuffed businessmen. It was a dim and musty basement with a heavy canvas bag, darkened around the middle by countless punches thrown by sweat-soaked gloves, a ring slightly smaller than regulation, its ropes wound with gauze, three creaking speed bags, and a broken horse. In one corner there were barbells made from different sizes of car and truck brake drums. A wan light filtered through dirty windows set high in the walls.

It was there, in a borrowed pair of blue trunks that clung precariously to his lean hips, and under them a suit of winter underwear rescued from a basement table by Gus Coe, that Tandy Moore began the process of learning to be a fighter. Their sole capital was a ten-dollar advance from a bored promoter, and five dollars Gus wheedled from a poolroom proprietor. Briggs, Gus's friend of the square face, leaned back against the wall with a watch in his hand, and Gus stood by while Tandy, bored and uncomfortable, looked at the heavy bag doubtfully.

"Now look," Gus said patiently, "you got a left hand but you don't use it right. Lift that left fist up to shoulder height an' hold it well out. When you hit, punch straight from the shoulder and step in with that left foot. Not much, just a couple of inches, maybe. But step in. Now try it."

Tandy tried it. His gloved fist smacked the bag solidly but without much force. Tandy looked unhappily at Gus.

"You mean like that? I couldn't break an egg!"

"You keep trying it. Shoot it straight out, make it snap. An' bring your fist back on the same line your punch traveled." He stepped up to the bag. "Like this—"

The left shot out and the bag jumped with the explosive force of the blow. Tandy Moore looked thoughtful.

It worked when Gus threw it, no question about that. Well, the least he could do was humor the guy. He was beginning to like Gus Coe. The big, easy-going ex-fighter was shrewd and thoughtful. And Briggs . . .

Briggs puzzled Tandy. He was quiet, so quiet you almost forgot he was around, but somehow he always gave Tandy the feeling of being dangerous. He was a man you would never start anything with. Tandy also knew that Briggs carried a gun. He had seen him with it, a small Browning automatic in a shoulder holster.

This training was nonsense. The exercise was okay, it got your muscles in shape, but as for the rest of it, Tandy shrugged mentally. You could either fight or you couldn't. Just let him get in the ring with one of those fancy Dans. He'd show them a thing or two!

II

THAT NIGHT TANDY stayed up late talking to his two new companions. He watched them closely, trying to figure out just what it was they were up to.

"What's the angle?" Tandy finally demanded. "I mean,

down there in the jungle, Briggs said something about maybe I was the guy?"

Gus dropped on the rooming-house bed opposite him. "It's like this, kid. A guy gave me an awful jobbing a while back. The guy is a big-shot manager and he's got money. The Portland and Seattle gamblers are with him, and that means a lot of muscle men, too. He got to one of my fighters, and one way and another, he broke me an' got me run out of town. Briggs knows all about it."

"But where do I come in?" Tandy asked.

"Both of us figured we might get a fighter and go back an' try him again. The best way to get to him is to whip his scrapper . . . take his money on the bets."

"Who's his fighter?" Tandy asked.

Gus grinned at him. "A Portland boy, Stan Reiser," he said.

"*Reiser!*" Tandy Moore came off the chair with a jump.

"Sure." Gus nodded. "He's probably one of the three top men on the coast right now, but you don't take him on your first fight." He looked at Tandy. "I thought you wanted to fight those guys? That you figured you could run any of them out of the ring?"

"It ain't that," Moore said, quieter now. "It's just that it isn't what I expected." His face turned grim and hard. "Yeah," he agreed, "I'll go along. I'd like to fight that guy. I'd like to lick him. I'd like to beat him until he couldn't move!"

Turning abruptly, Tandy walked out of the room and they heard his feet going down the stairs. Briggs stared at the door.

"What do you make of that?" Gus asked.

Briggs shrugged. "That kid's beyond me," he said. "Sometimes he gives me cold chills."

"You, too?" Gus looked understandingly at Briggs. "Funny, a kid like that making us feel this way."

Briggs rubbed out his cigarette. "Something's eatin' him, Gus. Something deep inside. We saw it this morning an' we may have just hit on it again, though what it has to do with Reiser or your situation I ain't gonna guess."

THEY WALKED INTO a hotel restaurant the night of the fight. It was early, late afternoon really. The wind whipping in off the Pacific in blasts that slammed the door closed as they came through. In these new surroundings, they looked shabby and out of place. This was blocks from the cheap rooming house where they lived, blocks from the beanery in which they had been eating.

They sat on stools at the restaurant counter, and a girl brought the menus. Tandy Moore looked up, looked into the eyes of the girl beyond the counter.

She smiled nervously and asked, "What can I get for you?"

Tandy jerked a thumb at Gus. "Ask him," he said, and stared down at his knuckles. He was confused for there had been something in the girl's eyes that touched him. It made him feel scared and he hated it.

She looked from Gus to Briggs. "Who is this guy?" she asked. "Can't he order for himself? What do you do, poke it to him with a stick?"

Tandy looked up, his eyes full of sullen anger. That closed-in feeling was back. Gus dropped a hand on his arm.

"She's ribbin' you, kid. Forget it." He glanced down

at the menu and then looked up. "A steak for him, an' make it rare. And just coffee for us."

When she turned away, Tandy looked around and said, low-voiced, "Gus, that'll take all the dough we've got! You guys eat, too. I don't need that steak."

"You fight tonight, not us," Gus replied, grinning. "All we ask is that you get in there and throw them."

The waitress came back with their coffee. She had caught the word "fight."

"You're fighting tonight?" she asked Tandy.

He did not look up. "Yeah," he said.

"You'd not be bad-looking," she said, "if you'd shave." She waited for a response, then glanced over at Gus, smiling. "Is he always like this?"

"He's a good kid," Gus said.

She went off to take another order but was back in a moment and, glancing around cautiously, slid a baked potato onto his plate. "Here's one on the house. Don't say I never gave you anything."

He didn't know how to reply so he mumbled thanks and started to eat. She stood there watching him, the tag on her uniform said "Dorinda."

"Come back and tell me about it." She looked at Tandy. "If you're able," she added.

"I'll be able!" he retorted. Their eyes met, and he felt something stir down deep within him. She was young, not over nineteen, and had brown hair and blue eyes. He looked at her again. "I'll come," he said, and flushed.

When they finished dinner, they walked around the block a couple of times to start warming up, then headed for the dressing room.

An hour and a half later Gus Coe taped up Tandy's hands. He looked at the young man carefully.

"Listen, kid, you watch yourself in there. This guy Al Joiner can box and he can punch. I would've got you something easier for your first fight, but they wanted somebody for this Joiner. He's a big favorite in town, very popular with the Norskies."

He cleared his throat and continued.

"We're broke, see? We get fifteen bucks more out of this fight; that's all. It was just twenty-five for our end, and we got ten of it in advance. If we win, we'll get another fight. That means we'll be a few bucks ahead of the game.

"I ain't goin' to kid you; you ain't ready. But you can punch, and you might win.

"You're hungry, kid. You're hungry for things that money can buy, an' you're mad." His eyes bored into Tandy's. "Maybe you've been mad all your life. Well, tonight you can fight back. Dempsey, Ketchell, lots of hungry boys did it in there. You can, too!"

Tandy looked down at Gus's big, gnarled hands. He knew the kindly face of the man who spoke to him, knew the worn shirt collar and the frayed cuffs. Gus had laundered their clothes these last days, using a borrowed iron for pressing.

Suddenly he felt very sorry for this big man who stood over him, and he felt something stirring within him that he had never known before. It struck him suddenly that he had a friend. Two of them.

"Sure," he said. "Okay, Gus."

IN THE CENTER of the ring, he did not look at Joiner. He saw only a pair of slim white legs and blue boxing trunks. He trotted back to his corner, and looked down at his feet in their borrowed canvas shoes.

Then the bell rang and he turned, glaring across the ring from under his heavy brows and moving out, swift and ready.

Al Joiner was taller than he was with wide, powerful shoulders. His eyes were sharp and ready, his lips clenched over the mouthpiece. They moved toward each other, Joiner on his toes, Tandy shuffling, almost flat-footed.

Al's left was a darting snake. It landed, sharp and hard, on his brow. Tandy moved in and Al moved around him, the left darting. A dozen times the left landed, but Tandy lunged close, swinging a looping, roundhouse right.

The punch was too wide and too high, but Joiner was careless. It caught him on the side of the head like a falling sledge and his feet flew up and he hit the canvas, an expression of dazed astonishment on his face. At seven he was on his feet and moving more carefully.

He faded away from Tandy's wild, reckless punches. Faded away, jabbing. The bell sounded with Tandy still coming in, a welt over his left eye and a blue mouse under the right.

"Watch your chance an' use that left you used on me," Gus suggested. "That'll slow this guy down. He's even faster than I thought."

The bell sounded and Tandy walked out to meet a Joiner who was now boxing beautifully, and no matter where Tandy turned, Joiner's left met him. His lips were cut and bleeding, punches thudded on his jaw. He lost the second round by an enormous margin.

The third opened the same way, but now Joiner began to force the fighting. He mixed the lefts with hard right crosses, and Tandy, his eyes blurred with blood, moved in, his hands cocked and ready. Al boxed carefully, aware of those dynamite-laden fists.

The fourth started fast. Tandy went out, saw the left move and threw his right, and the next thing he knew he was flat on his back with a roaring in his head and the referee was saying "Six!"

TANDY CAME OFF the canvas with a lunge of startled fury. A growl exploded from him as he swept into the other fighter, smashing past that left hand and driving him to the ropes. His right swung for Joiner's head and Al ducked, and Tandy lifted a short, wicked left to the liver and stood Joiner on his tiptoes.

Tandy stabbed a left at Joiner's face, then swung a powerful right. Joiner tried to duck and took the punch full on the ear. His knees sagged and he pitched forward on his face.

The referee made the count, then turned and lifted Tandy's hand. The fighter on the floor hadn't moved.

In the dressing room, Tandy stared bleakly at his battered face. "For this I get twenty-five bucks!" he said, grinning with swollen lips.

"Don't worry, kid!" Gus grinned back at him. "When you hit me with your left that day in the woods, I knew you had it. It showed you could think on your feet. You'll do!"

When they came out of the dressing room suddenly Gus stopped and his hand on Tandy's arm tightened. Two men were standing there, a small man with a tight white face and a big cigar, and a big younger man.

"Hello, Gus," the man with the cigar said, contempt in his voice. "I see you've got yourself another punk!"

Tandy's left snaked out and smashed the cigar into

the small man's teeth, knocking him sprawling into the wall, and then he whirled on the big man, a brawny blond whose eyes were blazing with astonishment.

"Now, you!" he snarled. His right whipped over like an arrow, but the big man stepped back swiftly and the right missed. Then, he started to step in, but Briggs stopped him.

"Back up, Stan!" he said coldly. "Back up unless you want lead for your supper! Lift that scum off the floor. It's lucky the kid didn't kill him!"

Stan Reiser stooped and lifted his manager from the floor. The black cigar was mashed into the blood of his split lips and his face was white and shocked, but his eyes blazed with murderous fury.

"I'll get you for this, Coe!" His voice was low and vicious. "You an' that S.O.—" His voice broke off sharply as Tandy Moore stepped toward him.

Moore glanced at Reiser. "Shut him up, Stan. I don't like guys who call me names!"

Reiser looked curiously at Tandy. "I know you from somewhere," he said thoughtfully, "I'll remember . . ."

Tandy's face was stiff and cold. "Go ahead!" he said quietly. "It will be a bad day for both of us when you do!"

OUTSIDE ON THE street, Gus shook his head. "What the hell is up with you?" he asked. "You shouldn't have done it, but nothin' ever did me so much good as your hittin' that snake. I don't believe anybody ever had nerve enough to sock him before, he's been king of the roost so long." Both Gus and Briggs looked at him quizzically.

"It's my business," Tandy growled and would say no more.

He said nothing but he was thinking. Now they had

met again, and he did not know if he was afraid or not. Yet he knew that deep within him, there was still that memory and the hatred he had stifled so long, it was a feeling that demanded he face Reiser, to smash him, to break him.

"How would I do with Reiser?" he asked suddenly.

Gus looked astonished. "Kid, you sure don't know the fight game or you'd never ask a question like that. Stan is a contender for the heavyweight title."

Tandy nodded slowly. "I guess I've got plenty to learn," he said.

Gus nodded. "When you know that, kid, you've already learned the toughest part."

III

THREE WEEKS LATER, after conniving and borrowing and scraping by on little food, Tandy Moore was ready for his second fight. This one was with a rough slugger known as Benny Baker.

The day of the fight, Tandy walked toward the hotel. There would be no steak today, for they simply hadn't money enough. Yet he had been thinking of Dorinda, and wondering where she was and what she was doing.

She was coming out of the restaurant door as he walked by. Her eyes brightened quickly.

"Why, hello!" she greeted him. "I wondered what had happened to you. Why don't you ever come in and see me?"

He shoved his hands in the pockets of the shabby trousers. "Looking like this? Anyway, I can't afford to eat in there. I don't make enough money. In fact"—he grinned, his face flushing—"I haven't any money at all!"

She put a hand on his arm. "Don't let it bother you, Tandy. You'll do all right." She looked away, then back at him. "You're fighting again, aren't you?"

"Tonight. It's a preliminary." His eyes took in the softness of her cheek, the lights in her dark brown hair. "Come and see it. Would you?"

"I'm going to be there. I'll be sure to be there early to see your fight."

He looked at her suddenly. "Where are you going now? Let's take a walk."

Dorinda hesitated only an instant. "All right."

They walked along, neither of them saying much, until they stopped at a rail and looked down the sloping streets to the confusion of canneries and lumber wharves along the riverfront. Off to the northwest the sun slanted through the clouds and threw a silver light on the river, silhouetting a steam schooner inbound from the rough water out where the Columbia met the Pacific.

"You worked here long?" he asked suddenly.

"No, only about two months. I was headed to Portland but I couldn't find a job. I came from Arizona. My father has a ranch out there, but I thought I'd like to try singing. So I was going to go to school at night, and study voice in my spare time."

"That's funny, you being from Arizona," he said. "I just came from there!"

"You did?" She laughed. "One place is all sun, the other all rain."

"Well, I grew up here. In St. John's, over near Portland. My dad worked at a box-shuck factory there. You know, fruit boxes, plywood an' all."

"Is he still there"—she looked into his eyes—"in Portland?"

"No." Tandy had to look away. "Not anymore."

Dorinda suddenly glanced at her watch and gave a startled cry.

"Oh, we've got to go! I'm supposed to be back at work!"

They made their way along the street and down the hill. He left her at the door of the restaurant.

"I probably won't get a chance to see you after the fight," she said. "I've been invited to a party at the hotel."

Quick jealousy touched him. "Who's giving?" he demanded.

"The fellow who is taking me, Stan Reiser."

He stared at her, shocked and still. "Oh . . ."

He blinked, then turned swiftly and walked away, trembling inside. Everywhere he turned it was Stan Reiser. He heard her call after him, heard her take a few running steps toward him, but he did not stop or turn his head.

He was burning with that old deep fury in the ring that night. Gus looked at him curiously as he stood in the corner rubbing his feet in the resin. In a ringside seat were Dorinda and Reiser, but Gus had not seen them yet. Briggs had. Briggs never missed anything.

"All right, kid," Gus said quietly, "you know more this time, and this guy ain't smart. But he can punch, so don't take any you can miss."

The bell sounded and Tandy Moore whirled like a cat. Benny Baker was fifteen pounds heavier and a blocky man, noted as a slugger. Tandy walked out fast and ᵒnny sprang at him, throwing both hands.

Almost of its own volition, Tandy's left sprang from his shoulder. It was a jab, and a short one, but it smashed Benny Baker on the nose and stopped him in his tracks. Tandy jabbed again, then feinted, and when Baker lunged he drilled a short right to the slugger's chin.

Benny Baker hit the canvas on the seat of his pants, his eyes dazed. He floundered around and got up at six, turning to meet Tandy. Baker looked white around the mouth, and he tried to clinch, but Tandy stepped back and whipped up a powerful right uppercut and then swung a looping left to the jaw.

Baker hit the canvas on his shoulder blades. At the count of ten, he had not even wiggled a toe.

Tandy Moore turned then and avoiding Dorinda's eyes looked squarely at Reiser. It was only a look that held an instant, but Stan's face went dark and he started half to his feet, then slumped down.

"Go back to Albina Street, you weasel," Tandy said. "I'll be coming for you!" Then he slipped through the ropes and walked away.

Gus Coe watched the interchange. The big ex-fighter took his cigar from his mouth and looked at Stan thoughtfully. There was something between those two. But what?

WITH THEIR WINNINGS as a stake they took to the road. The following week, at the armory in Klamath Falls, Tandy Moore stopped Joe Burns in one round, and thereafter in successive weeks at Burns and Eugene he stopped Glen Hayes in two, Rolph Williams in one, Pedro Sarmineto in five, and Chuck Goslin in three.

Soon the fans were beginning to talk him up and the sportswriters were hearing stories of Tandy Moore.

"How soon do I get a chance at Reiser?" Tandy demanded, one night in their room.

Gus looked at him thoughtfully. "You shouldn't fight Reiser for a year," he said, and then added, "You've got something against him? What is it?"

"I just want to get in there with him. I owe him something, and I want to make sure he gets it!"

"Well," Gus said, looking at his cigar, "we'll see."

A little later, Gus asked, "Have you seen that girl lately, the one who used to work in the restaurant?"

Tandy, trying not to show interest, shrugged and shook his head.

"No. Why should I see her?"

"She was a pretty girl," Gus said. "Seemed to sort of like you, too."

"She went to the fights with Reiser."

"So what? That doesn't make her his girl, does it?" Gus demanded. "Did you ask her to go? I could have snagged a couple of ducats to bring her and a friend."

Tandy didn't answer.

Gus took the cigar from his teeth, changed the subject abruptly.

"The trouble is," he said, "you got Reiser on your mind, and I don't know just how good you are. Sometimes when a man wants something awful bad, he improves pretty fast. In the short time we've been together, you've learned more than any scrapper I ever knew. But it's mighty important right now that I know how good you are."

Tandy looked up from the magazine he was thumbing. "Why now?"

"We've got an offer. Flat price of five grand, win, lose, or draw, for ten rounds with Buster Crane."

"Crane?" Tandy dropped the magazine he was holding to the tabletop. "That guy held Reiser to a draw. He had him on the floor!"

"That's the one. He's good, too. He can box and he can hit, and he's fast. The only thing is, I'm kind of suspicious."

Briggs, who had been listening, looked up thoughtfully. "You mean you think it's a frame?"

"I think Bernie Satneck, Reiser's manager, would frame his own mother," Gus answered. "I think he's gettin' scared of the kid here. Tandy wants Reiser, an' Satneck knows it. He's no fool, an' the kid has been bowling them over ever since he started, so what's more simple than to get him a scrap with Crane when the kid is green? If Crane beats him bad, he is finished off and no trouble for Satneck."

Conscious of Tandy Moore's intent gaze, he turned toward him. "What is it, kid?"

"Satneck, I want to take him down too! Him and his brother."

"I didn't know he had a brother," Briggs said.

"He may have a dozen for all I know," Gus said.

"Go ahead," Tandy said, "take that fight. I'll be ready." He grinned suddenly. "Five thousand? That's more than we've made in all of them, so far."

He walked out and closed the door. Briggs sat still for a while, then he got up and started out himself.

"Where you goin'?" Gus asked suspiciously.

"Why," Briggs said gently, "I'm getting very curious. I thought I'd go find out if Satneck has a brother and what they have to do with our boy here."

"Yeah," Gus said softly, "I see what you mean."

———

THE MONTH THAT followed found Tandy Moore in Wiley Spivey's gym six days a week. They were in Portland now, across the river from downtown and back in Tandy's home territory, although he mentioned this to no one. He worked with fighters of every size and style, with sluggers and boxers, with skilled counterpunchers. He listened to Gus pick flaws in their styles, and he studied slow-motion pictures of Crane's fights with Reiser.

He knew Buster Crane was good. He was at least a hundred percent better than any fighter Tandy had yet tackled. Above all, he could hit.

Briggs wasn't around. Tandy commented on that and Gus said, "Briggs? He's away on business, but will be back before the fight."

"He's quiet, isn't he? Known him long?"

"Twelve years, about. He's a dangerous man, kid. He was bodyguard for a politician with enemies, then he was a private dick. He was with the O.S.S. during the war, and he was a partner of mine when we had that trouble with Satneck and Reiser."

IV

TANDY MOORE STOPPED on the corner and looked down the street toward the river, but he was thinking of Buster Crane. That was the only thing that was important now. He must, at all costs, beat Crane.

Walking along, he glimpsed his reflection in a window and stopped abruptly. He saw a tall, clean-shaven, well-built young man with broad shoulders and a well-groomed look. He looked far better, he decided, than the rough young man who had eaten the steak that day in the restaurant and looked up into the eyes of Dorinda Lane.

Even as his thoughts repeated the name, he shied violently from it, yet he had never forgotten her. She was always there, haunting his thoughts. Remembering her comments, he never shaved but that he thought of her.

He had not seen her since that night when she came to the fight with Stan Reiser. And she hadn't worked at the restaurant in Astoria anymore after he returned from Klamath Falls.

Restlessly, Tandy Moore paced the streets, thinking first of Dorinda and then of Stan Reiser and all that lay behind it.

It was his driving urge to meet Reiser in the ring that made him so eager to learn from Gus. But it was more than that, too, for he had in him a deep love of combat, of striving, of fighting for something. But what?

GUS COE WAS sitting in the hotel lobby when Tandy walked in. Gus seemed bigger than ever, well, he was fatter, and looked prosperous now. He grinned at Tandy and said something out of the corner of his mouth to Briggs, who was sitting, and the Irishman got up, his square face warm with a smile.

"How are you, Tandy?" he said quietly.

"Hey, Briggsie, welcome back." He glanced at Gus. "Say, let's go to a nightclub tonight. I want to get out and look around."

"The kid's got an idea," Briggs said. "We'll go to Nevada Johnson's place. He's putting on the fight and it'll be good for the kid to be seen there. We can break it up early enough so he can get his rest. It would do us all good to relax a little."

Gus shrugged. "Okay."

The place was fairly crowded, but they got a table down front, and they were hardly seated before the orchestra started to play, and then the spotlight swung onto a girl who was singing.

Gus looked up sharply, and Tandy's face was shocked and still, for the girl outlined by the spotlight was Dorinda Lane.

Tandy stared, and then he swallowed a sudden lump in his throat. Her voice was low and very beautiful, and he had never dreamed she could look so lovely. He sat entranced until her song ended, and then he looked over at Gus.

"Let's get out of here," he said.

"Wait—" Gus caught his wrist, for the spotlight had swung to their table and the master of ceremonies gestured toward him.

"We have a guest with us tonight, ladies and gentlemen! A guest we are very proud to welcome! Tandy Moore, that rising young heavyweight who meets Buster Crane tomorrow night!"

Tandy looked trapped but took an uneasy bow. The spotlight swung away from him, and Gus leaned over.

"Nice going, kid," he said. "You looked good. Do you still want to go?"

They started for the door, and then Tandy looked over and saw Bernie Satneck sitting at a table on the edge of the floor. Reiser was with him, and another man who was a younger tougher version of the manager! Tandy locked his eyes forward and walked toward the lobby.

At the door he was waiting for Gus and Briggs to get their hats, when he heard a rustle of silk and looked around into Dorinda's face.

"Were you going to leave without seeing me?" she asked, holding out her hand.

He hesitated, his face flushing. Why did she have to be so beautiful and so desirable? He jerked his head toward the dining room.

"Stan Reiser's in there," he said. "Isn't he your boyfriend?"

Her eyes flashed her resentment. "No, he's not! And he never was! If you weren't so infernally stubborn, Tandy Moore, I'd have . . ."

"So, how did you get this job?"

Her face went white, and the next thing, her palm cracked across his mouth. The cigarette girl turned, her eyes wide, and the headwaiter started to hurry over, but Gus Coe arrived just in time. Catching Tandy's arm, he rushed him out the door.

Tandy was seething with anger, but anger more at himself than her. After all, it was a rotten thing for him to say. Maybe that hadn't been the way of it. And if it had, well, he'd been hungry himself. He was still hungry, no longer for food now, but for other things. And then the thought came to him that he was still hungry for her, Dorinda Lane.

THE CROWD WAS jammed to the edge of the ring when he climbed through the ropes the next night. His face was a somber mask. He heard the dull roar of thousands of people, and ducked his head to them and hurried to his corner.

In the center of the ring during the referee's briefing, he got his first look at Buster Crane, a heavyweight with twenty more pounds than his own one-ninety, but almost an inch shorter, and with arms even longer.

When the bell rang, he shut his jaws on his mouth-piece and turned swiftly. Crane was moving toward him, his eyes watchful slits under knitted brows. Crane had a shock of white blond hair and a wide face, but the skin was tight over the bones.

Crane moved in fast, feinted, then hooked high and hard. The punch was incredibly fast and Tandy caught it on the temple, but he was going away from it. Even so, it shook him to his heels, and with a queer kind of thrill, he realized that no man he had ever met had punched like Buster Crane. He was in for a battle.

Tandy jabbed, then jabbed again. He missed a right cross and Crane was inside slamming both hands into his body. He backed up, giving ground. He landed a left to the head, drilled a right down the center that missed, then shook Buster up with a short left hook to the head.

From there on, the battle was a surging struggle of two hard-hitting young men filled with a zest for combat. The second round opened with a slashing attack from Crane that drove Tandy into the ropes, but his long weeks of schooling had done their job and he covered up, clinched, and saved himself. He played it easy on the defensive for the remainder of the round.

The third, fourth, and fifth rounds were alike, with vicious toe-to-toe scrapping every bit of the way. Coming out for the sixth, Tandy Moore could feel the lump over his eye, and he was aware that Crane's left hook was landing too often. Thus far, Crane was leading by a margin, and it was that hook that was doing it.

A moment later the same left hook dropped out of nowhere and Tandy's heels flew up and he sat down hard.

Outside the ring, the crowd was a dull roar and he

rolled over on his hands and knees, unable to hear the count. He glanced toward his corner and saw Gus holding up four, then five fingers. He waited until the ninth finger came up, and then he got to his feet and backed away.

Crane moved in fast and sure. He had his man hurt and he knew it. He didn't look so good or feel so good himself, and was conscious that he wanted only one thing, to get this guy out of action before he had his head ripped off.

Crane feinted a left, then measured Moore with it, but Tandy rolled inside the punch and threw a left to the head, which missed. Crane stepped around carefully and then tried again. This time he threw his left hook, but Tandy Moore was ready. He remembered what he had been taught, and when he saw that hook start, he threw his own right inside of it.

With the right forearm partially blocking, his fist crashed down on Crane's chin with a shock that jarred Tandy to the shoulder!

Buster Crane hit the canvas on his face, rolled over, and then climbed slowly to his knees. At nine he made it, but just barely.

Tandy walked toward him looking him over carefully. Crane was a puncher and he was hurt, which made him doubly dangerous. Tandy tried a tentative left, and Crane brushed it aside and threw his own left hook from the inside. Tandy had seen him use the punch in the newsreel pictures he had studied, and the instant it started, he pulled the trigger on his own right, a short, wicked hook at close range.

Crane hit the canvas and this time he didn't get up.

When he was dressed, Tandy walked with Gus Coe to

the promoter's office to get the money. Briggs strolled along, his hands in his pockets, just behind them.

When they opened the door, Tandy's skin tightened, for Stan Reiser and Bernie Satneck were sitting at a table with a tall, gray-haired man whom Tandy instantly recognized as "Nevada" Johnson, the biggest fight promoter in the Northwest.

The rest of the room was crowded with sportswriters.

"Nice fight, tonight, Moore," Johnson said. "We've been waiting for you. How would you like to fight for the title?"

"The championship?" Tandy was incredulous. "Sure, I'd like to fight for it! But don't I get to fight him first?"

He gestured at Reiser and saw the big heavyweight's eyes turn ugly.

"See?" Nevada Johnson said to Satneck. "He's not only ready, but anxious to fight your boy. You say that Reiser deserves a title bout. Six months ago, I would have said the same thing, but now the situation has changed. Moore has made a sensational rise from nothing, although knowing Coe was his manager, I'm not surprised."

"This kid isn't good enough," Satneck protested. "The fans won't go for it. They'll think he's just a flash in the pan and it won't draw!"

Johnson looked around at the sportswriters and asked, "What about that?"

"If Bernie will forgive me," Hansen of the *Telegraph* said quietly, "I think he's crazy! A Tandy Moore and Stan Reiser fight will outdraw either of them with the champ, as long as we mention that the winner goes for the title. It's a natural if there ever was one."

"Frankly," Coe said quietly, "I can understand how Satneck must feel. After all, he's brought Reiser a long way, and it seems a shame to get his fighter whipped when the title is almost in his hands."

"Whipped?" Satneck whirled on Coe. "Why, that stinking little . . ." He looked at Tandy and his voice faded out and he flushed.

"I'd *like* to fight him," Tandy said, pleasantly enough. "I'd like nothing better than to get Reiser where he could take a poke at me when my back's not turned!"

Johnson and several of the sportswriters sat forward.

Reiser's face went dead-white but his eyes were thoughtful. He turned to his manager.

"Sign it!" he snapped. "Let's get out of here!"

Satneck glanced from Stan's face to Tandy's, and then at Gus, who was grinning mysteriously.

"What was that about?" the reporters asked, but Tandy just shook his head. Without another word, he grabbed the fountain pen that Johnson offered and signed.

AT THE HOTEL that night, when Tandy was in bed, Briggs and Gus sat in Gus's room. Neither of them spoke for a moment.

"I dug it up," Briggs said quietly. "An' don't worry, Tandy's okay. His old man was a rummy, he worked down here at the factory by the bridge. He was a better than fair street-scrapper when sober. Satneck's brother got lippy with him once, an' Tandy's old man mopped up the floor with him. Then, one night when he was tight, an' all but helpless, two of them held him while Reiser beat him up. It was an ugly mess. The kid came up on them and they slugged him."

"What about the kid?" Gus said, impatient.

"I was coming to that," Briggs said. "They knocked him out. Reiser did it, I think, with a sap. But when the kid came out of it, his old man was all bloody and badly beaten. Tandy got him home and tried to fix him up. When his old man didn't come to, Tandy called a doctor. The kid's father had a bad concussion and never was quite right after that. The slugging they gave him affected his mind and one side of his body. He could never work again."

"Did it go to court?"

"Uh-huh, but Tandy was one against a dozen witnesses, and they made the kid out a liar and he lost the case. The father died a couple of years ago. The kid's not quite ten years younger than Reiser, and couldn't have been more than a youngster when it all happened. I guess he's been on the bum ever since."

"The kid's hungry to get Stan Reiser into a ring with him," Gus said slowly.

"It's easy to see why Reiser didn't recognize him," Briggs said. "Tandy must have changed a lot since then. As far as that goes, look how much he's changed since we met him. You'd never know he was the same person. He's filled out, hardened up, and he looks good now."

"Well, I'm glad that's all there was," Gus said thoughtfully. "I was worried."

Briggs hesitated. "It isn't quite all, Gus," he said. "There is more."

"More?"

"That wasn't the first time the kid and Reiser met. They had a scrap once. Reiser was always mean, and he teased Tandy once when the kid was selling papers on a corner out here on Albina Street. The kid had spunk and swung on him, and I guess the punch hurt, because Stan darn near killed him with his fists. I think that's what started the row with his father."

Gus Coe scowled. "That's not good. Sometimes a beating like that sticks in the mind, and this one might. Well, all we can do is to go along and see. Right now, the kid's shaping up for this fight better than ever.

"You know, one of us has got to stay with him, Briggsie. Every minute!"

"That's right." Briggs sat down. "Bernie won't stand for this. We just blocked him from the championship and no matter what Reiser thinks, Bernie is scared. He's scared Tandy can win, and as he used every dirty trick in the game to bring Stan along, he certainly won't change now."

Gus nodded.

"You're right. He'll stop at nothing. The kid got under Reiser's skin tonight, too, and once in that ring, it will be little short of murder . . . for one or the other of them."

Briggs nodded. "You know, Gus, maybe we should duck Reiser."

Gus was thoughtful for a moment, and then he said, "I know. The kid may not be afraid of Reiser. But frankly, I am. I wanted to get even with Satneck and Reiser for the one they pulled on us, but that's not important anymore. Tandy is. I like him and he's goin' places."

"Yeah," Briggs agreed. "I like the kid too."

TANDY MOORE, HIS cuts healed, went back to the gym under Spivy's Albina Street Pool Room with a will. In meeting Reiser, he would be facing a man who wanted to maim and kill. Reiser had everything to lose by this fight and Tandy had all to gain. Reiser was the leading contender for the title, and was acknowledged a better man than the current champion. If he lost now, he was through.

Going and coming from the gym, and in his few nights around town, Tandy watched for Dorinda. He wanted to call and apologize for the nightclub scene, but was too proud, and despite his wish, he could see no reason for thinking he might not be right. It was possible he could be mistaken, yet it looked too obvious, and so much of that sort of thing was going on. Yet he didn't want to believe it, and deep within himself, he did *not* believe it.

As the days drew on and the fight came nearer, Tandy was conscious of a new tension. He could see that Gus Coe and Briggs were staying close to him; that Coe's face had sharpened and grown more tense, that Briggs was ever more watchful, and that they always avoided dark streets and kept him to well-lighted public thoroughfares.

To one who had been so long accustomed to the harsh and hard ways of life, it irritated Tandy even while he understood their feelings and knew they were thinking of him. He was realist enough to know that Bernie Satneck was not going to chance losing a fighter worth a million dollars without putting up a battle.

Bernie Satneck would stop at nothing. Nor would Stan Reiser, when it came to that.

Come what may between now and the day of the fight, Tandy Moore knew that all would be settled in the ring. He also knew that although Reiser was a hard puncher and a shrewd, dangerous fighter who took every advantage, he was not afraid of him. This was his chance to get some revenge both for himself and his father . . . and it was legal.

V

ONE DAY, HANSEN, the reporter, dropped around to the second-floor hotel where they were staying. Tandy was lying on the bed in a robe, relaxing after a tough workout. The smell of Chinese food from the café downstairs drifted in through the window. The sportswriter dropped into a chair and dug out his pipe; he lit it up.

"I want to know about you and Stan Reiser," he suggested suddenly. "You knew him when you were a kid, didn't you? Out in St. John's? Wasn't there bad blood between you?"

"Maybe." Tandy turned his head. "Look, Hansen, I like you. I don't want to give you a bum steer or cross you up in any way. Whatever you learn about Stan or myself is your business, only I'm not telling you anything. Whatever differences we have, we'll settle in the ring."

"I agree." Hansen nodded, sucking on his pipe. "I've looked your record over, Tandy. Actually, I needn't have. I know Gus, and there isn't a straighter guy in this racket than Gus Coe. And Briggs? Well, Briggs is not a good man to get in the way of, not even for Bernie Satneck."

His eyes lifted, testing him with the name, and Tandy kept his face immobile.

"You've got a record since taking up with Coe that's as straight as a die," the reporter said. "If there ever was anything in your past, you have lived it down. I wouldn't say as much for Stan Reiser."

"What do you mean?" Tandy demanded.

"Just this. Bernie Satneck is running a string of illegal enterprises that touches some phase of every kind of crookedness there is. I've known about that for a long time, but it wasn't until just lately that I found out who was behind him—that he's not the top man himself."

"Who is?" Tandy didn't figure it really mattered, he wasn't after anything but a settling of old accounts.

"Stan Reiser." Hansen nodded as he said it. "Sure, we know; Bernie Satneck is his manager, and the manager is supposed to be the brains. Well, in this case that isn't so. Bernie is just a tool, a front man."

Hansen drew thoughtfully on his pipe. "I've been around the fight game a long time, had thirty years' experience around fighters. Once in a while, you strike a wrong gee among them. I think less so than in most professions or trades, because fighting demands a certain temperament or discipline. Despite their associations, most fighters are pretty square guys."

"You say Reiser isn't?"

"I *know* he isn't. I want to get him completely out of the fight game, and so do some others we know. If you put him down, get him out of the running for the championship, we'll keep him down. Don't underestimate the power of the press. Are you sure you don't want to tell me your story?"

"I'll fight him in the ring, that's all," Tandy said quietly. "Whatever there is between Reiser and me can be settled inside the ropes."

"Sure. That's the way I figured it." Hansen stopped as he was leaving. "I know about your father, but I won't write that story unless you give me the go-ahead."

GUS LEFT TANDY in the room on the day of the fight and went off on an errand across town. Briggs was around somewhere, but where Tandy did not know.

He removed his shirt and shoes and lay down on the bed. He felt anything but sleepy, so he opened a magazine and began to read.

There was a knock on the door and when it opened it was Dorinda Lane.

She was the last person he expected to see and he hastily swung his feet to the floor and reached for a shirt.

"Is it all right for me to come in?"

"Sure," he said. "You . . . well, I wasn't expecting anybody."

She dropped into a chair. "Tandy, you've got to listen to me! I've found out something, something I've no business to know. I overheard a conversation last night. Bernie Satneck and Stan Reiser were talking."

"Look." He got up and walked across the room. "If you shouldn't, don't tell me. After all, if Reiser is a friend of yours."

"Oh, don't be silly!" Dorinda declared impatiently. "You're so wrong about that! I never had but one date with him. He had nothing at all to do with my coming to the city. Long before I met you, I had found an agent and was trying to get a singing job through him. Reiser didn't even recommend me to Nevada Johnson, I've just run into him there. But that's not important, Tandy." She stepped closer to him. "It's what Reiser and Satneck have planned!"

"You mean you know? You overheard?"

Dorinda frowned. "Not exactly, I did hear them talking in the club. Stan Reiser believes he can beat you. He was furious when he found that Bernie Satneck wasn't sure, but he did listen, and Satneck has suggested that they should take no chances. What they have planned, I don't know, as I missed part of it then, but it has something to do with the gloves, something to get in your eyes."

Tandy shrugged. "Maybe it could be resin. But they always wipe off the gloves after a man goes down, so it couldn't be that. Did you hear anything more?"

"Yes, I did. They had quite an argument, but finally I heard Reiser agree that if he hadn't stopped you by the ninth round, he would do what Bernie wanted."

Tandy Moore's eyes grew sharp. He looked down at his hands.

"Thanks, Dory," he said at last. "That'll help."

She hesitated, looking at him, tenderness and worry mingled in her eyes. Yet he was warned and he would be ready. It was nice to know.

AS HE CRAWLED into the ring, Tandy Moore stared around him in amazement at the crowd. It rolled away from the ring in great banks of humanity, filling the ball park to overflowing. The blowing clouds parted momentarily and the sun blasted down on the spotless white square of canvas as he moved across to his corner.

Gus, in a white sweater, was beside him and Briggs stood at the edge of the ring, then dropped back into his seat. An intelligent-looking man with white brows was in the corner with Gus. He was a world-famed handler of fighters, even more skillful than Gus himself.

The robe was slid from his shoulders, and as Tandy peered from under his brows at Gus, he grinned a little and smiled.

"Well, pal, here we are," he said softly.

"Yeah." Gus stared solemnly across the ring. "I wish I knew what they had up their sleeves. They've got something, you can bet on it. Neither Bernie Satneck nor Stan Reiser ever took an unnecessary chance."

Tandy stared down at his gloved hands. He had an idea of what they had up their sleeves, but he said nothing. That was his problem alone. He hadn't mentioned it to Gus and he was no nearer a solution now than ever. They might not try anything on him, but if they did he would cope with it when the time came.

The referee gave them their instructions and he and Reiser returned to their corners, and almost instantly the bell sounded.

Tandy whirled and began his swift, shuffling movement to the center of the ring. His mouth felt dry and his stomach had a queer, empty feeling he had never known before. Under him the canvas was taut and strong, and he tried his feet on it as he moved and they were sure.

Stan Reiser opened up with a sharp left to the head. It landed solidly and Tandy moved away, watching the center of Reiser's body where he could see hands and feet both at the same time.

Reiser jabbed and Tandy slipped the punch, the glove sliding by his cheekbone, and then he went in fast, carrying the fight to the bigger man.

He slammed a right to the ribs, then a left and right to the body. Stan backed up and he followed him.

Reiser caught him with a left to the head, and Tandy landed a right. He felt the glove smack home solidly in Stan's body, and it felt good. They clinched, and he could feel the other man's weight and strength, sensing his power.

He broke and Stan came after him, his left stabbing like a living thing. A sharp left to the mouth, then another.

Both men were in excellent shape and the murderous punches slid off their toughened bodies like water off a duck's back.

Just before the bell, Reiser rushed him into the ropes and clipped him with a wicked right to the chin.

Tandy was sweating now and he was surprised to see blood on his glove when he wiped his face.

When the bell rang for the second, he went out, feinted, and then lunged. Reiser smashed a right to the head that knocked him off balance, and before he could get his feet under him, the bigger man was on him with a battering fury of blows.

Tandy staggered and retreated hastily, but to no avail. Stan was after him instantly, jabbing a left, then crossing a right. Tandy landed a right uppercut in close and Stan clipped him with two high hooks.

Sweaty and bloody now, Tandy bored in; lost to the crowd, lost to Gus, to Dorinda, and to Briggs, living now only for battle and the hot lust of combat. It lifted within him like a fierce, unholy tide. He drove Stan back and was in turn driven back, and they fought, round after round, with the tide of battle seesawing first one way and then another, bloody and desperate and bitter.

In the seventh round, they both came out fast. The crowd was in a continuous uproar now. Slugging like mad, they drove together. Stan whipped over a steaming right uppercut that caught Tandy coming in and his knees turned to rubber. He started to sink and Stan closed in, smashing a sharp left to the face and then crossing a right to the jaw that drove Tandy to his knees.

His head roaring, Tandy came up with a lunge and dove for a clinch, but Stan was too fast. He stepped back and stopped the attempt with a stiff left to the face that cut Tandy's lips, and then he rushed Tandy, smashing and battering him back with a furious flood of blows, driving him finally into the ropes with a sweeping left that made Tandy turn a complete somersault over the top rope!

His head came through them again and he crawled inside, with Reiser moving in for the kill.

Retreating, Tandy fought to push his thoughts through the fog from the heavy punches. He moved back warily, circling to avoid Reiser. The big man kept moving in, taking his time, more sure of himself now, and set for a kill.

Tandy Moore saw the cruel lips and the high cheekbones, one of them wearing a mouse, he saw a thin edge of a cut under Stan's right eye, and his lips looked puffed. His side was reddened from the pounding Tandy had given it, and Tandy's eyes narrowed as he backed into the ropes. That eye and the ribs!

Reiser closed in carefully and stabbed a left. More confident now, Tandy let the punch start, then turned his shoulders behind a left jab that speared Stan on the mouth. It halted him and the big fighter blinked.

Instantly, Tandy's right crossed over the left jab to the mouse on the cheekbone.

It landed with a dull thud and Stan's eyes glazed. His nostrils alive with the scent of sweaty muscles and blood, Tandy jabbed, then crossed, and suddenly they were slugging.

Legs spread apart, jaws set, they stood at point-blank range and fired with both hands!

The crowd came up roaring. The pace was too furious to last and it finally became a matter of who would give ground first. Suddenly Tandy Moore thrust his foot forward in a tight, canvas-gripping movement. Tandy saw his chance and threw a terrific left hook to the chin but it missed and a right exploded on his own jaw and he went to the canvas with a crash and a vast, roaring sound in his skull.

He came up swinging and went down again from a wicked left hook to the stomach and a crashing right to the corner of his jaw.

Rolling over, he got to his knees, his head filled with that roaring sound, and vaguely he saw Stan going away from him and realized with a shock that he was on his feet and that the bell ending the round was clanging in his ears!

One more round! It must be now or never! Whatever Reiser and Bernie had planned, whatever stratagem they had conceived, would be put into execution in the ninth round, and in the next, the eighth, he must win. He heard nothing that Gus Coe said. He felt only the ministering hands, heard the low, careful tone of his voice, felt water on his face and the back of his neck, and then a warning buzzer sounded and he was on his feet ready for the bell.

VI

THE BELL RANG and Tandy went out, a fierce, driving lust for victory welled up within him until he could see nothing but Stan Reiser. This was the man who had beaten his father, the man who had whipped him, the man who was fighting now to win all he wanted, all he desired. If Tandy could win, justice was at hand.

He hurled himself at Reiser like a madman. Toughened by years of hard work, struggle, and sharpened by training, he was ready. Fists smashing and battering he charged into Reiser, and the big heavyweight met him without flinching. For Stan Reiser had to win in this round, too. He must win in this round or confess by losing that he was the lesser man. Hating Tandy with all the ugly hatred of a man who has wronged another, he still fought the thought of admitting that he must stoop to using other methods to beat this upstart who would keep him from the title.

Weaving under a left, Tandy smashed a right to the ribs, then a left, a right, a left. His body swayed as he weaved in a deadly rhythm of mighty punching, each blow timed to the movements of Stan Reiser's body.

The big man yielded ground. He fell back and tried to sidestep, but Tandy was on him, giving no chance for a respite.

Suddenly the haze in Tandy's head seemed to clear momentarily and he stared upon features that were battered and swollen. One of Stan's eyes was closed and a raw wound lay under the other. His lips were puffed and his cheekbone was an open cut, yet there was in the man's eyes a fierce, almost animal hatred and something else.

It was something Tandy had never until that moment seen in a boxer's eyes. It was fear!

Not fear of physical injury, but the deeper, more awful fear of being truly beaten. And Stan Reiser had never been bested in that way. And now it was here, before him.

It was an end. Reiser saw it and knew it. Nothing he could do could stop that driving attack. He had thrown his best punches, used every legitimate trick, but there was one last hope!

Tandy feinted suddenly and Reiser struck out wildly, and Tandy smashed a right hand flush to the point of his chin!

Stan hit the ropes rolling, lost balance, and crashed to the floor. Yet at seven he was up, lifting his hands, half blind, but then the bell rang!

THE NINTH ROUND. Here it was. Almost before he realized it, the gong sounded and Tandy was going out again. But now he was wary, squinting at Stan's gloves.

Were they loaded? But the gloves had not been slipped off. There was no time, and no chance for that under the eyes of the crowd and the sportswriters. It would be something on the gloves.

He jabbed and moved away. Stan was working to get in close and there was a caution in his eyes. His whole manner was changed. Suddenly Reiser jabbed sharply for Tandy's head, but a flick of his glove pushed the blow away and Tandy was watchful again.

The crowd seemed to sense something. In a flickering glimpse at his corner, Tandy saw Gus Coe's face was scowling. He had seen that something in Reiser's style had changed; something was wrong. But what?

Stan slipped a left and came in close. He hooked for Tandy's head and smeared a glove across his eye. The glove seemed to slide on the sweat, and Tandy lowered his head to Stan's shoulder and belted him steadily in the stomach. He chopped a left to the head and the referee broke them. His right eye was smarting wickedly.

Something on the gloves! And in that instant, he recalled a story Gus had told him; *it was mustard oil!* So far he'd gotten little of it, but if it got directly in his eyes—

He staggered under a left hook, blocked a right, but caught a wicked left to the ribs. Sliding under another left, he smashed a right to the ribs with such force that it jerked Reiser's mouth open. In a panic the bigger man dove into a clinch, and jerking a glove free ground the end of it into Tandy's eye! He gritted his teeth and clinched harder.

"You remember me; the newsboy?" Tandy hissed as they swung around in a straining dance.

The referee was yelling, *"Break!"*

Stan hooked again but Tandy got his shoulder up to take the blow. "I'm going to take you down and if I don't I'll tell my story to anyone who'll listen!" Panic and fear haunted Stan Reiser's eyes and then something in him snapped; there was no longer any thought of the future just a driving, damning desire to punish this kid who would dare to threaten him.

Tandy jerked away and Stan hooked viciously to the jaw. Staggering, he caught the left and went to the canvas. He rolled over and got up, but Stan hooked another wicked left to his groin, throwing it low and hard with everything he had on it!

Tandy's mouth jerked open in a half-stifled cry of agony and he pitched over on his face, grabbing his crotch and rolling over and over on the canvas!

Men and women shouted and screamed. A dozen men clambered to the apron of the ring; flashbulbs popped as the police surged forward to drag everyone back. Around the ring all was bedlam and the huge arena was one vast roar of sound.

Tandy rolled over and felt the sun on his face, and he knew he had to get up.

Beyond the pain, beyond the sound, beyond everything was the need to be on his feet. He crawled to his knees and while the referee stared, too hypnotized by Tandy's struggle to get up to stop the fight, Tandy grabbed the ropes and pulled himself erect.

Blinded with pain from his stinging eyes, his teeth sunk into his mouthpiece with the agony that gnawed at his vitals, Tandy brushed the referee aside and held himself with his mind, every sense, every nerve, every ounce of strength, concentrated on Stan Reiser. And Reiser rushed to meet him.

Smashing Reiser's lips with a straight left, Tandy threw a high hard one and it caught Reiser on the chin as he came in. Falling back to the ropes, fear in every line of his face, Stan struggled to defend against the tide of punches that Tandy summoned from some hidden reserve of strength.

With a lunge, Reiser tried to escape. As he turned Tandy pulled the trigger on a wicked right that clipped Stan flush on the chin and sent him off the platform and crashing into the cowering form of Bernie Satneck!

Stan Reiser lay over a chair, out cold and dead to the world. Bernie Satneck struggled to get out from beneath him.

Then, Gus and Briggs were in the ring and he tried to see them through eyes that streamed with tears from the angry smart of the mustard oil.

"You made it, son. It's over." Gus carefully wiped off his face. "You'll fight the champ, and I think you'll beat him, too!"

Dory was in the ring, her eyes bright, her arm around his shoulders.

"It's just a game now, Gus." He sank to the mat, gasping. "I'll do whatever you say."

"Your poor face." Dorinda's eyes were full of tears, her hand cool on his cheek.

"Just don't complain about my beard." He grinned. "It could be weeks before I can shave."

Gus and Briggs got him to his feet. "Hell," he grumbled, "I hope it isn't weeks before I can walk."

Supported by his two friends, trailed by Dorinda, who had caught up his robe and towel, Tandy limped toward the dressing rooms.

"I wish my dad could have seen," he whispered. "I wish my dad could have seen me fight."

IT'S YOUR MOVE

OLD MAN WHITE was a checker player. He was a longshoreman, too, but he only made his living at that. Checker playing was his life. I never saw anybody take the game like he took it. Hour after hour, when there was nobody for him to play with, he'd sit at a table in the Seaman's Institute and study the board and practice his moves. He knew every possible layout there could be. There was this little book he carried, and he would arrange the checkers on the board, and then move through each game with an eye for every detail and chance. If anybody ever knew the checkerboard, it was him.

He wasn't a big man, but he was keen-eyed, and had a temper like nobody I ever saw. Most of the time he ignored people. Everybody but other checker players. I mean guys that could give him a game. They were few enough, and with the exception of Oriental Slim and MacCready, nobody had ever beat him. They were the best around at the time, but the most they could do with the old man was about one out of ten. But they gave him a game and that was all he wanted. He scarcely noticed anybody else, and you couldn't get a civil word out of him. As a rule he never opened his face unless it was to talk the game with somebody who knew it.

Then Sleeth came along. He came down from Frisco and began hanging around the Institute talking with the guys who were on the beach. He was a slim, dark fellow with a sallow complexion, quick, black eyes, and he might have been anywhere from thirty to forty-five.

He was a longshoreman, too. That is, he was then. Up in Frisco he had been a deckhand on a tugboat, like me. Before that he had been a lot of things, here and there. Somewhere he had developed a mind for figures, or maybe he had been born with it. You could give him any problem in addition, subtraction, or anything else, and you'd get the answer just like that, right out of his head. At poker he could beat anybody and was one of the best pool shots I ever saw.

We were sitting by the fireplace in the Institute one night when he came in and joined us. A few minutes later, Old Man White showed up wearing his old pea jacket as always.

"Where's MacCready?" he said.

"He's gone up to L.A., Mr. White," the clerk said. "He won't be back for several days."

"Is that other fellow around? That big fellow with the pockmarked face?"

"Slim? No, he's not. He shipped out this morning for Gray's Harbor. I heard he had some trouble with the police."

Trouble was right. Slim was slick with the cards, and he got himself in a game with a couple of Greeks. One of the Greeks was a pretty good cheat himself, but Oriental Slim was better and cashing in from the Greek's roll. One word led to another, and the Greek went for a rod. Well, Oriental Slim was the fastest thing with a chiv I ever saw. He cut that Greek, then he took out.

Old Man White turned away, growling something into his mustache. He was a testy old guy, and when he got sore that mustache looked like a porcupine's back.

"What's the matter with that guy?" Sleeth said. "He acts like he was sore about something?"

"It's checkers," I said. "That's Old Man White, the best checker player around here. Mac and Slim are the only two who can even make it interesting, and they're gone. He's sour for a week when he misses a game."

"Hell, I'll play with him!"

"He won't even listen to you. He won't play nobody unless they got some stuff."

"We'll see. Maybe I can give him a game."

Sleeth got up and walked over. The old man had his book out and was arranging his men on the board. He never used regular checkers himself. He used bottle tops, and always carried them in his pocket.

"How about a game?" Sleeth says.

Old Man White growled something under his breath about not wanting to teach anybody; he didn't even look up. He gets the checkers set up, and pretty soon he starts to move. It seems these guys that play checkers have several different openings they favor, each one of them named. Anyway, when the old man starts to move, Sleeth watches him.

"The Old Fourteenth, huh? You like that? I like the Laird and Lady best."

Old Man White stops in the middle of a move and looks up, frowning. "You play checkers?" he said.

"Sure, I just asked you for a game!"

"Sit down, sit down. I'll play you three games."

Well, it was pitiful. I'm telling you it was slaughter. If the old man hadn't been so proud, everything might have been different, but checkers was his life, his religion; and Sleeth beat him.

It wasn't so much that he beat him; it was the way he beat him. It was like playing with a child. Sleeth beat him five times running, and the old man was fit to be tied. And the madder he got, the worse he played.

Dick said afterward that if Sleeth hadn't talked so much, the old man might have had a chance. You see, Old Man White took plenty of time to study each move, sometimes ten minutes or more. Sleeth just sat there gabbing with us, sitting sideways in the chair, and never looking at the board except to move. He'd talk, talk about women, ships, ports, liquor, fighters, everything. Then, the old man would move and Sleeth would turn, glance at the board, and slide a piece. It seemed like when he looked at the board, he saw all the moves that had been made, and all that could be made. He never seemed to think; he never seemed to pause; he just moved.

Well, it rattled the old man. He was sort of shoved off balance by it. All the time, Sleeth was talking, and sometimes when he moved, it would be right in the middle of a sentence. Half the time, he scarcely looked at the board.

Then, there was a crowd around. Old Man White being beat was enough to draw a crowd, and the gang all liked Sleeth. He was a good guy. Easy with his dough, always having a laugh on somebody or with somebody, and just naturally a right guy. But I felt sorry for the old man. It meant so much to him, and he'd been kingbee around the docks so long, and treating everybody with contempt if they weren't good at checkers. If he had even been able to make it tough for Sleeth, it would have been different, but he couldn't even give him a game. His memory for moves seemed to desert him, and the madder he got and the harder he tried, the more hopeless it was.

It went on for days. It got so Sleeth didn't want to play him. He'd avoid him purposely, because the old man was so stirred up about it. Once Old Man White jumped up in the middle of a game and hurled the board clear across the room. Then he stalked out, mad as a wet hen, but just about as helpless as an Armenian peddler with both arms busted.

Then he'd come back. He'd always come back and insist Sleeth play him some more. He followed Sleeth around town, cornering him to play, each time sure he could beat him, but he never could.

We should have seen it coming, for the old man got to acting queer. Checkers was an obsession with him. Now he sometimes wouldn't come around for days, and when he did, he didn't seem anxious to play anymore. Once he played with Oriental Slim, who was back in town, but Slim beat him too.

That was the finishing touch. It might have been the one game out of ten that Slim usually won, but it hit the old man where he lived. I guess maybe he figured he couldn't play anymore. Without even a word, he got up and went out.

A couple of mornings later, I got a call from Brennan

to help load a freighter bound out for the Far East. I'd quit my job on the tug, sick of always going out but never getting any place, and had been longshoring a little and waiting for a ship to China. This looked like a chance to see if they'd be hiring; so I went over to the ship at Terminal Island, and reported to Brennan.

The first person I saw was Sleeth. He was working on the same job. While we were talking, another ferry came over and Old Man White got off. He was running a steam winch for the crew that day, and I saw him glance at Sleeth. It made me nervous to think of those two guys on the same job. In a dangerous business like longshoring—that is, a business where a guy can get smashed up so easy—it looked like trouble.

It was after four in the afternoon before anything happened. We had finished loading the lower hold through No. 4 hatch, and were putting the strong-backs in place so we could cover the 'tween decks hatchway. I was on deck waiting until they got those braces in place before I went down to lay the decking over them. I didn't want to be crawling down a ladder with one of those big steel beams swinging in the hatchway around me. Old Man White was a good hand at a winch, but too many things can happen. We were almost through for the day as we weren't to load the upper hold 'til morning.

A good winch-driver doesn't need signals from the hatch-tender to know where his load is. It may be out of sight down below the main deck, but he can tell by the feel of it and the position of the boom about where it is. But sometimes on those old winches, the steam wouldn't come on even, and once in a while there would be a surge of power that would make them do unaccountable things without a good hand driving. Now Old Man

White was a good hand. Nevertheless, I stopped by the hatch coaming and watched.

It happened so quick that there wasn't anything anyone could have done. Things like that always happen quick, and if you move, it is usually by instinct. Maybe the luckiest break Sleeth ever got was he was light on his feet.

The strong-back was out over the hatch, and Old Man White was easing it down carefully. When it settled toward the 'tween decks hatchway, Sleeth caught one end and Hansen the other. It was necessary for a man to stand at each end and guide the strong-back into the notch where it had to fit to support the floor of the upper hold. Right behind Sleeth was a big steel upright, and as Old Man White began to lower away, I got nervous. It always made me nervous to think that a wrong move by the winch-driver, or a wrong signal from the hatch-tender spotting for him, and the man with that post at his back was due to get hurt.

Sleeth caught the end of the strong-back in both hands and it settled gradually, with the old winch puffing along easylike. Just then I happened to glance up, and something made me notice Old Man White's face.

He was as white as death, and I could see the muscles at the corner of his jaw set hard. Then, all of a sudden, that strong-back lunged toward Sleeth.

It all happened so quick, you could scarcely catch a breath. Sleeth must have remembered Old Man White was on that winch, or maybe it was one of those queer hunches. As for me, I know that in the split second when that strong-back lunged toward him, the thought flashed through my mind, "Sleeth. It's your move!"

And he did move, almost like in the checker games. It

was as if he had a map of the whole situation in his mind. One moment he was doing one thing and the next . . .

He leaped sideways and the end of that big steel strong-back hit that stanchion with a crash that you could have heard in Sarawak; then the butt swung around and came within an eyelash of knocking Hansen into the hold, and I just stood there with my eyes on that stanchion thinking how Sleeth would have been mashed into jelly if he hadn't moved like Nijinsky.

The hatch-tender was yelling his head off, and slowly Old Man White took up the tension on the strong-back and swung her into place again. If it had been me, I'd never have touched that thing again, but Sleeth was there, and the strong-back settled into place as pretty as you could wish. Only then could I see that Sleeth's face was white and his hand was shaking.

When he came on deck, he was cool as could be. Old Man White was sitting behind that winch all heaped up like a sack of old clothes. Sleeth looked at him then, grinned a little, and said, sort of offhand, "You nearly had the move on me that time, Mr. White!"

OFF THE MANGROVE COAST

———————————

THERE WERE FOUR of us there, at the back end of creation, four of the devil's own, and a hard lot by any man's count. We'd come together the way men will when on the beach, the idea cropping up out of an idle conversation. We'd nothing better to do; all of us being fools or worse, so we borrowed a boat off the Nine Islands and headed out to sea.

DID YOU EVER cross the South China Sea in a forty-foot boat during the typhoon season? No picnic certainly, nor any job for a churchgoing son; more for the likes of us, who mattered to no one, and in a stolen boat, at that.

Now, all of us were used to playing it alone. We'd worked aboard ship and other places, sharing our labors with other men, but the truth was, each was biding his own thoughts, and watching the others.

There was Limey Johnson, from Liverpool, and Smoke Bassett from Port au Prince, and there was Long Jack from Sydney, and there was me, the youngest of the lot, at loose ends and wandering in a strange land.

Wandering always. Twenty-two years old, I was, with five years of riding freights, working in mines or lumber camps, and prizefighting in small clubs in towns that I never saw by daylight.

I'd had my share of the smell of coal smoke and cinders in the rain, the roar of a freight and the driving run-and-catch of a speeding train in the night, and then the sun coming up over the desert or going down over the sea, and the islands looming up and the taste of salt spray on my lips and the sound of bow wash about the hull. There had been nights in the wheelhouse with only the glow from the compass and out there beyond the bow the black, glassy sea rolling its waves up from the long sweep of the Pacific . . . or the Atlantic.

In those years I'd been wandering from restlessness but also from poverty. However, I had no poverty of experience and in that I was satisfied.

It was Limey Johnson who told us the story of the freighter sinking off the mangrove coast; a ship with fifty thousand dollars in the captain's safe and nobody who knew it was there anymore . . . nobody but him.

Fifty thousand dollars . . . and we were broke. Fifty thousand lying in a bare ten fathoms, easy for the taking. Fifty thousand split four ways. A nice stake, and a nice bit of money for the girls and the bars in Singapore or Shanghai . . . or maybe Paris.

Twelve thousand five hundred dollars apiece . . . if we all made it. And that was a point to be thought upon, for if only two should live . . . twenty-five thousand dollars . . . and who can say what can or cannot happen in the wash of a weedy sea off the mangrove coast? Who can say what is the destiny of any man? Who could say how much some of us were thinking of lending a hand to fate?

Macao was behind us and the long roll of the sea began, and we had a fair wind and a good run away from land before the sun broke upon the waves. Oh, it was gamble enough, but the Portuguese are an easygoing people. They would be slow in starting the search; there were many who might steal a boat in Macao . . . and logically, they would look toward China first. For who, they would ask themselves, would be fools enough to dare the South China Sea in such a boat; to dare the South China Sea in the season of the winds?

She took to the sea, that ketch, like a baby to a mother's breast, like a Liverpool Irishman to a bottle. She took to the sea and we headed south and away, with a bearing toward the east. The wind held with us, for the devil takes care of his own, and when again the sun went down we had left miles behind and were far along on our way. In the night, the wind held fair and true and when another day came, we were running under a high overcast and there was a heavy feel to the sea.

As the day drew on, the waves turned green with white beards blowing and the sky turned black with clouds. The wind tore at our sheets in gusts and we shortened sail and battened down and prepared to ride her out. Never before had I known such wind or known the world could breed such seas. Hour by hour, we fought it out, our poles bare and a sea anchor over, and though none of us were praying men, pray we did.

We shipped water and we bailed and we swore and we worked and, somehow, when the storm blew itself out, we were still afloat and somewhat farther along. Yes, farther, for we saw a dark blur on the horizon and when we topped a wave, we saw an island, a brush-covered bit of sand forgotten here in the middle of nothing.

We slid in through the reefs, conning her by voice and hand, taking it easy because of the bared teeth of coral so close beneath our keel. Lincoln Island, it was, scarcely more than a mile of heaped-up sand and brush, fringed and bordered by reefs. We'd a hope there was water, and we found it near a stunted palm, a brackish pool, but badly needed.

From there, it was down through the Dangerous Ground, a thousand odd miles of navigator's nightmare, a wicked tangle of reefs and sandy cays, of islands with tiny tufts of palms, millions of seabirds and fish of all kinds . . . and the bottom torn out of you if you slacked off for even a minute. But we took that way because it was fastest and because there was small chance we'd be seen.

Fools? We were that, but sometimes now when the fire is bright on the hearth and there's rain against the windows and the roof, sometimes I think back and find myself tasting the wind again and getting the good old roll of the sea under me. In my mind's eye, I can see the water breaking on the coral, and see Limey sitting forward, conning us through, and hear Smoke Bassett, the mulatto from Haiti, singing a song of his island in that deep, grand, melancholy bass of his.

Yes, it was long ago, but what else have we but memories? For all life is divided into two parts: anticipation and memory, and if we remember richly, we must have lived richly. Only sometimes I think of them, and wonder what would have happened if the story had been different if another hand than mine had written the ending?

Fools . . . we were all of that, but a tough, ruddy lot of fools, and it was strange the way we worked as a team;

the way we handled the boat and shared our grub and water and no whimper from any man.

There was Limey, who was medium height and heavy but massively boned, and Long Jack, who was six-three and cadaverous, and the powerful, lazy-talking Smoke, the strongest man of the lot. And me, whom they jokingly called "The Scholar" because I'd stowed a half-dozen books in my sea bag, and because I read from them, sometimes at night when we lay on deck and watched the canvas stretch its dark belly to the wind. Smoke would whet his razor-sharp knife and sing "Shenandoah," "Rio Grande," or "High Barbaree." And we would watch him cautiously and wonder what he had planned for that knife. And wonder what we had planned for each other.

THEN ONE MORNING we got the smell of the Borneo coast in our nostrils, and felt the close, hot, sticky heat of it coming up from below the horizon. We saw the mangrove coast out beyond the white snarl of foam along the reefs, then we put our helm over and turned east again, crawling along the coast of Darvel Bay.

The heat of the jungle reached out to us across the water and there was the primeval something that comes from the jungle, the ancient evil that crawls up from the fetid rottenness of it, and gets into the mind and into the blood.

We saw a few native craft, but we kept them wide abeam wanting to talk with no one, for our plans were big within us. We got out our stolen diving rig and went to work, checking it over. Johnson was a diver and I'd been down, so it was to be turn and turn about for us . . .

for it might take a bit of time to locate the wreck, and then to get into the cabin once we'd found it.

We came up along the mangrove coast with the setting sun, and slid through a narrow passage into the quiet of a lagoon where we dropped our hook and swung to, looking at the long wall of jungle that fronted the shore for miles.

Have you seen a mangrove coast? Have you come fresh from the sea to a sundown anchorage in a wild and lonely place with the line of the shore lost among twisting, tangling tentacle roots, strangling the earth, reaching out to the very water and concealing under its solid ceiling of green those dark and dismal passages into which a boat might make its way?

Huge columnar roots, other roots springing from them, and from these, still more roots, and roots descending from branches and under them, black water, silent, unmoving. This we could see, and beyond it, shutting off the mangrove coast from the interior, a long, low cliff of upraised coral.

Night then . . . a moon hung low beyond a corner of the coral cliff . . . lazy water lapping about the hull . . . the mutter of breakers on the reef . . . the cry of a night bird, and then the low, rich tones of Smoke Bassett, singing.

So we had arrived, four men of the devil's own choosing, men from the world's waterfronts, and below us, somewhere in the dark water, was a submerged freighter with fifty thousand dollars in her strongbox.

Four men . . . Limey Johnson—short, powerful, tough. Tattooed on his hands the words, one to a hand, *Hold—Fast*. A scar across the bridge of his nose, the tip of an ear missing . . . greasy, unwashed dungarees . . . and stories of the Blue Funnel boats. What, I wondered, had become of the captain of the sunken ship, and the others who must have known about that money? Limey Johnson had offered no explanation, and we were not inquisitive men.

And Long Jack, sprawled on the deck looking up at the stars? Of what was he thinking? Tomorrow? Fifty thousand dollars, and how much he would get of it? Or was he thinking of the spending of it? He was a thin, haggard man with a slow smile that never reached beyond his lips. Competent, untiring . . . there was a rumor about Macao that he had killed a man aboard a Darwin pearl fisher . . . he was a man who grew red, but not tan, with a thin, scrawny neck like a buzzard, as taciturn as Johnson was talkative. Staring skyward from his pale gray eyes . . . at what? Into what personal future? Into what shadowed past?

Smoke Bassett, powerful tan muscles, skin stretched taut to contain their slumbering, restless strength. A man with magnificent eyes, quick of hand and foot . . . a dangerous man.

And the last of them, myself. Tall and lean and quiet, with wide shoulders, and not as interested in the money. Oh, yes, I wanted my share, and would fight to have it, but there was more than the money; there was getting the money; there was the long roll of the ketch coming down the China Sea; there was the mangrove coast, the night and the stars . . . there were the boat sounds, the water sounds . . . a bird's wing against the wind . . . the distant sounds of the forest . . . these things that no man can buy; these things that get into the blood; these things that build the memories of tomorrow; the hours to look back upon.

I wanted these more than money. For there is a time

for adventure when the body is young and the mind alert and all the world seems there for one's hands to use, to hold, to take. And this was my new world, this ancient world of the Indies, these lands where long ago the Arab seamen came, and where the Polynesians may have passed, and where old civilizations slumber in the jungles; awaiting the explorations of men. Where rivers plunge down massive, unrecorded falls, where the lazy sea creeps under the mangroves, working its liquid fingers into the abysmal darkness where no man goes or wants to go.

What is any man but the total of what he has seen? The sum of what he has done? The strange foods, the women whose bodies have merged with his, the smells, the tastes, the longings, the dreams, the haunted nights? The Trenches in Shanghai, Blood Alley, Grant Road in Bombay, and Malay Street in Singapore . . . the worst of it, and the best . . . the temples and towers built by lost, dead hands, the nights at sea, the splendor of a storm, the dancing of dust devils on the desert. These are a man . . . and the solid thrill of a blow landed, the faint smell of opium, rubber, sandalwood, and spice, the stink of copra . . . the taste of blood from a split lip.

Oh, yes, I had come for things other than money but that evening, for the first time, no man gave another good night.

Tomorrow there would be, with luck, fifty thousand dollars in this boat . . . and how many ways to split it?

No need to worry until the box was aboard, or on the line, being hoisted. After that, it was every man for himself. Or was I mistaken? Would we remain friends still? Would we sail our boat into Amurang or Jesselton and leave it there and scatter to the winds with our money in our pockets?

That was the best way, but with such men, in such a place, with that amount of money . . . one lives because one remains cautious . . . and fools die young.

AT THE FIRST streaks of dawn, I was out of my blankets and had them rolled. While Smoke prepared breakfast, we got the diving outfit up to the side. We were eating when the question came.

"I'll go," I said, and grinned at them. "I'll go down and see how it looks."

They looked at me, and I glanced up from my plate and said, "How about it, Smoke? Tend my lines?"

He turned to me, a queer light flicking through his dark, handsome eyes, and then he nodded.

A line had been drawn . . .

A line of faith and a line of doubt . . . of the three, I had chosen Smoke Bassett, had put in him my trust, for when a man is on the bottom, his life lies in the hands of the man who tends his lines. A mistaken signal, or a signal ignored, and the diver can die.

I had given my life to Smoke Bassett, and who could know what that would mean?

JOHNSON WAS TAKING soundings, for in these waters, chart figures were not to be trusted. Many of the shores have been but imperfectly surveyed, if at all, and there is constant change to be expected from volcanic action, the growth of coral, or the waves themselves.

When we anchored outside the reef, I got into the diving dress. Limey lent me a hand, saying to me, "Nine or ten fathoms along the reef, but she drops sharp off to fifty fathoms not far out."

Careful . . . we'd have to be careful, for the enemies of

a diver are rarely the shark or the octopus, but rather the deadline and constant danger of a squeeze or a blowup. The air within the suit is adjusted to the depth of the water and its pressure, but a sudden fall into deeper water can crush a man, jamming his entire body into his copper helmet. Such sudden pressure is called a squeeze.

A blowup is usually caused by a jammed valve, blowing a man's suit to almost balloon size and propelling him suddenly to the surface where he lies helpless until rescued. While death only occasionally results from a blowup, a diver may be crippled for life by the dreaded "bends," caused by the sudden change in pressure, and the resulting formation of nitrogen bubbles in the bloodstream.

When the helmet was screwed on, Limey clapped me on the top and I swung a leg over to the rope ladder. Smoke Bassett worked the pump with one arm while he played out the hose and rope. Up—down. *Chug-chug*. A two-stroke motion like a railroad hand car. It didn't take much energy but each stroke was a pulse of oxygen . . . like a breath, or the beating of your heart. The big mulatto grinned at me as he worked the handle.

Clumsy, in the heavy shoes and weighted belt, I climbed down and felt the cool press of water rise around me. Up my body . . . past my faceplate.

It was a slow, easy descent . . . down . . . down . . . and on the bottom at sixty feet.

In the dark water, down where the slow weeds wave in the unstirring sea . . . no sound but the *chug-chug-chug* of the pump, the pump that brings the living air . . . down in a green, gray, strange world . . . cowrie shells . . . a big conch . . . the amazing wall of the reef, jagged, broken, all edges and spires . . . a stone fish, all points and poison.

Leaning forward against the weight of the water, I moved like some ungainly monster of the deep, slowly along the bottom. Slowly . . . through the weeds, upon an open sand field beneath the sea . . . slowly, I walked on.

A dark shadow above me and I turned slowly . . . a shark . . . unbelievably huge . . . and seemingly uninterested . . . but could you tell? Could one ever know?

Smell . . . I'd heard old divers say that sharks acted upon smell . . . and the canvas and rubber and copper gave off no smell, but a cut, a drop of blood in the water, and the sharks would attack.

Chug-chug-chug . . . I walked on, turning slowly from time to time to look around me. And the shark moved above me, huge, black, ominous . . . dark holes in the reef where might lurk . . . anything. And then I saw . . . something.

A blackness, a vast deep, opening off to my right, away from the reef. I looked toward it, and drew back. Fifty fathoms at some places, but then deeper, much deeper. Fifty fathoms . . . three hundred feet.

A signal . . . time for me to go up. Turning, I walked slowly back, and looking for the shark, but he had gone. I had failed to hold his interest . . . and I could only hope that nothing in my personality would induce him to return.

When the helmet was off, I told them. "Probably the other way. But when you go down, Limey, keep an eye open for that shark. I don't trust the beggar."

ON THE THIRD day, we found the hulk of the freighter. At the time, I was below, half asleep in my bunk. Bassett was in the galley cooking, and only Long Jack was on deck, handling the lines for Limey. Dozing, I heard him bump against the vessel's side and I listened, but there was nothing more, only a sort of scraping, a sound I could not place, as if something were being dragged along the hull.

When I heard the weighted boots on the deck, I rolled over and sat up, kicking my feet into my slippers. Johnson was seated on the rail and his helmet was off and Long Jack was talking to him. When they heard my feet on the deck, they turned. "Found it!" Limey was grinning his broken-toothed smile. "She's hanging right on the lip of the deep. She's settin' up fairly straight. You shouldn't have much trouble gettin' the box."

THERE WAS A full moon that night, wide and white; a moon that came up over the jungle, and standing by the rail, I looked out over the lagoon and watched the phosphorescent combers roll up and crash against the outer reef. When I had been standing there a long time, Smoke Bassett walked over.

"Where's Limey?"

"Fishin'," he said, "with a light."

"Tomorrow," I said, "we'll pick it up."

"Anson Road would look mighty good now. Anson Road, in Singapore . . . an' High Street. You know that, Scholar?"

"It'll look better with money in your pocket."

"Look good to me just anyway." Smoke rolled a cigarette. "Money ain't so important."

We watched the moon and listened to the breakers on the reef. "You be careful down there," Smoke Bassett told me suddenly. "Mighty careful." He struck a match and lit his cigarette, as he always did, one-handed.

Lazily, I listened to the sea talking to the reef and then

listened to the surf and to the jungle beyond the line of mangroves. A bird shrieked, an unhappy, uncanny sound.

"Them two got they heads together," Smoke Bassett said. "You be careful."

Long Jack . . . a queer, silent man around whom one never felt quite comfortable. A taciturn man with a wiry strength that could be dangerous. Only once had we had words and that had been back in Macao when we first met. He had been arrogant, as if he felt he could push me around. "Don't start that with me," I told him.

His eyes were snaky, cold, there were strange little lights in them, and contempt. He just looked at me. I didn't want trouble so I told him, "You could make an awful fool of yourself, Jack," I said.

He got up. "Right now," he said, and stood there looking at me, and I know he expected me to take water.

So, I got up, for this was an old story, and I knew by the way he stood that he knew little about fistfighting, and then a fat man, sitting in a dirty singlet and a blue dungaree coat, said, "You *are* a fool. I seen the kid fight in Shanghai, in the ring. He'll kill you."

Long Jack from Sydney hesitated and it was plain he no longer wanted to fight. He still stood there, but I'd seen the signs before and knew the moment was past. He'd had me pegged for a kid who either couldn't or wouldn't go through.

That was all, but Long Jack had not forgotten, I was sure of that. There had been no further word, nor had we talked much on the trip down the China Sea except what was necessary. But it had been pleasant enough.

The next morning when I got into the suit, Limey came up to put on the copper helmet. There was a look in his eyes I didn't like. "When you get it out of the desk," he said, "just tie her on the line and give us a signal."

But there was something about the way he said it that was wrong. As I started into the water, he leaned over suddenly and stroked his hand down my side. I thought he wanted something and turned my faceplate toward him, but he just stood there so I started down into the water.

When I was on the deck of the freighter, I started along toward the superstructure and then saw something floating by my face. I stepped back to look and saw it was a gutted fish. An instant, I stood there staring, and then a dark shadow swung above me and I turned, stumbled, and fell just as the same huge shark of a few days before whipped by, jaws agape.

On my feet, I stumbled toward the companionway, and half fell through the opening just as the shark twisted around and came back for another try.

And then I knew why Limey Johnson had been fishing, and what he had rubbed on my arm as I went into the water. He had rubbed the blood and guts of the fish on my suit and then had dumped it into the water after me to attract the shark.

Sheltered by the companionway, I rubbed a hand at my sleeve as far around as I could reach, trying to rub off some of the blood.

Forcing myself to composure, I waited, thinking out the situation.

Within the cabin to the right, I had already noticed the door of the desk compartment that held the cash box stood open to the water. That meant the money was already on our boat; it meant that the bumping I'd heard along the side had been the box as it was hoisted aboard. And letting me go down again, rubbing the blood and corruption on my sleeve had been a deliberate attempt at murder.

Chug-chug-chug . . . monotonously, reassuringly, the steady sound of the pump reached me. Smoke was still on the job, and I was still safe, yet how long could I remain so under the circumstances?

If they had attempted to kill me they would certainly attempt to kill Smoke, and he could not properly defend himself, even strong as he was, while he had to keep at least one hand on the pump. Outside, the shark circled, just beyond the door frame.

Working my way back into the passage, I fumbled in the cabin, looking for some sort of weapon. There was a fire ax on the bulkhead outside, but it was much too clumsy for use against so agile a foe, even if I could strike hard enough underwater. There was nothing . . . suddenly I saw on the wall, crossed with an African spear of some sort, a whaler's harpoon!

Getting it down, I started back for the door, carefully freeing my lines from any obstructions.

Chug . . . chug . . . chug . . .

The pump slowed, almost stopped, then picked up slowly again, and then something floated in the water, falling slowly, turning over as I watched, something that looked like an autumn leaf, drifting slowly down, only much larger.

Something with mouth agape, eyes wide, blood trailing a darkening streamer in the green water . . . it was Long Jack, who had seen the last of Sydney . . . Long Jack, floating slowly down, his belly slashed and an arm cut across the biceps by a razor-edged knife.

An instant I saw him, and then there was a gigantic swirl in the water, the shark turning, doubling back over,

and hurling himself at the body with unbelievable feroc-
ity. It was my only chance; I stepped out of the door and
signaled to go up.

There was no response, only the *chug-chug-chug* of
the pump. Closing my valve only a little, I started to rise,
but desperately as I tried, I could not turn myself to watch
the shark. Expecting at any moment that he would see
me and attack, I drifted slowly up.

Suddenly the ladder hung just above me although the
hull was still a dark shadow. I caught the lower step and
pulled myself slowly up until I could get my clumsy feet
on the step. Climbing carefully, waiting from moment to
moment, I got to the surface and climbed out.

Hands fumbled at the helmet. I heard the wrench, and
then the helmet was lifted off.

Smoke Bassett had a nasty wound over the eye where
he had been struck by something, and where blood stained
his face it had been wiped and smeared. Limey Johnson
was standing a dozen feet away, only now he was drawing back, away from us.

He looked at the harpoon in my hands and I saw him
wet his lips, but I said nothing at all. Bassett was helping
me out of the helmet, and I dared not take my eyes from
Johnson.

His face was working strangely, a grotesque mask of
yellowish-white wherein the eyes seemed unbelievably
large. He reached back and took up a long boat hook.
There was a driftwood club at my feet, and this must have
been what had struck Bassett. They must have rushed him
at first, or Long Jack had tried to get close, and had come
too close.

When I dropped the weight belt and kicked off the
boots, Smoke was scarcely able to stand. And I could

see the blow that had hit him had almost wrecked the side of his face and skull. "You all right? You all right, Scholar?" His voice was slurred.

"I'm all right. Take it easy. I'll handle it now."

Limey Johnson faced me with his new weapon, and slowly his courage was returning. Smoke Bassett he had feared, and Smoke was nearly helpless. It was Limey and me now; one of us was almost through.

Overhead the sun was blazing . . . the fetid smell of the mangroves and the swamp was wafted to the ketch from over the calm beauty of the lagoon. The sea was down, and the surf rustled along the reef, chuckling and sucking in the holes and murmuring in the deep caverns.

Sweat trickled into my eyes and I stood there, facing Limey Johnson across that narrow deck. Short, heavy, powerful . . . a man who had sent me down to the foulest kind of death, a man who must kill now if he would live.

I reached behind me to the rail and took up the harpoon. It was razor sharp.

His hook was longer . . . he outreached me by several feet. I had to get close . . . close.

In my bare feet, I moved out away from Smoke, and Limey began to move warily, watching for his chance, that ugly hook poised to tear at me. To throw the harpoon was to risk my only weapon, and risk it in his hands, for I could not be sure of my accuracy. I had to keep it, and thrust. I had to get close. The diving dress was some protection but it was clumsy and I would be slow.

There was no sound . . . the hot sun, the blue sky, the heavy green of the mangroves, the sucking of water among the holes of the coral . . . the slight sound of our breathing and the rustle and slap of our feet on the deck.

He struck with incredible swiftness. The boat hook

darted and jerked back. The hook was behind my neck, and only the nearness of the pole and my boxer's training saved me. I jerked my head aside and felt the thin sharpness of the point as it whipped past my neck, but before I could spring close enough to thrust, he stepped back and bracing himself, he thrust at me. The curve of the hook hit my shoulder and pushed me off balance. I fell back against the bulwark, caught myself, and he lunged to get closer. Three times he whipped the hook and jerked at me. Once I almost caught the pole, but he was too quick.

I tried to maneuver . . . then realized I had to get *outside* of the hook's curve . . . to move to my left, then try for a thrust either over or under the pole. In the narrow space between the low deckhouse and the rail there was little room to maneuver.

I moved left, the hook started to turn, and I lunged suddenly and stabbed. The point just caught him . . . the side of his singlet above the belt started to redden. His face looked drawn, I moved again, parried a lunge with the hook, and thrust again, too short. But I knew how to fight him now . . . and he knew too.

He tried, and I parried again, then thrust. The harpoon point just touched him again, and it drew blood. He stepped back, then crossed the deck and thrust at me under the yard, his longer reach had more advantage now, with the deckhouse between us, and he was working his way back toward the stern. It was an instant before I saw what he was trying to do. He was getting in position to kill Bassett, unconscious against the bulwark beside the pump.

To kill . . . and to get the knife.

I lunged at him then, batting the hook aside, feeling it

rip the suit and my leg as I dove across the mahogany roof of the deckhouse. I thrust at him with the harpoon. His face twisted with fear, he sprang back, stepped on some spilled fish guts staining the deck. He threw up his arms, lost hold of the boat hook, and fell backward, arms flailing for balance. He hit the bulwark and his feet flew up and he went over, taking my harpoon with him . . . a foot of it stuck out his back . . . and there was an angry swirl in the water, a dark boiling . . . and after a while, the harpoon floated to the surface, and lay there, moving slightly with the wash of the sea.

THERE'S A PLACE on the Sigalong River, close by the Trusan waters, a place where the nipa palms make shade and rustle their long leaves in the slightest touch of wind. Under the palms, within sound of the water, I buried Smoke Bassett on a Sunday afternoon . . . two long days he lasted, and a wonder at that, for the side of his head was curiously crushed. How the man had remained at the pump might be called a mystery . . . but I knew.

For he was a loyal man; I had trusted him with my lines, and there can be no greater trust. So when he was gone, I buried him there and covered over the grave with coral rock and made a marker for it and then I went down to the dinghy and pushed off for the ketch.

SOMETIMES NOW, WHEN there is rain upon the roof and when the fire crackles on the hearth, sometimes I will remember: the bow wash about the hull, the rustling of the nipa palms, the calm waters of a shallow lagoon. I will remember all that happened, the money I found, the men that died, and the friend I had . . . off the mangrove coast.

THE CROSS AND THE CANDLE

WHEN IN PARIS, I went often to a little hotel in a narrow street off the Avenue de la Grande Armee. Two doors opened into the building; one into a dark hallway and then by a winding stair to the chambers above, the other to the café, a tiny bistro patronized by the guests and a few people of the vicinity.

It was in no way different from a hundred other such places. The rooms were chill and dank in the morning (there was little heat in Paris, even the girls in the Follies Bergère were dancing in goose pimples), the furnishings had that added Parisian touch of full-length mirrors running alongside the bed for the obvious and interesting purpose of enabling one, and one's companion, to observe themselves and their activities.

Madame was a Breton, and as my own family were of Breton extraction, I liked listening to her tales of Roscoff, Morlaix, and the villages along the coast. She was a veritable treasure of ancient beliefs and customs, quaint habits and interesting lore. There was scarcely a place from Saint-Malo to the Bay of Douarnenez of which she didn't have a story to tell.

Often when I came to the café, there would be a man seated in the corner opposite the end of the bar. Somewhat below medium height, the thick column of his neck spread out into massive shoulders and a powerful chest. His arms were heavy with muscle and the brown hands that rested on the table before him were thick and strong.

Altogether, I have seen few men who gave such an impression of sheer animal strength and vitality. He moved in leisurely fashion, rarely smiled, and during my first visits had little to say.

In some bygone brawl, his nose had been broken and a deep scar began over his left eye and ran to a point beneath a left ear of which half the lobe was gone. You looked at his wide face, the mahogany skin, and polished over the broad cheekbones and you told yourself, "This man is dangerous!" Yet often there was also a glint of hard, tough humor in his eyes.

He sat in his corner, his watchful eyes missing nothing. After a time or two, I came to the impression that he was spinning a web, like some exotic form of spider, but what manner of fly he sought to catch, I could not guess.

Madame told me he was a *marin,* a sailor, and had lived for a time in Madagascar.

One afternoon when I came to the café, he was sitting in his corner alone. The place was empty, dim, and cold. Hat on the table beside him, he sat over an empty glass.

He got up when I came in and moved behind the bar. I ordered *vin blanc* and suggested he join me. He filled the two glasses without comment, then lifted his glass. *"À votre santé!"* he said. We touched glasses and drank.

"Cold, today," he said suddenly.

The English startled me. In the two months past, I had spoken to him perhaps a dozen times, and he replied always in French.

"You speak English then?"

He grinned at me, a tough, friendly grin touched by a sort of wry cynicism. "I'm an American," he said, "or I was."

"The devil you say!" Americans are of all kinds, but somehow . . . still, he could have been anything.

"Born in Idaho," he said, refilling our glasses. When I started to pay, he shook his head and brought money from his own pocket and placed it under an ashtray for Madame to put in the register when she returned. "They call me Tomas here. My old man was an Irish miner, but my mother was Basque."

"I took it for granted you were French."

"Most of them do. My mother spoke French and Spanish. Picked them up around home from her parents, as I did from her. After I went to sea, I stopped in Madagascar four years, and then went to Mauritius and Indochina."

"You were here during the war?"

"Part of the time. When it started, I was in Tananarive; but I returned here, got away from the *Boche,* and fought with the maquis for a while. Then I came back to Paris."

He looked up at me and the slate-gray eyes were flat and ugly. "My girl was dead."

"Bombs?"

"No. A Vichy rat."

He would say nothing more on the subject and our talk drifted to a strange and little-known people who live in and atop a mountain in Madagascar, and their peculiar customs. I, too, had followed the sea for a time so there was much good talk of the ways of ships and men.

Tomas was without education in the accepted sense, yet he had observed well and missed little. He had read widely. His knowledge of primitive peoples would have fascinated an anthropologist and he had appreciation and understanding for their beliefs.

After talking with him, I came more often to the café, for we found much in common. His cynical toughness appealed to me, and we had an understanding growing from mutual experiences and interests. Yet as our acquaintance grew, I came to realize that he was a different man when we talked together alone than when others were in the room. Then his manner changed. He became increasingly watchful, talked less and only in French.

The man was watching for someone or something. Observing without seeming to, I became aware the center of his interests were those who came most often to the café. And of these, there were four that held his attention most.

Mombello was a slender Italian of middle years who worked in a market. Picard was a chemist, and Leon Matsys owned a small iron foundry on the edge of Paris and a produce business near The Halles. Matsys was a heavy man who had done well, had educated himself, and was inclined to tell everyone so. Jean Mignet, a sleek, catlike man, was supported by his wife, an actress of sorts. He was pleasant enough to know, but I suspected him of being a thief.

Few women came to the café. Usually the girls who

came to the hotel entered by the other door and went to the chambers above, and after a period of time, returned through the same door. To us, they existed merely as light footsteps in the dark hall and on the stairs.

Madame herself, a friendly, practical Breton woman, was usually around and occasionally one of the daughters Mombello would come in search of their father.

The oldest was eighteen and very pretty, but business-like without interest in the men of the café. The younger girl was thin, woefully thin from lack of proper food, but a beautiful child with large, magnificent dark eyes, dark wavy hair, and lips like the petals of a flower.

Someone among these must be the center of interest, yet I could not find that his interest remained long with any one of the four men. For their part, they seemed to accept him as one of themselves. Only one, I think, was conscious of being watched. That one was Jean Mignet.

On another of those dismal afternoons, we sat alone in the café and talked. (It always seemed that I came there only when the outside was bleak and unhappy, for on the sunny days, I liked being along the boulevards or in St. Germaine.) The subject again arose of strange superstitions and unique customs.

There was a Swede on one of my ships who would never use salt when there was a Greek at the table; an idea no more ridiculous than the fear some people have of eating fish and drinking milk in the same meal.

Tomas nodded. "I've known of many such ideas," he said, "and in some of the old families you will find customs that have been passed along from generation to generation in great secrecy for hundreds of years.

"I know of one"—he hesitated, describing circles on the dark tabletop with the wet bottom of his glass—

"that is, a religious custom followed so far as I know by only one family."

He looked up at me. "You must never speak of this around here," he said, and he spoke so sharply and with so much feeling, I assured him I'd never speak of it anywhere, if he so wished.

"In the family of my girl," he said, "there is an ancient custom that goes back to the Crusades. Her ancestor was a soldier with Saint Louis at Saint-Jean-d'Acre. No doubt you know more of that than I do. Anyway, when his brother was killed in the fighting, there was no shrine or church nearby, so he thrust his dagger into a log. As you know, the hilts of daggers and swords were at that time almost always in the form of a cross, and he used it so in this case, burning a candle before the dagger.

"It became the custom of a religious and fighting family, and hence whenever there is a death, this same dagger is taken from its wrappings of silk and with the point thrust into wood, a candle for the dead is burned before it.

"Marie told me of this custom after her mother's death when I came hurriedly into her room and surprised her with the candle burning. For some forgotten reason, a tradition of secrecy had grown around the custom, and no one outside the family ever knew of it.

"That night in the darkened room, we watched the candle slowly burn away before that ancient dagger, a unique dagger where on crosspiece or guard was carved the body of Christ upon the cross and the blade was engraved with the figure of a snake, the snake signifying the powers of evil fallen before God.

"I never saw the dagger again while she lived. It was put away among her things, locked carefully in an iron chest, never to be brought out again until, as she said, she herself died, or her brother. Then, she looked at me, and said, 'Or you, Tomas, for you are of my family now.' "

He looked at me, and underneath the scarred brows, there were tears in his eyes.

"She must have been a fine girl," I said, for he was deeply moved.

"She was the only thing in my life! Only a madman, a mad American, would return to France after the war broke out. But I loved her.

"Look at me. I'm not the kind of man many women could love. I'm too rough, too brutal! I'm a seaman, that is all, and never asked to be more. A good man at sea or in a fight, but I have no words with which to say nice things to a woman, and she was a beautiful girl with an education."

Tomas took out his wallet and removed a worn photograph. When I looked at it, I was frankly astonished. The girl was not merely a pretty girl, she was all he had said, and more. She *was* beautiful.

Furthermore, there was something in her eyes and face that let you know that here was a girl who had character, maybe one who knew what loyalty was.

"She is lovely," I said sincerely. "I never saw anyone more beautiful!"

He was pleased, and he looked at me with his face suddenly lighter. "She was magical!" he said. "The best thing in my life. I came first to her house with her brother, who had been my shipmate on a voyage from Saigon. She was a child then, and I thought of her as nothing else.

"So, when next I came to the house, I brought her a

present from Liverpool, and then others from Barcelona and Algiers. Simple things, and inexpensive, the sort of things a sailor may find in almost any port, but they had romance, I suppose, a color.

"I gave them simply because I was a lonely man, and this family had taken me as one of them, and because the giving of things is good for a lonely heart.

"One day, she was twelve then, I think, she had gone to a theater in the Boulevard de Clichy with her brother, and when they came out, she saw me with a girl, a girl from a café in the Pigalle. She was very angry and for days she would not speak to me.

"Her brother teased her, and said, 'Look! Marie thinks already she is a woman! She is jealous for you, Tomas!' "

He smiled at the memory. "Then, I was gone again to sea, and when I came again to the house, Marie was fourteen, taller, frightened, and skinny. Always she stared at me, and I brought her presents as before. Sometimes I took her to the theater, but to me she was a child. She was no longer gay, full of excitement and anger. She walked beside me very seriously.

"Four years then I was gone, and when I returned . . . you should have seen her! She was beautiful. Oh, I tell you, she was a woman now, and no doubt about it.

"I fell in love! So much that I could not talk for feeling it, but never did I think for a moment that it could matter.

"But did I have a choice? Not in the least! She had not changed, that one. She was both the little girl I knew first and the older one I knew later, and more besides. She laughed at me and said that long ago she had made up her mind that I was to be her man, and so it was to be whether I liked it or not! Me, I liked it. She was so much of what I wanted that she frightened me.

"Can you imagine what that did to me, m'sieu? I was a lonely man, a very lonely man. There had been the girls of the ports, but they are not for a man of soul, only for the coarse-grained who would satisfy the needs of the moment. Me, I wanted love, tenderness.

"I know." He shrugged. "I don't look it. I am a sailor and pleased to be one, and I've done my share of hard living. More than once, I've twisted my knife in the belly of a man who asked for it, and used my boots on them, too. But who is to say what feeling lives in the heart of a man? Or what need for love burns inside him?

"My parents died when I was young and the sea robbed me of my country. In such a life, one makes no close friends, no attachments, puts down no roots. Then, this girl, this beautiful girl, fell in love with me.

"Fell in love? No, I think the expression is wrong. She said she had always loved me even when she was a child and too young to know what it meant.

"Her mother and brother approved. They were good people, and I had lived long among them. Then the mother died, Pierre was away in the colonies, and Marie and I were to be married when he returned. So we lived together.

"Is this wrong? Who is to say what is right and what is wrong? In our hearts we understood and in France, well, they understand such things. What man is to live without a girl? Or a girl without a man?

"Then away I went to sea on my last trip, and while I was gone, the war came, and with it the Germans. When I returned, I joined the maquis to get back into France. Her letters were smuggled to me.

"Marie? She was a French girl, and she worked with the underground. She was very skillful, and very adept at fooling the *Boche*. Then, something happened.

"One of the men close to her was betrayed, then another, finally, it was her brother who was killed. The gestapo had them, but they died without talking. One night I came to her to plead that she come away with me, it had been three years that I had fought in the underground, for her, almost six. But she told me she could not go; that someone close to her was working with the Nazis, someone who knew her. She must stay until she knew who it was.

"Yet try as she could, there was no clue. The man was shrewd, and a very devil. He finally came to her himself, after her brother was caught. He told her what he knew of her underground activities and of mine. He told her unless she came to live with him that I would be tortured and killed.

"He had spied upon her. He had even discovered her burning the candle before the dagger for Pierre after he was killed. He told her of it, to prove how much he knew—to prove he knew enough to find me—and she had admitted the reason.

"In the letter in which all this was told, she could not tell me who he was. He had friends in the underground, and she was fearful that learning who she was writing about, they would destroy the letter if they saw his name, and then she would be cut off from me and from all help.

"She would give me his name, she said, when I came next to Paris. He had not forced himself on her, just threatened. We had to plan to do away with him quickly. Marie said, too, that she was afraid that if the invasion came, he would kill her, for she alone could betray him; she alone knew of his activities for the Nazis.

"The invasion a secret? Of course! But when orders began to come for the underground, come thick and fast, we knew it was coming. Then, the landings were made, and for days we were desperately busy.

"We rose in Paris, and they were exciting, desperate days, and bitter days for the collaborators and the men of Vichy. Their servitude to the Nazis had turned to bitterness and gall; they fled, and they begged, and they died.

"When I could, I hurried to the flat where Marie lived. It was near here, just around the corner. I found her dying. She had been raped and shot by this collaborator two days before and she had crawled to her apartment to wait for me. She died telling me of it, but unable before her last breath to give me his name."

"And there was no way you could figure out who he was?" I asked.

"How?" He spread his hands expressively. "No one suspected him. His desire for her was such that he had threatened her, and in threatening her he had boasted of what he had done. That was a mistake he rectified by killing her.

"Only one thing I know. He is one of our little group here. She said he lived in this neighborhood, that he was waiting here more than once when he accosted her. He thinks himself safe now. My girl has been dead for some time and her body buried. She is never mentioned here.

"Mombello? He is an Italian. Picard is a chemist, and has had traffic with Germany since the twenties. Matsys? An iron foundry owner who retained it all through the war, but who was active in the underground as were Picard and Mignet."

We were interrupted then by some others coming into the café, yet now the evening had added zest. Here was a deadly bit of business. Over the next two hours, as they trooped in, I began to wonder. Which was he?

The slender, shrewd Mombello with his quick, eager eyes? That lean whip of a man, Mignet? The heavy Matsys with blue and red veins in his nose, and the penchant for telling you he'd seen it all and done it all. Or was it dry, cold Picard who sipped wine through his thin lips and seemed to have ice water for blood?

Which man was marked to die? How long would Tomas sit brooding in his corner, waiting? What was he waiting for? A slip of the tongue? A bit of drunken talk?

None of these men drank excessively. So which one? Mombello whose eyes seemed to gloat over the body of every woman he saw? Mignet with his lust for money and power and his quick knife? Or big affable Matsys? Or Picard with his powders and acids?

How long would he wait? These five had sat here for months, and now . . . now there were six. I was the sixth. Perhaps it was the sixth to tip the balance. Here they were caught in a pause before death. Yet the man who killed such a girl, and who betrayed his country, should not go free. There was a story in this, and it had an ending, somewhere.

Over the following gray days, several in a row, the conversation ebbed and flowed and washed around our ears. I did not speak privately to Tomas again but there seemed an ongoing, silent communication between us. Then, in a quiet moment of discussion, someone mentioned the bazooka, and it came to me then that another hand had been dealt . . . mine.

"A strange weapon," I agreed, and then moved the tide of conversations along the subject of weapons and warfare. I spoke of the first use of poison gas by soldiers of Thebes when they burned sulfur to drive defenders from the walls of Athenian cities, then to the use of islands of defense; a successful tactic by the Soviets in this war, previously used by the Russians defending themselves against Charles XII of Sweden.

Then other weapons and methods, and somehow, but carefully, to strange knives.

Tomas ignored me, the spider in his web, but he could hear every word and he was poised, poised for anything.

Mignet told of a knife he had seen in Algiers with a poisoned barb in the hilt near the blade, and Mombello of a Florentine dagger he had once seen.

Tomas stayed silent, turning his glass in endless circles upon the table before him, turning, turning, turning. We locked eyes for a moment and before he looked away he seemed to sigh and give a nearly imperceptible nod.

"There was a knife I saw once," I said suddenly, "with engraving on it. A very old knife, and very strange. A figure of Christ on the cross rose above a fallen snake. The religious symbolism is interesting. I'd never seen its like before, the worksmanship was so finely wrought."

A moment passed, a bare breath of suspended time . . .

"It was not the only one, I think," Leon Matsys said. "Odd things, they were used in some custom dating back to the Crusades."

He looked up, about to say more, then slowly the life went from his face. He was looking at Tomas, and Tomas was smiling.

Jean Mignet's eyes were suddenly alive. He did not know, but he suspected something. He was keen, that one.

Leon Matsys's face was deathly pale. He was trapped now, trapped by those remarks that came so casually from his lips. In the moment he had certainly forgotten what they might imply, and could not know that it would matter. He looked to one side and then the other, and then he started to take a drink.

He lifted the glass, then suddenly put it down. He got up, and his face was flabby and haunted by terror. He seemed unable to take his eyes from Tomas.

I glanced at Tomas, and my muscles jumped involuntarily. He had the ancient knife in his hand and was drawing his little circles with its point.

Matsys turned and started for the entrance, stumbling in his haste. The glass in the tall door rattled as it slammed closed, leaving only a narrow view of the dimly lit street.

After a moment Tomas pushed his chair back and got up and his step was very light as he also went out the door.

THE DIAMOND OF JERU

THE PENAN PEOPLE of Borneo say that the forest and the earth will provide for you if only you will let them. I hadn't exactly found that to be true, but what did I know? I was an American, stopping briefly in their land and ignorant of their ways.

I WAS DOWN TO my last few coins when John and Helen Lacklan arrived in Marudi. I'd come down from Saigon to make my fortune but luck had not been with me. For over a year I'd been living like a beachcomber who had accidentally found his way inland. There was a longing in me to make my way back home but no money to do it with. I'd told myself it was better to stay where I was and wait for an opportunity. Around Sarawak, in those days, a white man could go a long way just on confidence and the color of his skin.

My luck paid off in this way: a friend in the government office offered to send me some tourists, Mr. and

Mrs. John Lacklan. He had set me up, time and again, with minor engineering and construction jobs and was responsible for my having been able to keep body and soul together over the last few months. The Lacklans were an American couple, in from Singapore. They were recently married and, most importantly, they were looking for a diamond.

Now they find diamonds around Bandak, around Kusan, and near Matapura, to name only a few places. They also find some rare colors in the Sarawak River. Most so-called "fancy" stones are found in Borneo, for diamonds come in a variety of colors, including black. But after looking over the possibilities they had come up the Baram River to Marudi or Claudtown, as some called it, and Vandover was going to send them to me.

It was late in the day and the wind picked up slightly, coming in over the river to where we sat on his porch near the old fort. "I told him about you." Vandover poured cold beer into my glass. "He wants to go up the Baram. You want enough money to get you home and . . ." He eyed me mischievously. "I suspect that you wouldn't mind having one more go at the river yourself. All the better if Mr. Lacklan is paying."

We toasted my good fortune and I let the beer slide back down my throat. Cold beer had been a rare and precious luxury in my world for too long. If everything worked out I would soon be done with Borneo and on my way back . . . back to the land of cold beer.

IT WAS DARK by the time I got home. I navigated my way across the room to the bed. Without lighting a lamp I undressed and lay back under the mosquito netting.

Above my head fireflies cruised lazy circles against the ceiling, flickering, on . . . off . . . on . . .

Money to go home. A buck or two to help get my feet back under me at the worst. At the best . . . ?

I too had come to Borneo hunting diamonds. If you were lucky you washed them out of a river just like panning for gold. I had found a fortune of them, in a pool just below a dried-up waterfall. I had spent a month in the bush digging them from the river, but ultimately, the river had taken them back.

Eager to return with my treasure and careless I'd put my canoe into a rapid at the wrong angle and almost lost my life. As it was I lost the boat, the diamonds, and most of my kit. A family of Iban pulled me from the water and took care of me until I was on my feet again. I was seven weeks getting back, nursing broken ribs and a persistent fever.

What money I had left had slowly trickled away; paid out to Raj, my houseboy, and for food, drink, and quinine. I've heard it said that, in the tropics, you rented your life from the devil malaria and quinine was the collector. After my disaster on the Baram the disease had become a most demanding landlord.

But now I would have another chance. We would go upstream of the pool where I found my diamonds, closer to the source, the find would be better this time and I'd have Lacklan's fee even if we didn't locate a single stone. With the good feeling of money in my pockets I drifted off to sleep.

MY PLACE WAS a deserted bungalow that I'd adopted and repaired. When Lacklan and his wife appeared, I was seated on the verandah idly reading from Norman Douglas's *South Wind*.

They turned in the path, and I got to my feet and walked to the screen door. "Come in," I called out, "it isn't often I have visitors."

As they came up on the porch, I noticed that Helen's eyes went at once to the book I had been reading. She glanced up quickly, and smiled. "It's rather wonderful, isn't it?"

She was tall and lean, with fine thin limbs and dark blue eyes that shone in the shadow of her wide-brimmed straw hat. She had a face like that of a model from one of those fashion ads but with more character, faint friendly lines around the corners of her eyes and mouth, no makeup. Her nose was large but perfectly shaped and her jaw betrayed strength, a strength that also was apparent in her body, beautifully formed but built for a lifetime of swimming and skiing. Her skin, where it disappeared under the fabric of her sundress, looked like it was taking on a healthy shade of copper from the equatorial sun.

She had commented on my book. . . . "It's an old friend," I said, smiling.

Lacklan looked from one to the other of us, irritated. "You're Kardec?" he demanded. "I'm John Lacklan." He was tall and slightly stooped. A thin blue vein pulsed in one of his temples as he peered at me from behind glasses with round, nearly black lenses. Vandover had told me he was an administrator at one of the big government labs back in the States. Atom bombs or something.

Lacklan pushed ahead, up the stairs. "I understand you're the authority on diamonds?" The way he said "authority" indicated that he doubted it.

"Well"—I hesitated because I was well aware of all that I didn't know—"maybe. Will you sit down? We'll have a drink."

Raj was already at my elbow. He was a Sea Dyak, not over sixteen, but his mind was as quick and intelligent as anyone I've ever encountered.

"Scotch," Helen said, "with soda . . . about half."

Raj nodded and glanced at Lacklan, who waved a careless hand. "The same," he said.

When Raj returned with our drinks, Helen sat there sipping hers and watching me. From time to time, she glanced at her husband, and although she said nothing, I had an idea that she missed nothing.

"You've been up the Baram, above Long Sali?" he asked.

"Yes." I saw no reason for explaining just how far I had gone. Marudi was a rough sixty miles from the mouth and Long Sali was a village a hundred fifteen miles farther upriver.

"Are there diamonds up there? Gemstones?"

"There are," I agreed, "but they are scattered and hard to find. Most of the stones are alluvial and are washed out of creeks back up the river. Nobody has ever located their source."

"But you know where diamonds can be found, and you can take us to them. We're not wasting our time?"

In this part of the world I had become used to the cultures of Chinese and Malay, Muslim and British, all of these groups had a sense of politeness or patience bred into them. In comparison the directness and force of Lacklan's questions was like an attack.

"You are not wasting your time," I assured him. "I've found diamonds. I can't promise, but with luck, I can find more. Whether they are bort or gem quality will be anyone's guess."

"You speak the language?" he asked.

"I speak marketplace Malay," I said, "and a scattering of Iban. Also," I added dryly, "I know that country."

"Good! Can you take us there?"

"Us?" I asked cautiously. "Your wife, too?"

"She will go where I go."

"It's our project, Mr. Kardec," Helen Lacklan said. She stretched out a long, firm hand to show me the ring on her finger. An empty setting stared up at me like a blind eye. "John gave me this ring five years ago. We're going to find the stone together."

It was a wonderful, romantic notion but far easier said than done.

"You know your business best," I said carefully, "but that's no country for a woman. It's jungle, it's miserably hot, and there are natives up there who have never seen a white man, let alone a white woman. Some of them can't be trusted."

I was thinking of one nefarious old codger in particular.

"We'll be armed." His manner was brusque and I could see his mind was made up. I suddenly had a vision that both amused me and made me very nervous: John Lacklan as Henry Stanley blasting his way through the forests of central Africa. His chin was thrust out in a way that told me he was primed for an argument . . . I knew to never come between a man and his weapons, especially when he's a client. I turned to her.

"I don't want to offend you, Mrs. Lacklan, but it is very rough country, bad enough for men alone, and with a woman along . . ." I could see I was going to have to give her a better argument. "There will be snakes and leeches. I'm not trying to scare you, it's just a fact. We'll be on the water and in the water all day, every day, and with the humidity we'll never get dry, not until we get back. We'll be eating mostly fish we catch ourselves and rice. There is the risk of infection from any cut or scrape and an infection while you're upriver can kill you."

She was quiet for a moment. "I believe I'll be all right," she said. "I grew up in Louisiana, so the heat and humidity . . . well, they are only a little bit worse here." She laughed and her teeth were white and perfect. "Really, Mr. Kardec, I'm quite strong."

"I can see that," I said, and then wished I'd said nothing at all.

Lacklan's head snapped up and for a moment he glared at me. This man was deeply jealous, though Helen didn't seem the kind of person who would give him reason. Of course, that very fact made her all the more attractive.

She caught his reaction to me and quickly said, "Perhaps it would be better if I stayed here, John. Mr. Kardec is right. I might make trouble for you."

"Nonsense!" he replied irritably. "I want you to go."

His eyes narrowed as they turned back to me and burned as they looked into mine. I couldn't tell if he was disturbed about my appreciation of his wife or because I'd made her consider not going upriver with him or, and I only thought of this later, because I'd made her consider staying in Marudi where she would be on her own while we were gone.

"We will both go, Mr. Kardec. Now what will it cost me and when can we leave?"

I explained what they would need in the way of clothing and camping gear. Warned them against wearing shorts, no reason to make life easy for the mosquitoes and leeches. And then told them my price.

"I get a thousand, American. The canoes, Raj, and four Iban crewmen will run you six-fifty. Kits, food, first-aid and mining supplies, maybe another three to three-fifty. Depends on whose palm I have to grease."

"Is that the best you can do?" he objected. "You're taking more than half for yourself!"

"Look, Mr. Lacklan, I've been where you need to go. I've found diamonds . . . lots of diamonds. I lost them all but I know where they were. If it was easy, or cheap, I'd be back there working that streambed right now instead of trying to make a deal with you."

I could see something behind his glasses. A calculation taking place, like in one of the computers he probably used at work, punch cards feeding in data, tubes glowing with orange light. "All right," he said. "But how are we going to split up our take? After all, I'm paying for this expedition. I should get a piece of whatever you dig out."

I guess I recoiled a bit. Anyway, Helen looked at me in concern and Lacklan leaned back in his chair smugly. I hadn't really given it much thought. I'd figured that I'd take them there and they'd work the river in one area and I'd find somewhere else. I could see that this might lead to problems, especially once he realized that he could enlist the boat crews in the digging and panning.

"We'll split what we find, fifty-fifty," I said. "With the best stone to be for Mrs. Lacklan's ring." He was still gazing at me, one eyebrow arched above the round steel rim of his dark glasses. I gave in a little more. "I'll give Raj and the boat crews a bonus from my share."

Helen Lacklan turned to him. "That's fair, darling, don't you think?"

"Yes, I suppose it is."

We settled on a date, ten days from then, to leave. They went to the door and Helen hesitated there. "Thank you," she said graciously. "I enjoyed the drink."

They walked away toward the town.

It's maybe only once in a lifetime that a man sees such a woman, and I confess I looked after them with envy for him. It made my throat dry out and my blood throb in my pulses just to look at her, and it was that as much as anything else that made me worry about taking the job. A man needed all his attention on such a trip as this . . . and no man could remain other than completely aware of such a woman when she was near him.

Nothing moves fast in the tropics, yet despite that I had lined up the boats, boatmen, and equipment within a week. Raj was instrumental in bringing everything together as always. Even when I had no money he stuck with me. "You make better job, boss," he'd say when I pushed him to look for work elsewhere. "We don't work much but we make lots money!" I'm not sure that I'd have liked the irregular pay if I had been in his place. But Raj seemed to come alive when trying to figure out something he'd never done before and the jobs we got were always a challenge of one kind or another.

Around Marudi I caught sight of John and Helen once or twice, it wasn't a big place. He was not one to take his attention from whatever he was doing to nod or say hello but once or twice I got a smile from her. Then for several days in a row I didn't see either of them.

The day before we were supposed to leave I spotted the Lacklans coming up the path from town. And something—their postures, the way they walked?—told me the plan had gone wrong.

"Kardec?" There was a bluster in his manner that seemed ready to challenge any response that I might have. "We've made other arrangements. I'll pay whatever expenses you've incurred so far." Helen did not meet my eyes.

"Other arrangements?" The answer was evasive. "You've decided not to go?"

"We'll be going, but with someone else. How much do I owe you?"

Frankly, it made me angry. The deal had been all set, and now . . . I stated my price and he paid me. Helen merely stood there saying nothing, yet it seemed she was showing a resentment or anger that I had not seen before.

"Mind telling me how you're going?"

"Not at all. But it doesn't really matter, does it?"

His very arrogance and coolness angered me, and also to have all my excellent planning go for nothing. "It matters a great deal," I told him. "There's one other man that would take you upriver who is trustworthy, a native named Inghai, and he's down with a broken leg. If you go back in there with another native, you're a fool!"

"You're calling me a fool?" He turned on me sharply, his eyes ugly. For a minute I thought he was going to swing on me and I'd have welcomed it. I'd have liked nothing so much as to help him lose a few teeth.

Then I had an awful premonition. Jeru was up to his old tricks again. "Look," I asked, "is it a native? Did he show you a diamond? A big stone? Something about twenty carats?"

They were surprised, both of them. "And what if he did?"

"You tried to buy it and he wouldn't sell. Am I right?"

"So what?"

"If I am right, then this was the same fellow who guided two parties up the Baram before, one group from Kuching, one came over from Sibu. None of them ever came back."

"You're implying that he had them killed? For what reasons? For the diamonds they found?"

"Diamonds mean nothing to him. I believe he used the one stone he has to lure them upriver so he could murder them for their possessions."

"Nonsense!"

"He was an old man, wasn't he? With a deep scar on his cheek?"

Their expressions cleared. "No." Lacklan was triumphant. "He was a youngster. No older than your houseboy."

So they had switched, that was all. The trick was the same. The stone was the same. And they were not the first to do it. It had been done by the Piutes in Colorado, eighty or ninety years ago, with gold nuggets for bait.

"Have it your own way, Lacklan. It wouldn't matter if you were going alone, but you're taking your wife along."

His face flamed and his eyes grew ugly. "My wife is my own concern," he said, "and none of your affair."

"You're right, of course, only I'd do a lot of thinking before I'd let bullheadedness risk my wife's life. Risk your own all you like."

"Nonsense!" Lacklan scoffed. "You're just trying to scare us to keep our business."

So they walked away and I could see Helen talking

with him as they went up the road toward town. Whatever she said, I heard him answer angrily.

WHAT THE LACKLANS were getting into had a certain smell to it. It was the smell of an old reprobate named Jeru who was hidden out upriver with a small band of renegades. Jeru was reputedly the last of the old-time Sea Dyak pirates and the story was that he had fled upriver from the Brook militia and was living like a tribal chief with a group of followers who had been outcasts from their own longhouses. No one really knew if this was true but it was known that Jeru had appeared in the cities along the coast and lured people, usually foreigners, into the backcountry. And once they disappeared they never returned.

It had been years since the last time this had happened and the story had been spreading that Jeru might be dead . . . nonetheless, it had me worried.

THAT NIGHT THERE were four of us there on the verandah of the resident officer's bungalow. Van apologized for the deal with the Lacklans falling through. "There's no accounting for people, I suppose."

I didn't mention John Lacklan's hair-trigger jealousy and the fact that I might have helped arouse it.

"I've got another possibility for you though," he said. "There's a canal job. It cuts through from one of the creeks about a mile above town. Hasn't been used in years but Frears wants it open again. I told him you could do it, bossing a native crew. It'll pay almost what Lacklan would but it will take longer. We'll get you home yet."

"Van," I said, "I'm worried. Their story sounded so familiar. Remember Carter? That was two years before my time, but he came down from Hong Kong on a vacation. He met some native on the coast who had a big diamond and wouldn't sell it. The native agreed to show him where there were more. He went upriver and was never heard of again.

"A few months later, the same thing happened to Trondly at Kuching. There was also that story about the two who went up-country from Sibu and Igan, and another from Bintulu."

"That was old Jeru. Word has it he's dead."

"Maybe. But this sounds like the same come-on. And it sounds like the same diamond. Huge thing, high quality, native won't sell but he will take them to where he found it. If it's not Jeru then it could be someone else playing the same game. If a native finds a gemstone and sells it, he spends the little he got, and that's the end of it. This way that stone represents a permanent income. Rifles, ammo, blankets, trinkets, food, clothing, tools, and trade goods . . . and every few months a new supply."

"Fantastic idea." Vandover rubbed his long jaw. "It sounds like that old blighter of a Jeru, or his ghost. Maybe he figured he was getting too well known to keep doing it himself."

"It could be," Fairchild agreed. "You'd better call Kuching on it. Sounds to me like a police matter."

My scotch tasted good, and the furniture on the verandah was comfortable. Turning the glass in my fingers, I looked over at Fairchild. "Using your outboard? It is a police matter but I don't think it can wait. That fathead can fry in his own juice for all I care, but I'd not like to see Helen Lacklan trapped because of him."

"Use it," Fairchild assented. "If Rector wasn't due in tomorrow I'd go with you."

BY DAYLIGHT THE native huts and banana and rubber plantations were behind us. Only Raj accompanied me. Although a Sea Dyak of the coast, his mother was Penan, one of the forest people. His uncles had occasionally taken him off on long migrations following the wild sego harvest and he spoke a number of the inland dialects. He knew of old Jeru as well and liked none of what he'd heard. From a *blotto*, the hollowed-out tree trunk that is the native boat, he learned from three natives that the boy and his two white clients were six hours ahead of us.

Raj sat up in the bow of the canoe, on the other side of my quickly loaded supplies. The strong brown stream was muddy and there were occasional logs, but this outboard was a good one and we were making better time than Lacklan would be making. I did not attempt to overtake them because I neither wanted them to think me butting in nor did I want their guide to know I was following.

I was carrying a Mauser big-game rifle, a beautiful weapon. It gave me a comforting feeling to have the gun there as I watched the boat push its way up the Baram. The river trended slightly to the south-southeast and then took a sharp bend east, flowing down from among a lot of eight-thousand-foot peaks. Mostly jungle, yet there were places where stretches of tableland waved with grass. This was wild country, rarely visited, and there were small herds of wild pigs and a good many buffalo.

We avoided villages as the necessary social activity that would accompany our stopping would slow us down considerably. I made camp on a small island cut off from shore by a few yards of rushing water. We slung our hammocks, draped mosquito netting over them, and slid into our dry clothes to sleep.

As WE PRESSED on the river narrowed and grew increasingly swift. We were well into the Kapuas Mountains, the rugged chain that is the spine of Borneo and terminates in the thirteen-thousand-foot dome of Kinabalu. The air was clear and the heat less oppressive at the increased altitude. At times we pushed through patches of water flowers miles long and so thick it looked like we could have gotten out of the boat and walked.

I put on a bit more speed for the motor would soon be useless in the rocks and shallower rapids and I wanted to be able to catch up when necessary. We ascended cascades, the easier ones with the outboard howling at full throttle, the more difficult by shoving and hauling the boat through torrents of water streaming between the rocks and over low falls.

I wondered how the Lacklans were making out; I couldn't really imagine John Lacklan in chest-deep water pushing a canoe ahead of him. And though she might be willing to try, I couldn't imagine him allowing Helen to do such a menial job. How they were negotiating the river was a question that worried me because if neither of the Lacklans were doing the physical work, then there had to be more natives helping out besides just the one guide. The crew of the *blotto* had not mentioned the number in the crew and I'd heard no mention of an outboard like mine . . . that meant oarsmen and probably two boats to split the weight of both the men and supplies into manageable amounts. So that meant four to eight natives, I hesitated to guess at their tribe and if they were from Jeru's group, that was probably a moot point.

"Raj," I called forward, "how many boats do you think they have?" We were stopped in a shallow sandy part of the stream at the top of a rocky cascade. I was bailing the water from the canoe and Raj was carefully wiping off our equipment. We were both soaking wet.

"Two, boss."

"And how many men on paddles, four?"

"Six. Two paddle in each boat, one rests."

I looked up at him narrowly. "How the hell do you know that?"

"I can see them!" He grinned at me and pointed . . .

In the distance, through some trees and across the river, two boats were turning into the shore. I sloshed around for a better look. It was midafternoon and it looked like they were going to camp. There were two big dugouts each with four people in them and as I watched the men in the bows jumped out and dragged the hollowed-out logs up onto the shore. In one boat was a slender figure in a wide straw hat, that must be Helen, and in the other sat John Lacklan, wearing a cork sun helmet. For an instant his glasses flashed in the sun as he rose from the boat.

"We'd better pull out here and camp ourselves. I don't want to be seen."

We hauled the boat to shore, built a smoky fire to keep the sand flies away, and as Raj began to make camp I took my field glasses and crept along the bank to a spot across the river from the Lacklan camp. I slid in behind a decomposing log covered in plates of bracket fungus and focused my binoculars on the beach across the river. Two of the tattooed natives were cooking a pot of what had to be rice and another had walked upstream and dropped a line into the water, patiently waiting for a fish to strike. The three others had vanished into the forest. Lacklan was sitting on the sand jotting notes in a book or journal and Helen was tying up their hammocks. I put down the glasses and glanced around. My spot was back within the tree line and relatively dry, even so it wouldn't be long before the leeches got at me. The air over the river was thick with brightly colored butterflies, some as big as my hand. They fluttered in and out of patches of sunlight like continuously falling leaves. I squinted through the lenses again. Lacklan looked comfortable on his small crescent of beach. The fisherman and one of the cooks looked to be in their mid-thirties, hard capable men, though small. Each had a *parang* at his side and near the kit of one of the natives that I assumed had gone into the jungle was an old single-barreled shotgun, its stock held together with copper wire.

The fisherman looked up suddenly and the two other members of the boat crews came wandering back into camp. With them was a slight younger man whose posture was somehow more assertive than the older men, tough as they might be. This would be the boy I'd been told about. He wore a button-down shirt that was missing most of its buttons and was tucked into an old pair of dungarees. The clothes were castoffs from someone down in the settlements but he wore them with a certain flair. Unlike the others, he did not have the traditionally pierced ears. Over his eyes he had on a set of sunglasses, the type that aviators tended to wear. The returning men sat close around the rice pot and the fisherman returned to his chore.

I was getting set to pull back into the trees and make

my way back to our camp when I saw Helen walk away from the spit of beach across the river. She had obviously been waiting for the other men to come back, because as soon as they sat down she walked over to the place where Lacklan was sitting and spoke to him, then she picked up a small pack and walked away.

She headed downriver and in a moment was out of sight, lost in a tangle of vines and tree trunks. I slid back a ways, then moved through the forest on my side of the river, trying to catch up. If she went too far I was afraid she'd see our camp. Unless the two of them ran into trouble I was not of a mind to try explaining what I was doing there to a paranoid little tyrant like John Lacklan. I moved downstream as quickly as I could without being seen. Noise wasn't a problem here because the river would drown out anything short of a gunshot.

I dodged back toward the water and crouched down. I couldn't see anything. Then, I noticed some movement on the bank upstream of where I had been looking. It was a piece of fabric moving in the breeze. The khaki blouse that Helen Lacklan had been wearing hung from a branch near a calm backwater. Now, what . . . ?

Alarmed, I almost stood up. Then there was a bursting spray of silver as Helen's head appeared above the surface and shook the water from her hair. She swam for the bank and I would like to say that I was gentleman enough to avert my eyes when she climbed out but that in all honesty would not be true.

She fumbled with a pile of gray fabric on the sand that I now realized was the pants that she had been wearing, and then splashed back into the water with a bar of soap in her hand and began to wash.

The idea of a bath reminded me that I might not get

one myself until I got back to Marudi, unless I could share Helen Lacklan's soap. An entertaining but not very realistic thought. Before I was tempted to watch when Helen climbed out again and got dressed, I slipped away from the riverbank and made my way back to camp.

THE NEXT DAY, travel was harder. We had to creep our way slowly upriver, cautiously coming around every bend, always alert for the chance that John Lacklan's canoes had stopped or that there would be a stretch of river long enough for them to look back and see us trailing them. To make matters worse, although they were heavily loaded, there was an extra man to switch off paddling in each of their boats and in the rougher spots all of them, including John and Helen, helped out. We had the outboard but I was afraid to start the damned thing because of the noise. It had enabled us to catch up but now we merely had its weight to contend with.

Mountains loomed up around us and the way was narrower. Somewhere, hidden in these peaks, I had heard there were huge caves. We were nearing the place where I had originally found my diamonds, a long day or two and we'd be there.

That gave me an idea. What would happen if I dropped into the Lacklan camp some afternoon and let them know my old diamond placer was nearby? John would almost certainly object but I wondered if he wouldn't be tempted to take a day or two out to see what might be found there. With luck I could derail the whole plan, if there was a plan at all. I leaned forward to speak to Raj. "Jeru's camp, does anyone know where it is?"

"No, boss. Very far upriver." He paused for a moment. "If I was Jeru I would not be on river. Police mans, they do not like to get out of the boat. They do not like jungle because their rifles are no good."

He was right, the limited light, limited range, and plentiful cover in the forest did reduce the effectiveness of firearms considerably.

"I have heard on the coast that the pirate Jeru went to a longhouse where all mans dead of sickness. He took longhouse for those who follow him. They are all very bad. They take heads, even now they take heads."

If Borneo is famous for one thing it is its native head-hunters. As romantically gruesome as the practice is it has been dramatically curtailed in recent years, at least along the coast. In the interior, the severed heads of tribal enemies are still kept for their magical power, and a freshly taken head has the most power.

The sun was just touching the rim of the mountains when Lacklan's boats tucked into the shore and Raj and I stopped paddling and let the current carry us back downstream about half a mile before finding a place to camp.

As was becoming my habit I took my field glasses and started upriver, out of camp. At the last moment Raj's voice stopped me for a moment.

"Boss?" I turned to where he was standing by the fire. "If there no trouble, we hunt for diamonds, okay?"

"Sure, Raj," I said. "We're up here, might as well." He was right. I'd given up the canal job to come after the Lacklans; we were using up the supplies I'd bought for them and nothing lucrative awaited us back in Marudi. On the day after tomorrow I would drop in on my favorite tourists and find out if I could get them away from their guides. Then we'd see if we could dig some diamonds. I didn't want to return from this fool's errand with nothing. On top of it all I had a sixteen-year-old

Dyak kid who thought I was just enough off my rocker that he had to remind me occasionally to keep my eyes on the target.

THE RIVER WAS wide here, and though I was farther away than the first time I had spied on the Lacklans, the water was slow enough that I could hear some of what was going on in their camp. There was a clank of pots as one of the older men laid out his cooking supplies, the hard bark of an ax as someone back in the forest chopped wood.

Helen Lacklan sat in a patch of sunlight reading a book. From its bright red cover and small size I recognized it as a popular guidebook on Indonesia and Malaysia. John Lacklan sat in the boat cleaning his gun. It looked from this distance to be a bolt-action Winchester; with an ebony cap on the forestock I figured that it was one of the fancier models. From its long barrel and scope and the fact that the Lacklans came from New Mexico I assumed that it was his prized gun for deer or bighorn sheep . . . whichever, it wasn't the best weapon for the jungle. This was a place where speed and maneuverability counted most. As I watched he carefully depressed the stop and slid the bolt back into the rifle, then pressed five long cartridges back into its magazine. For the first time I was glad he was armed.

He tucked his cleaning supplies into a small pack and then stalked over to a mound of supplies and set the rifle down. He paused and made a comment to Helen but she barely looked up. He stood there, tension building up in him, for a moment, but then broke off and went to the other end of the camp. I realized that I was witnessing an argument or the aftermath of one.

Over the wash of the river, slow and quiet at this point, I heard a man's voice raised in anger. Then John Lacklan was standing over Helen yelling and gesticulating wildly. His thin face was turning a dark red under the fresh burn he'd been getting, and although I couldn't understand the words, his voice was hoarse. Suddenly, Helen threw her book at him and leaped to her feet. The red-covered guidebook bounced off of his shoulder and he backed up a step. She advanced toward him and it almost looked like she was daring him to hit her. They paused and he backed away. In some way, she had called his bluff.

I squirmed back into the shadows of the forest. At the last minute as I headed back to my camp I noticed the flamboyantly dressed Iban boy and two of the men from the boat crew standing in the tree shadows across from me. The older crewmen had averted their gazes with expressions of shock and embarrassment on their faces; such outbursts of emotion as they had just witnessed were not considered at all acceptable in Malaya, but the boy studied them carefully and with a knowing smirk from behind his dark glasses.

I LAY IN MY hammock that night wondering what would happen tomorrow afternoon when I faced them again. It was going to be awkward and I was going to have to act like there was never any problem between us. I didn't know if they would accept the story I was going to make up about deciding to use their supplies to look for diamonds, but it probably made more sense than what I was actually up to.

Had I really followed them hoping for the worst so that I could step in and rescue Helen Lacklan and make her husband look the fool that I took him to be? And if that was true how much of a fool was he? He had chosen another guide to keep his wife and I apart. I had thought the idea amusing at the time, then I'd thought it dangerous. I had had one short opportunity to appreciate Helen Lacklan and I doubted if she had given much thought, if any, to me. But here I was, following them through the bush and rapidly developing a case that would do a sophomore proud on a married woman I hardly knew. Paranoid he might be but I was beginning to guess few people called John Lacklan stupid.

Well, I would follow along for one more day, until we reached my old diamond placer, then I would do my best to divert them from whatever this Iban boy had planned. If they didn't want to follow me I would leave them to their destiny.

For better or for worse, I thought, I was back upriver. Even though it had cost me all the supplies that Lacklan had paid for, supplies that I might have sold, and losing the canal-cleaning job. I realized I'd better make the best of it. This was what I'd wanted all along: another chance at the diamonds. I drifted off to sleep as a soft rain began tapping at the shelter half strung over my mosquito net. Somehow I'd gotten what I'd wanted all along.

A HIGH-PITCHED CRACK OF thunder brought me awake just before dawn. I lay listening, waiting for the echoes to roll back from the mountains or down the river canyon. Through some trick of the rain or the forest vegetation the echo didn't come. I thought about returning home with the money from a diamond find in my pocket . . . I thought about returning home with enough to explain my having disappeared into the Far East for almost two years.

An hour later when the gibbon monkeys began to noisily greet the sun, Raj rolled out of his hammock and made up some breakfast. We didn't take long to get packed. I walked up the riverbank, the water running slightly higher because of last night's rain, just far enough to see if the Lacklans had left camp yet. Their boats were gone so we pushed out into the stream and dug our paddles in against the current.

Around us the forest released great plumes of steam as the sun's heat cut into the trees. Trunks, some two hundred feet tall, leaned out over the water leaving only the narrowest slot of sky overhead. In the jungle itself one rarely could see more than sixty yards without the view being blocked by the growth. Even the tops of the trees were obscured by a much lower canopy with only the massive trunks hinting at the true size of the forest giants.

We pushed past the Lacklans' campsite from the night before. They must have had an early start because their fire was cold, not even a thin line of smoke rising from behind the piled-up rocks they had used as a hearth. The shadows between the boles of the trees behind their camp were black as night, the few penetrating rays of the morning sun overshooting this area to glance off the emerald leaves of the higher forest.

Suddenly I stopped paddling. The canoe lost momentum and Raj looked around quickly.

"Boss? What's wrong?"

Hidden under the trees, deep within the shadows but not quite deep enough to keep the morning light from revealing it, was the stern of a *blotto*.

"Turn in!" I commanded, and we made for the shore.

Leaving Raj to haul our boat out of the water I grabbed up my gun and splashed up onto the rocky beach. I hit the darkness of the forest and froze, letting my eyes adjust.

The two dugouts rested in narrow lanes between the trees, back along the shore were drag marks from where they had been pulled out of the water and across the mud flat to the jungle. Everything, supplies, mining equipment, camping gear, everything but the paddles were gone!

Could they have headed away from the river to a legitimate place to placer for diamonds? Had they hidden the canoes or just pulled them away from the rising waters of the river? I walked back out to their campsite.

The fire was dead and there was no sign it had been doused with water. They had not had breakfast.

Then I saw it. Shining brightly in a patch of sunlight; the answer to my questions . . . the worst answer to my questions. A long thin cylinder of brass. I picked it up and turned it over. It was stamped .30-06. The empty cartridge casing smelled powerfully of gunpowder even in this dampness. It had not been thunder I had heard just before dawn. It had been John Lacklan's rifle!

I HAD TRACKED ANIMALS while hunting in Arizona and Nevada but following a trail in the jungles of Borneo was a different experience altogether. Luckily, the Lacklans and their captors had left camp after the rain stopped and they were not trying to hide their trail. The fact that there were ten of them heavily laden with the goods from the canoes helped also.

Raj and I were burdened only with water, light packs, our *parangs*—Raj's being more along the lines of a traditional headhunting sword, thus larger than mine—and my rifle.

They left occasional slip marks in the mud, breaks or machete cuts on protruding branches and vines. The trail was not hard to follow. But another problem soon became apparent.

Away from the river we found ourselves climbing a tall ridge cut by many small streams. The trail then followed the top of the ridge as it switchbacked along between the Baram River on one side and a deeply cut canyon on the other. Visibility was so limited and the landscape so broken that although I could easily follow the trail or backtrack my own path I had no idea which direction was north, south, east, or west. I could barely tell which way was up- or downriver unless I could see the water close up and by now we were hundreds of feet above the banks. To make matters worse it was dark, dark as deep twilight, and the humidity had increased tremendously. I was overheated, slick with sweat, and making far too much noise as I pushed along the trail.

Raj was doing better than I and it wasn't only because of his youth. Although he had lived his life in Marudi he often went with his uncles to the forest and had some of the natural ease of the jungle peoples. He seemed to be able to instinctively place his feet in the most solid spots whether we were climbing over rocks covered with wet moss or skirting a deep bog of leaf mold. I dropped our pace to the point where I could follow him more exactly, and in relative silence, we pressed on.

By noon we seemed no closer to our quarry and I was down to the last of my canteen. We stopped by a brook that cascaded down the dim mountainside and had some dried pork while I boiled water on a tiny gas stove I had bought for the Lacklans. I didn't always purify my water when I was in the bush but this would be a disastrous time to get sick so we waited while the stove hissed and the pot finally boiled. Raj harvested a vine growing nearby and after pounding it with a rock he made a paste that we rubbed on our legs. *"Kulit elang,"* he said. "Will help a couple hours, leeches don't like." We pressed on.

THE DIM LIGHT under the tree canopy was fading and the black cicadas had started their rasping, throbbing chorus when we reached what seemed to be our destination. We were on another river, much smaller than the Baram, and tucked back in the trees at the edge of a gravel bank was a decrepit longhouse. Dugouts were pulled up on the bank and all around the main dwelling stretched a wasteland of squalor such as I had only seen in the native villages that had become ghettos because of their closeness to the large coastal cities.

The last of the sunlight was striking the overgrown slopes of the nearby mountains and the river valley was in shadow but I could barely make out overgrown fields and collapsed farm huts behind the ring of trash that had been ejected over the years from the longhouse. In most cases a Dyak longhouse is a fascinating structure; built up, off the ground and out of the flood plains on stilts, sometimes as much as twenty feet high, the interior of the building is twenty feet from floor to ceiling and often over one hundred feet long. Its roof and sides are made of a kind of native thatch or sheathed in tin, where available. Although surrounded by farming huts and storehouses it is the communal dwelling for the entire village.

This longhouse was one of the smaller ones and obviously very old. One corner was drooping dangerously on poorly repaired stilts and in this and other areas the verandah had all but given way. Across the distance I could hear harsh laughter and a slight strain of *sapeh* music on the wind, lights could be seen coming on through the doors and breaks in the walls.

Raj edged closer, he seemed jumpy, his fingers toyed with the hilt of his *parang*.

"You were right, boss." He whispered, although we were a good half mile away. "This is the longhouse of *Tuan* Jeru."

I was surprised by his use of the term *"Tuan,"* which indicates respect, and by his nervous whisper. I had seen Raj stand calmly by and thrust the same *parang* he was now nervously tapping deep into the side of a boar that attacked one of our workmen on a construction job. He had then pivoted like a matador and finished the enormous animal off when it turned to attack him instead. He had been barely fifteen at the time.

"Are you afraid of going in there? Tell me why?" I wasn't feeling too good about it myself but I figured I better know as much as possible.

Raj's chin came up and the dying light in the sky glinted in his eyes. "I am not afraid of any man!" he stated flatly. "But it is said that *Tuan* Jeru is a *bali saleng,* a black ghost, that he has killed many mans and taken their blood to bless the buildings of the English and Dutch and now for the oil companies."

"Do you believe that?" I demanded. "You've worked with me on many buildings. Have you ever seen a foreigner take the time to make a sacrifice of blood or anything else?"

"No . . ."

I wasn't sure that this was really the right argument to use and I actually had a fair amount of respect for the beliefs of Raj and his people, but if he went in there scared, witch doctor or not, Jeru would take advantage of the situation.

"How many do you think are down there?"

"If the stories are true, twenty mans, maybe ten womans, maybe more."

"What else do the stories say?" I asked.

"The mans of *Tuan* Jeru are *sakit bati;* they are killers and rapists from the oil camps and towns on the coast. No village would have them. They are collectors of blood and they take heads to make magic."

"Do you want to stay here, guard our backs?" I gave him a chance to get out with honor.

"I will go with you, boss," the boy said.

"Good. Now, what do you think is going on down there?"

"I think they have big *arak* party. Everyone get very drunk. They have all new trade goods, shotgun shell, fancy rifle. I think we wait."

"What about the Lacklans? Will they be all right?"

Raj paused, he wanted to tell me what he thought I wanted to hear but he knew I would press him for the truth. "I don't know, boss," he said. "I think maybe they cut off man's head. The woman, I don't know . . . These people, they not Iban, not Kayan, not Kelabit," he named off the three major tribal groups, "they something different now . . . outlaws, you know. I bet they get drunk like Iban though, you'll see."

I hoped so, because outlaws or not I was betting that just like a normal village they had plenty of dogs and roosters. The typical longhouse celebration in Sarawak was a roaring drunk and I hoped that was what they were building up to because otherwise we weren't going to get in there without raising an alarm.

I wanted to be ready when the moment came, so we moved in closer, carefully waded through the rushing waters of the stream, and circled away downwind of the skeletal silhouette of the longhouse. We settled down just inside the secondary tree line and waited to see what would happen. The noise from inside was getting louder and I was sure that Raj had been right about them working themselves up to an all-night drunk. I just wasn't sure what was going to happen to John and Helen . . . or when.

They might be dead already and I couldn't wait much longer without trying to find out. I decided to split the difference; wait another hour but if I heard a commotion I'd go in with the rifle and hope for the best. If there were twenty men in the longhouse, at least five would have the cheap single-shot shotguns that were common in the backcountry of Borneo. Someone in there had possession of Lacklan's deer rifle and certainly there would be a full complement of spears, blowpipes, and machetes. My only hope was to get in and get as many of them covered as possible before anyone thought to grab a weapon. It wasn't much of a plan; get in fast, get out fast, and put my confidence in the local *arak*'s potency.

Now, in my experience, *arak* has the punch of the best (or worst, depending on your expectations) moonshine. It seemed to have the chemical properties of torpedo fuel or the infamous "Indian whiskey" that was made in the old days in Oklahoma. One shot would make you stagger, a couple more would make you stupid. Imbibing further could leave one blind or even dead. Waiting for a level of intoxication that would give me an edge was a risky business.

About a half hour later two men staggered out on the verandah and hung over the railing. They alternated between what sounded like telling jokes and laughing hysterically with being violently ill. After three or four rounds of this odd combination of social interaction they parted, one going back into the light and noise of the longhouse, the other slumped, snoring, against the railing. The sound of the crowd inside had taken on a harsher tone and I figured I'd better move in before something bad happened . . . if it hadn't already.

Touching Raj on the shoulder I slipped past him and made my way down toward the river. We crept in past the outer circle of trash and one of my worst fears came suddenly true.

Three dogs rushed us out of the darkness under the longhouse. Barking and snarling they rushed through the moonlight like dark missiles, low to the ground . . . missiles with pale flashing teeth.

I took a swipe at the first with my rifle butt and connected heavily. It backed off yelping. Raj moved quickly, snatching up the smallest of them by grabbing a fist of flesh on either side of the dog's neck just below the ears. He spun in a tight circle with the frantic beast snapping in his outstretched arms and let go, hurling the dog far out into the river. I clubbed with my rifle again, and drawing his *parang*, Raj swatted an animal with the flat of the blade. The two remaining dogs backed up, growling but no longer willing to attack. I was just beginning to curse our luck and wonder if we should either hide or charge the ladder to the longhouse when a door above us slammed open and a man staggered out onto the verandah and called out into the night in what sounded like Iban.

Instantly Raj answered in an angry adult tone I'd never heard him use before. The man above us muttered something and then whistled sharply and called out some kind of command. We stood frozen in the darkness as he wandered back inside and closed the door.

Raj heaved a sigh of relief and I turned to peer into the darkness where he was standing. "What, in the name of God, was that all about?" I demanded.

He laughed, a giddy, semihysterical cackle. "I told him to call off his damn dogs!"

WE WERE A moment getting our wind back, then we worked our way under the longhouse and edged toward the back where, because of the slope of the gravel, the stilts were not so long. The ground beneath the building stank from garbage and worse. Above us feet tramped rhythmically on the ancient plank floor and shrill voices cried out. Toward the back the floor was low over our heads and then I was boosting Raj onto the verandah, and swinging up myself. Moving carefully on the weathered boards we eased up to a crack in the wall and peered in.

The light was probably dim, but with our pupils dilated by hours in the darkness it was blinding. Raj backed up for a moment and I blinked and squinted. In the center of a seated group a dancer leaped and whirled, his moves theatrically depicting . . . something, I couldn't tell what. There were men and women in the room, but fewer women than I had thought. Bottles, mostly old beer and wine, were lying about. Some were obviously empty, others still in use. I knew from past experience that they no longer held beer or wine; they had been filled and refilled time and again with *arak*.

The dancer disappeared from view and another took his place. He was a thin old man but he moved with an energy that, while not youthful, was surprisingly vigorous. He whirled and stomped, spinning a *parang* over his head with a glittering flash of steel. I suddenly saw that the dark area that I had noticed on one side of his face was not a shadow or a tattoo but a deep and twisted mass of scar tissue. He mimed climbing onto something higher than himself, something that moved unsteadily. He fought, he carried something away. He was raiding a ship or a boat . . . this must be Jeru! Not only was he here, still alive after all these years, but he was telling his story in a dance.

I bent to Raj's ear. "Is that him?"

The boy nodded, his body alive with fear and excitement.

"You watch our backs," I told him. I didn't want him working up a scare by watching this man that he believed to be a witch and I didn't want both of us to be night blind.

When I turned back to the crack Jeru was hacking his way through the forest and then something . . . he mimed men marching and everyone laughed. He was showing them he'd been chased by soldiers, paddled up a river, cut off men's heads with his *parang*. He stepped out of sight for a moment and came back with a long Japanese military rifle. He shook it in the air and then after handing it to someone, mimed cutting off what I surmised to be the Japanese soldier's head. He pointed to the roof with a harsh cry and, crouching, I could see a cluster of dark spheres hanging from the rafters. Severed heads. No doubt the unfortunate Jap was one of them.

The story continued with Jeru finding something in a stream. He held the imaginary something up to the light, turning it this way and that. He reached for his neck and pulled a leather strap off, over his head. In a setting or basket of leather there gleamed a stone.

This was it. The huge diamond that he had used for many years to lure men upriver, never to return. A diamond of fabulous size and quality, so the story went; from where I was all I could tell was that it was large and wrapped in braided strings of leather. It glowed rather than flashed, for this was a raw stone with none of the facets of a cut one, but there was a white fire hiding deep within it.

The old man took on a posture of humility, he moved stiffly, portraying a sense of age that obviously was not his natural state. Again, he got a laugh. He was showing the stone to someone, offering it, walking away as if disinterested, then leading them on. He took an old stove-in pith helmet from the place it hung on the wall and wore it for a moment as he paddled an imaginary boat. Then he was himself again and beating his companion to the ground he drew his *parang* and cut off the man's head.

The audience was silent now and a sense of tension penetrated the wall and clutched at my heart. Even Raj, eyes turned to the night, could feel it and he moved closer to me, his hand on his knife.

JOHN LACKLAN STAGGERED into view, pushed along by the rough shoves of the boy who had been his guide. His hands were tied, his clothing torn, his body scratched and bruised. How badly he had been treated I didn't know; the trip through the jungle might have left him in the condition that he was in. I admired him in that moment, though, for he held his head high, in his eyes was the hollow look of fear but he didn't beg, or cry, or even tremble. He was keeping himself together although I thought I could tell that it was a near thing.

Without looking away I ran a shell into the chamber of my rifle and set the safety. I wasn't at all sure about my original plan of barging in and spiriting them away; there were easily as many shotguns in the room as I had expected plus the Japanese rifle and the boy carried Lacklan's Winchester over his shoulder. Not only were there more guns than I would have liked but several were cradled in the hands of Jeru's outlaws, held casually but ready for use.

The boy stepped in behind Lacklan and kicked the back of his left knee, knocking him to a kneeling position. Lacklan started to get back up but the boy unlimbered the rifle and poked him hard in the kidney with the muzzle. John Lacklan gave a choking cough of pain and collapsed back to the floor. Old Jeru whirled his *parang* and then tested the edge against his thumb.

"Find me a door!" I whispered to Raj. "Damn quick!"

Now there was a commotion somewhere in the room. "Get off me!" I heard Helen call out. Then she lurched into view, a portly Iban trying to drag her down by one arm. She shook him off; he was surprised, I think, by that same physicality that had caught my attention. She was bigger than he was and lithely powerful.

"Stop it! You stop this!" she yelled at them. Raj was back tugging at my sleeve but the boy, sunglasses pushed up on his forehead, stepped in quickly and pressed the rifle barrel against Helen's throat . . . even if John Lacklan got his head cut off I wasn't going in there if it risked Helen's getting killed.

The boy yelled at her in Iban, then in English. "Sit, missy. You sit or I kill you." He jabbed at her with the gun barrel. "Everybody die, you don't sit down."

She didn't even move.

"You can't kill him. Take our things, our money. You can't kill him!" she cried.

"We're Americans, damn it. Let us go or you'll regret this." John's voice wavered.

In my travels around the world I've noticed that identifying yourself as an American never helps, it just makes the locals get violent or want more money.

The boy shrugged, "We kill Englang, Dutch . . . America, who cares." He suddenly spoke in his own tongue for a moment and everyone laughed. Old Jeru the hardest.

"You don't want John's head." Helen spoke in a manner that let me know she wanted all to hear. "I know that Dyak tribesmen only take the heads of powerful enemies, of warriors. The head of a strong man is magic but a weak man . . . a weak man is nothing. My husband is not a warrior, he's not even a strong man. Did he walk here? No. You had to carry him over the last hill . . ."

"Be quiet, Helen!" John hissed. "Don't make this any worse than it is."

But she ignored him. "He's a scholar. What are you going to say? There are the heads of the Japanese soldiers, we fought their machine guns with knives but we won. There is the head of the man who read books, aren't we brave!"

The boy turned to Jeru and they spoke quietly for a moment. Others in the crowd seemed a bit nervous. The bottles started being passed around again but with them there started a low mutter of conversation.

Jeru spoke and the boy turned to Helen with a smirk. He spoke in Iban to the crowd and there was scattered laughter but it sounded forced. He said to her, "We cut off head; see what happens. No magic, we throw out!"

"No!" she cried and started to say something else but John bellowed at her.

"Helen, shut up! Just shut up!" He was almost crying in fear or frustration. He lurched to his feet and the boy smashed the butt of the rifle into the pit of his stomach. I was ready to move and Raj was even tugging me toward the door when Helen threw herself on the boy. Jeru knocked her to the floor but John charged him. With his hands tied all he could have done would have been to knock Jeru down but the old man deftly rapped John Lacklan on the head with the butt of his *parang* and Lacklan went to the floor, out cold.

Jeru hawked and spat. Then with a further growl of disgust he dragged Lacklan into a corner and dropped him. He motioned to the boy and the young man led the quietly sobbing Helen to the same spot, then they both stepped forward to the seated group and took up *arak* bottles.

I got the feeling that there had been a reprieve of sorts and I'd better make the best of it. Pulling myself away from the scene beyond the crack in the wall I let my eyes readjust to the darkness. When my vision started to come back I motioned Raj ahead of me. "Let's get on the ground, we've got to get to work."

We dropped down under the longhouse and I made my way back to the spot where the broken floor sagged toward the mud. This whole corner of the building was ready to collapse and I figured that it would be unlikely that anyone would be using it for anything. I shrugged out of my pack and dug out my mountaineer stove. I pumped up the pressure and fired it. Using the light from the flame I found a place where several broken logs and a piece of the *attap* thatch wall all lay together. I wedged the stove into the broken wood just under the thatch and let the plume of fire bite into the thatch.

I grabbed Raj and led him back to the spot where we had climbed onto the longhouse verandah.

"You stay here. When I come back I'm going to be coming fast, if anyone needs help getting off the porch you help. If you run into any of Jeru's people . . ."

"I know what to do, boss." He tapped the hilt of his *parang.*

"Right. If I'm not with you go straight up the hill and follow the crest east, okay?"

I pulled myself up onto the aging boards again, and careful to walk along a crosspiece so as to make less noise, I slid up to the wall and took a fast glance through the crack. Heavily tattooed bodies moved back and forth, momentarily obscuring my vision. Nothing much was going on but more people were up and around. Well, that couldn't be helped.

I moved along the wall to the door that Raj had found. I breathed deep and waited for the fire to catch. Suddenly there was an excited burst of Iban from inside the building, the sound of running feet and a breaking bottle. It was only then that I smelled smoke. There was a rush of feet and a door in the front of the place crashed open. I couldn't see what was happening but I figured someone was going for water. I didn't move until I heard the crash of the floor giving way.

I HIT THE DOOR and came into the big room with the Mauser up, sling around my left arm. The long room was filled with smoke and the back, where I had started the fire, was listing. Flames were beginning to take the roof. An older man stood right in front of me with a bottle in his hand, he seemed to be standing back, bemused, while the main crowd moved toward the blaze. I dropped the rifle from my shoulder and clipped him on the side of the head as I went past.

A woman tore by me and in the confusion didn't even notice that I was there. Someone seemed to have fallen through the burning floor and that was fine with me. I dropped beside the Lacklans pulling my knife.

Lacklan twisted around in panic and kicked at me with both feet as I reached for his arms. Helen got it first.

"John, stop! It's help."

I grabbed one of the kicking feet and cut off the ropes that bound them, when they had tied his feet I didn't know. She extended her hands to me and I quickly swiped the blade between them catching the bindings by luck. Then there was the roar of an explosion and a scattering of bird shot tore into my boot and ankle like a swarm of angry bees. I dropped the knife and turned bringing the rifle up.

A short, tattooed native struggled to reload his crude shotgun. Others stood behind him frozen, but they were all looking at me. Suddenly one of the men in back came up with the Japanese rifle, I didn't even know I had him in my sights until I squeezed the trigger.

The concussion in the long room was even louder than the shotgun. The rifleman went down and all hell broke loose. Men and women scattered, two shotguns belched fire in the light of the roaring flames, throwing huge plumes of white smoke. I wasn't hit but burning paper and powder smoldered in my clothes. I put three shots into the crowd as fast as I could work the bolt and then I was pushing Lacklan toward the door and praying that Helen was following. In my last look the room was an inferno of flame, burning thatch falling from the ceiling. Around the cluster of heads hanging from the rafters wasps swarmed in panic, driven from their nests in the empty eyes and mouths by the heat and smoke.

We crashed out into the fire-streaked night. Lacklan stumbled and a man dropped a bucket of water and came at me with a knife. I deflected it with my rifle barrel and kicked him hard on the hip. He fell and I gave him another in the face. The gun was empty and I had no time to reload.

I pulled Helen past me, pointed to the end of the verandah, and yelled, "Go! Find Raj!"

I turned, knowing that to run at that moment would be the end of me. Three men rushed forward in the shifting light and I went to meet them. I clubbed and punched and kicked and bit. One cut me across the back. Then I was on the wooden floor slamming my knee into his midsection. My rifle flopped uselessly, its sling still entwined with my arm.

There was a flare of light and an explosion of wood. One of my attackers threw himself off of me and there was Jeru, standing over me holding a pistol so ancient it must have come to Sarawak with the first white rajah. I twisted sharply, Jeru fired again, missing. He struggled to cock the enormous relic, twisting the cylinder by hand. I scrambled sideways, put a knee into someone's stomach; suddenly I was fighting with one of the men who attacked me again. We struggled, turned, and then hit the railing of the verandah. With a splintering crash at least twenty feet of it let go and we were falling.

In midair I pushed away from the man I was fighting, hit the ground, and rolled. My rifle, still bound to my arm by a twist of the sling, rapped me on the back of the head. My vision went gray but I heard Jeru's gun bellow and the hard bite of black powder hit my nostrils. He was leaning over the railing peering into the darkness, the torn side of his face a dark knot of rage. I grabbed my rifle and ran underneath the burning longhouse.

Flames licked along the floor above me. The structure groaned as walls twisted and buckled. In back, the corner where I had started the fire was dark. Someone had managed to put out the flames, a futile gesture for the fire had spread to the rest of the building.

I made it to the darkness and looked back. The dim forms of Jeru's men began to appear in the firelight. Some ran off toward the river, probably for more water, but four or five of them started forward under the building, coming after me.

I'd had just about enough. I snapped four fresh cartridges into the magazine of the Mauser and dropped a fifth into the chamber. I backed up farther into the darkness and brought the rifle up. I took aim at the first man, then shifted to one of the pilings beside him. I fired and splinters flew. They dropped to the ground but then came on, worming their way forward through the debris under the longhouse. The first had a shotgun and the second man carried a long blowpipe with a spear blade bound to one end. I squinted, fired, and the heavy bullet took the blowpipe man along the top of the shoulder as

I had intended, then burned the back of his calf. He screamed, and I ran, blindly, uphill into the jungle.

I NEARLY TOOK A header into some kind of hole, leaves whipped my face, and I slowed down. I cursed myself for not killing both of the men I'd shot at under the long-house. I had a total of nine bullets left, three in the gun and six jingling in my pocket, I couldn't afford to waste them.

I had to find Raj and the Lacklans. If they hadn't made it out I'd have to go back . . . I wasn't looking for-ward to suicide.

I cut left along the hillside, heading in the direction they would have taken if they had gone straight up the hill. I stopped to catch my breath and found I couldn't keep my knees from shaking. I squatted down, sucking air, and felt the prickles of adrenaline recede from my limbs. I had shot a man. Several actually, but one of them I had killed for sure. Unbidden, a phrase that my father had used came to mind, "If you fool around with a bandwagon, you're liable to get hit with a horn." It wasn't as amusing as it had been but I was realizing that it didn't only apply to me getting into this situation, it applied to those poor chaps I'd shot, too.

Those men down there had lived as traditional Iban and Kayan or whatever. Some, perhaps many, had trav-eled to the cities and oil fields to try a different kind of life. But somewhere, something had gone wrong. Instead of staying on to collect their paychecks, instead of re-turning home to farm and fish, they had come here. In a country that was virtually without violent crime they joined with a man who made a living robbing tourists and diamond hunters. A man who was continuing to take heads not of his enemies in war, a practice, if not what I would call civilized, then at least honored by Iban tradition.

Helen had thought quickly back there. She'd confronted that old witch doctor with his own hypocrisy, given other circumstances it might have been funny. It was something else too, though. Some of those men in there had believed in what she'd said. There was magic in the head of a brave enemy. To take a man's head was, in a strange way, actually an honor. If you had a vision of yourself as a warrior you didn't kill tourists. Helen might have planted a seed of doubt in a few of the men down there. Either old Jeru might have fewer followers come morning or they'd all be coming after me, the more honorable enemy.

I started up the hill again, going slowly in order to make as little noise as possible. In the dark phosphorescent mushrooms glowed dimly. The sounds of insects and animals filled the night, covering the noises that I made but also covering the sounds of anyone who might be following me. It felt like hours since Raj and I had the fight with the dogs but I could still occasionally see the moon through gaps in the trees; I didn't know what time it was but it had been headed down as we approached the longhouse. Higher and higher I climbed, pulling myself along using the trunks of the smaller trees and rocks and handfuls of undergrowth. I was exhausted, my legs were shot, and my arms and lower legs were covered with leeches.

Finally I reached the bare crest of the ridge and looked out across a vast panorama, dimly lit by the setting moon. I turned east and started climbing again.

When the landscape was left in blackness, when the

last of the silver light had faded from the sky, I rested. I carefully cleaned the leeches off by feel. One leg was puckered with bird shot but most of it had not penetrated my boot. I stopped myself from touching it. I knew Borneo, it was going to get infected and the less I scared myself the better. I got up and pressed on and it was only a few hundred yards farther when I heard voices ahead.

It was Raj and the Lacklans, and they had collapsed at the foot of a rock outcropping, half dead from exhaustion. "Raj?" I called out; I didn't want him taking a swipe at me in the dark.

"Boss?"

"Yeah. Hold on, I'll be over there in a minute." I picked my way across the rocks toward them.

It was a subdued reunion. We were all dead tired from running and climbing over a thousand feet of mountain. I'm not sure that Helen and John had realized what was going on yet. They were just happy to be away from Jeru's longhouse and all in one piece.

Not long after I got my breath back, I began to notice that it was cold. Now, there's not too many places on the island of Borneo where you could say that but we were well over eight thousand feet and we were all dressed for the heat. To make things worse we were worn-out and the clouds were beginning to pile up against the mountain range, I could feel the moisture on my cheek and lips and when I looked up the stars were dimmer. Raj's teeth were chattering and the Lacklans were huddled together strangely; though Helen was curled up close to him, John was positioned almost as if he was trying to pretend she wasn't there. Well, whatever they were going through was their problem. I was worried about the cold.

"Let's get up," I told them. "We're going to go on a bit farther."

They looked at me uncomprehendingly, but Raj stumbled to his feet and picked up our packs; he had brought mine along from the longhouse somehow.

"Mr. Kardec?" Helen was sitting up. "I don't know if my husband can . . . he hurt his leg before we got to that village."

"Let me see it," I said. "We have to go on. We need some shelter or at least a fire and some food."

Lacklan pulled away from me as I squatted down beside him. "I can make it. I don't need help." Then he said, "I don't need your help."

WE HELD TO the ridge and we kept climbing. I needed someplace to camp and this was probably not the place to find it but the slopes on either side of us were too steep to negotiate in the dark, especially given our condition. I was beat, every muscle hurt, and my body begged to stop moving. John had turned his ankle and could walk only with difficulty but he and Helen were managing the altitude the best; after all, they lived near Santa Fe, over a mile above sea level. Raj was cold and something else was bothering him but he wasn't ready to talk about it. He helped John Lacklan along and kept his mouth shut.

Something was going on between John and Helen; she had tried to help him at first but he was having none of that. Finally, she gave up and he was on his own for a while but then, because he was stumbling badly, Raj offered to help and he'd accepted. Helen came up to me in the dark; she took my hand and pressed the haft of my knife into it. I returned it to its sheath.

"Thank you," she said. After that she walked with me more and more, and while I liked that in some ways, it disturbed me too.

During a pause to rest I got Raj aside and questioned him on what went on before I joined them. "Nothing," he said. "They just act like they having big fight but they don't fight, they don't talk."

"Did they ask what we were doing here?"

He laughed softly. "Oh, yes. I tell them that you come to save them from the *bali saleng*."

For a Dyak, a people who tend to tell you only what you want to hear, Raj is sometimes too straightforward.

We came to the rocky upthrust of another peak, its blackness vaguely defined in the starlight, but there was shelter here, a bowl of rocks and, within it, the black mouth of a cave. From the sounds in the jungle below I could tell it was still a couple of hours until dawn. Huddled just inside the entrance we rested and I emptied my rucksack onto a rock. I used some peroxide on my leg and poured some across the cut in my back, then got up. With the empty bag I headed back into the night.

"Mr. Kardec, where are you going?" Helen's voice spoke out of the darkness.

"To find some fuel, I'll have to go down into the forest a ways."

"Are we still in danger?"

"I don't know. Come morning I expect they'll be after us."

"And they'll find us, too," Lacklan mumbled softly.

"But will they come up here?" she asked. "I read that

many of the tribes feel that there are spirits in the mountains, especially the peaks, and will never go there."

I had heard the same. The natives were very aware of the *Toh*, the spirits of the forest and mountains. An area that was rarely visited was often considered to have dangerous *Toh* and was therefore avoided. It was Sarawak's version of our own self-fulfilling fear of the unknown. The high mountains were reputed to be the home of powerful *Toh*.

I didn't reply as I thought about it. I hoped she was right.

"So, maybe this place is safe. At least that's what I read." She was looking for some reassurance but she didn't get it from her husband.

"You and that confounded guidebook," he snapped. "We don't know that will work!"

"Well if that confounded guidebook is where she learned about headhunting, it probably saved your life." I said I'd had enough of Lacklan's attitude and he wasn't a potential client anymore. "Jeru wasn't even going to sharpen his *parang*."

"I'm glad you enjoyed that at my expense. I'll have you know that the weapons I've made could blow this miserable island off the map."

I was amazed. He was fuming because she had told that bunch of renegades he wasn't a warrior. He was an egomaniac and a fool. Or maybe just a brilliant man who was so small inside that he had become lost in the forest.

"Mr. Lacklan," I told him. "I don't know if you're suicidal or exactly what your problem is but I look at life this way—an adventure is something you return home to tell about. If you don't make it back, it's just an exotic funeral. Be happy Helen did what she did. I am. If she hadn't I might have died because I was stupid enough to try and help you."

"And why did you come after us? Because you are the good Samaritan? Or because you are after my wife?"

"John!" Helen flinched and I could see that he'd aimed that barb more at her than me.

"I don't know," I said, "but this late in the game I'd be a fool to try to figure it out." I grabbed up the knapsack and headed out into the darkness. I started down the slope and Raj came scrambling after me. I hadn't planned on his coming but was just as happy; I knew he would be very uncomfortable if the Lacklans decided to continue the fight.

The purple light of predawn was just coming to the sky as we made our way along the mountainside about one hundred feet above the forest. I was headed toward an area below us that I had glimpsed from the ridge; it was lighter in color and I was sure it was a rock slide. Where it had hit the trees we might find some downed wood.

Sure enough, it was a slide. A huge lip of rock had flaked off and gone crashing down into the jungle. Underneath the scar were the dark mouths of several caves, probably connected to the cave above where the Lacklans waited. Thirty feet into the tree line we found all the wood we wanted, picking out the dry pieces was easy for little of it was damp. I figured that we were so high that we were above most of the rain that soaked the lower elevations, either that or we were just lucky.

We gathered as much wood as we could fit in our packs and turned to go back up the mountain. For an instant Raj froze and so did I. Between ourselves and the brightening sky was a moving, flickering black cloud. There were bursts of darkness against the sky, a sound like water rushing up a shallow sandy beach; wings, thousands and thousands of wings. The dawning sky was darkened with bats. A thin cloud rising over the jungle, they coalesced into a dense riot of swooping, dodging confusion directly over us. Their wings cupping the thin air they streamed toward the mountainside. Under the scar of the fallen brow of rock, they flew, pouring into the cave mouths just above us.

Then from above us I heard a thin scream. Raj and I looked at each other, then I grabbed up my rifle and took off up the hill. The gun and the wood and the previous twenty-four hours of clambering up and down hillsides slowed me down. However, we made it to the top without having to ditch our loads and I eased around the rocks, rifle at the ready.

The Lacklans were well out of the circle of rocks and away from the cave, crouched behind the rocks and harried-looking. I almost laughed but couldn't summon the energy; a miniature tornado of bats fluttered and turned around the tunnel entrance, the last stragglers of the mass from below using the back door.

I'd had enough alarms for one day. Leaving Raj to start a fire in a small pocket in the rocks I went back into the cave and refilled my pack with its supplies. I ducked and shook my head as the last of the bats flew past but I got my rope, stove fuel, first-aid kit, and most importantly the little food I'd been able to bring along.

We warmed ourselves silently around the fire; the Lacklans didn't seem to feel like talking and I didn't feel comfortable conversing with them either. I shared our dried pork and heated two cans of condensed soup over the fire. It wasn't much and it wasn't very good but it was all I had and we needed anything we could get. When we were done I put out the fire. I hated to do it as we were all chilled but the sun was coming up and our smoke might have been visible. In the treetops below us the gibbons began their whooping cries, staking out their territory for the day.

"We're going to have to keep going," I said. "We're not safe until we're back on the river and we won't be safe even then." I looked in their eyes and was afraid of what I saw.

John, with his leg barely capable of bearing his weight, was nearly finished. Helen would go on without complaining but she couldn't go farther without rest. Raj could do what was necessary, he'd shut his mind down and go at it like a Chinese coolie, he'd survive if he could, regardless of the suffering. I hoped I could do the same but I wasn't sure.

"We'll be okay," I said, standing up. I looked out across the high ridge and the forest and clouds that swept away in both directions and I realized we weren't going to make it.

All we needed was rest. All we needed was to move slowly and accommodate John's injury. All we needed was time and I saw then that we were out of time.

Off down the backbone of the mountains, three miles away but plainly visible as the sunlight poured across a low shoal of clouds to the east, was a group of men. They were coming up the ridge toward us and there was an easy dozen of them . . . more men than I had bullets, more men than I cared to engage even with my pockets full of ammunition.

"Raj!" I called. "I think we've got trouble." Instantly

he was beside me, John and Helen not far behind. I pointed. "Is that Jeru?"

"Yeah, boss."

"What are we going to do?" This question was from Helen but there was no panic in her voice. She stood there, dirty, clothing torn, having had no sleep, and little rest . . . it was an honest question, she was ready to get started.

"I hold them off as long as possible. You get out of sight; retreat into the cave. Take my rope, I believe there's a way out down below."

"You believe?" John was belligerent.

I shrugged. "With any luck they'll be satisfied with me and they won't know where you've gone."

"You'll be killed!" Helen grabbed my arm and turned me toward her. Her eyes searched mine, for what I didn't know; it was one of those moments when men and women have different things in mind.

"I might be. With luck I can kill enough of them that they decide I'm not worth it."

John shifted on his bad leg. "How much ammunition have you got?"

"Nine rounds."

"She's right, you'll be killed."

"You got a better idea?"

Nobody said anything. The men on the distant ridge were getting closer.

I turned. "Let's start by getting out of sight." I ripped open my pack and pulled out the bottle of stove fuel. Going to where we'd had our fire I picked up a fair-sized branch and blew on the white coals at one end. Ash flew away on my breath and deep in the darker cracks flickers of red glowed. I poured a bit of the fuel on the branch right up near the sparks and I blew again. In a minute I had a flaming torch.

The cave angled down, turned, and then dropped off abruptly, a black shaft corkscrewing downward. It would be a nasty climb but that in itself might save us. Bats skittered nervously on the ceiling, they didn't like the smoke from my torch.

"Raj," I called. "Get me my rope." He wasn't behind me, only the distant forms of the Lacklans peering in from the entrance. "Raj?"

I cursed and tossed my torch down the shaft. It fell, bounced, flared, and went out. In the darkness I could see reflected daylight deep in the shaft. Well, the lower cave *was* a way out, that was something in our favor. We could run, or they could. It wouldn't be much of a lead, but it would hold off the inevitable an hour, three? It would hold off the inevitable for them, not me. I headed back out of the cave. "Damn it, Raj, where's my rope?"

When I got to the entrance he was holding it in his hands but that was all. He looked at me strangely.

"Come on!" I insisted. We had to get him and the Lacklans started or this would all be for nothing.

"I stay with you, boss."

"This is no time for loyalty or bravery or whatever it is, Raj. If you don't go with them they'll never find the boats. Get going!"

He shuffled forward, hesitated . . . he was scared! Scared of the cave.

I moved over to him and spoke softly, "What's wrong?"

"I go. But this not good. You think *Toh* big joke. I hope you right."

Suddenly I had an inkling of an idea. Maybe we could get out of this, all of us. If it worked it was going to take brains, and luck, and courage. But I'm better at courage when I think I've got a chance.

"Raj, if you're worried about the spirits, what about them?" I pointed out at the ridge. Jeru and his men were out of sight, negotiating a low spot, but I doubted we had more than half an hour. "Is Jeru afraid of *Toh*?"

He frowned. "Maybe . . ." Then he looked up at me, squinting. "His mans, they afraid, I think. Jeru he make *obat,* a spell, he say he *bali saleng.* He say what he does okay, but all mans still afraid."

"Good," I said. "Come with me." I snatched the coil of rope out of his hand and I ran to get my stove fuel.

"What's going on?" John Lacklan grabbed at me but I avoided him.

"I've got an idea!" I said and tossed him my rifle. "If they get within five hundred yards shoot once, I'll be back."

"Tell me what you're up to, damn it!"

I didn't tell him, I was already headed down the slope toward the mouth of the lower caves. I hoped he would show good judgment because as soon as I was over the edge I could no longer see the oncoming men.

RAJ AND I put our backs into it. We pulled three big partly rotten logs up the hill to the caves, both of us straining like a team of oxen on the rope. We laid a fire just inside where the tunnels converged and got it burning, then tossed every branch we could find up into a pile alongside it. We worked, getting everything into position and doing a fair job of it until I heard the boom of the Mauser.

I tossed the fuel bottle to Raj and took off running. "Don't do anything until you hear me whistle," I yelled back. I hit the mountainside and scrambled, arms and legs tearing at the earth and rock. I must have had my second wind but my muscles felt strange and hollow, it was not a good feeling.

I paused just under the lip to get a lungful of air then, hugging the ground, my leg throbbing, I slipped over the top. John was down inside the pocket of rocks where we'd had our fire and Helen was right behind him.

"What's happened?" I whispered.

"They're close. I shot and they went to ground."

"Okay. Give me the rifle. Stay clear of the cave mouth but if anything happens to me get back in the cave and stay there no matter what happens."

"What are you going to do?"

"Put on a show," I said and taking a deep breath, I stepped out.

"*TUAN* JERU! COME out and face me!" I stood there, the Mauser slung diagonally across my back. I would have rather left it with Lacklan but if they hadn't seen it on me they would have suspected an ambush. As it was I'd be lucky not to get a bullet or a blowgun dart.

After a moment there was a motion in the brush and the slight form of Jeru appeared with the boy in the aviator glasses at his side. They started for me across the last few feet of the rocky ridge. Jeru wore a wood-sheathed *parang* on one hip and the ancient pistol on the other. The boy carried Lacklan's rifle. They stopped a short distance away.

"You speak poorly," sneered Jeru, commenting on my fragmentary Malay.

"I speak this language no better than I have to," I said loudly, my main audience was Jeru's followers, "but I speak the language of the spirits well. My *obat* is as good as yours in this place. Go away from here. Go and leave us to ourselves. The gods of this mountain do not want you!" I pinched my fingers together, placed them between my lower lip and upper teeth, and whistled as loud as I could.

The boy took a step back and shook his head in shock. He brought up the long rifle but I didn't move. I tried to calmly stare him down . . . I was sure I was going to die.

Then there came a sound from the cave like a sudden rush of wind. In the boy's glasses I saw reflected a momentary flash of orange flame in the tunnel mouth. Raj, on my signal, had poured the entire bottle of stove fuel on the fire.

With a rush like a great wave crashing on a reef the bats vomited from the cave. They came piping and flapping blindly into the morning sunlight driven by the smoky fire that Raj was now stoking with all the wood he could find. With the lower entrances to the tunnels blocked by smoke and flame they sought the upper opening in numbers that were terrifying to behold. They were a great disoriented black cloud that shot from the hole in the mountaintop as if from a high pressure hose. They fluttered and dove and poured into the sky above our heads.

Jeru crouched in surprise and I stepped in and before the boy could pull the rifle's trigger I slapped the barrel aside and kicked him in the groin. He went down, leaving me with the gun, and I saw two of Jeru's men racing away down the ridge, their tattooed backs glistening with the sweat of exertion and fear.

I turned to the old man and with a whining growl he

drew his *parang*. He cut at me with such speed that I barely could move in time, shoving the rifle sideways into the blade. There was a ringing of steel and Lacklan's gun was torn from my grasp, falling to the rocks at my feet. Jeru reversed and I leaped back, the blade slicing air near my belly. He was fast; for an old man he was awfully fast.

I got my knife out and took a cut at him but he thrust along my arm, his blade leaving a trace of fire and a line of blood . . . he was better at this than I was. Better by a long shot.

He stabbed and cut. We fought back and forth there on that high ridge with a clear sweep of forest below us on one side and the white glare of the clouds beneath us on the other. And then he cut me, the knife grazing my chest, the blade momentarily catching on the Mauser's leather strap, and it was all over. His blade snagged and I caught his arm and was behind him in one movement. It was my fight then and for him it was hopeless. As good as he was with a knife, he was an old man. I was stronger than he was and I was heavier too. I broke his arm but there was no give in him so I clipped him on the jaw, a punch that would have put away a much bigger man, and I'm not proud to say that I broke that too.

He was unconscious. I was down, the world spinning around me, my chest bloody, my arm bloody, too bloody. The boy scrambled away, sobbing. There was the sound of gunfire. Helen was standing over me working the bolt on John's fancy rifle. Brass flew, bright against the sky. Men fled downhill, disappearing into the trees.

They broke open the first-aid kit, poured something in my wounds that hurt more than the knife had. Raj was getting me on my feet and my head was clearing; I had never really been out, just gray for a while, like I'd held my breath too long.

We were at the edge of the slope when I remembered. I pulled away from Raj's hands and went back. Jeru moaned when I turned him on his back. He looked at me, eyes no longer full of anger but neither was there fear. He waited for me to do whatever I had to do. It took only a moment.

"Thank you, *Tuan* Jeru," I told him. "Go to a village where no one knows you, live your days as an old man should. Cross my path again and I'll take *your* head and hang it on my porch."

I left him there, bats circling above, and I staggered off after the others. We went down past the cave where the fire still burned but was now low and dying. Then we were in the jungle and soon it was darker and hotter.

IT WAS TWO days back to the boats. Two days of struggle and pain. John Lacklan and I setting our pitiful pace. His leg was swollen and my cuts and the places where the buckshot hit me had become infected. As much as I disliked the man he had a certain kind of toughness. It was the toughness of the littlest kid on the team or perhaps the brainy child that nobody liked . . . but he wasn't going to let that leg stop us. I had to make myself keep pace with him.

The boats were intact. In this I was surprised for I was sure that even if we got to the river without another fight I thought they would have stolen or destroyed the boats. I guess with their burned longhouse, several dead, and wounded leader they had enough to deal with. Raj took us downriver in the bigger dugout with Fairchild's motor jury-rigged to the stern. On the trip downriver I got sicker and they tell me when I arrived in Marudi I was unconscious and running a high fever. For the second time in two years I had returned from upriver barely alive. But this time I had the difference.

I LAY IN BED and got better. Vandover came down and brought the doctor. He shot me with penicillin, cleaned my wounds and dusted them with sulfa, then they sat on the verandah and drank the last of my scotch. I stared at the peeling paint on the ceiling.

She came to visit me an hour before the mail boat left for Singapore. The room was closed and dark but sunlight blazed through every crack in the shutters. She was dressed in a white traveling outfit and as she stood in the doorway she was a vague figure beyond the patched mosquito netting. I sat up.

"Mr. Kardec?" She came into the room, taking off a large pair of dark glasses. "I just came to thank you. You saved our lives." I could see that the wedding ring, with its empty socket, was missing from her finger.

I wanted to make some kind of smart comment but I didn't really know what it would be. "How's your husband?" I asked.

"He's got a bad sprain. All that walking we did made it worse. We're leaving today . . ." She stopped for a moment, holding on to some kind of feeling, I couldn't tell what.

"He won't talk to me," she said. "It's like I did something unforgivable back there but I don't see that I really had a choice."

"I think he's trying too hard to be a strong man." I thought this was right, it felt right. "Something inside of him is desperate. He's barely holding on to something but I don't know what it is. He'd of rather died back there than be saved by you."

"John was so brilliant. You should have seen him when we met. They all listened when he spoke, Dr. Teller, even General LeMay."

"This is a different world, Helen. You knew that, I could see it. Sometimes when there is nothing between you and nature you find out things you wish you didn't know . . . sometimes when you look at yourself you are smaller in the scheme of things than you thought you were." I shifted, sitting up a little farther, leaning back against the headboard. "There's been a time or two when I found myself in the middle of a dark forest praying for God to save me. You have to accept your fear and survive. It's not about your image of yourself, it's just about getting back in one piece."

"I guess so," she said.

We were both silent for a moment. Then she straightened up, all business.

"We should pay you, at least what we were going to for guiding us. We owe you that, and more."

I carefully moved the mosquito net aside and swung my feet to the floor. The cut under my bandages pulled tightly and it burned, but it was a healing pain.

"I don't want any money," and then before I could take it back, I said, "I did it for you. I don't want to lose that."

She crossed the room and bending down, she kissed me. For just a moment she held my face in her hand. "What will you do?" she asked. "How will you ever get home?"

I didn't really wonder how she knew this, I expect Vandover or Fairchild must have told her . . . it didn't matter. I sat straighter, trying to feel the strength in my body. It was there, not much, but coming back. I opened the nightstand drawer.

"Never underrate a man who has lived as I have, Helen. Just as a man who has lived as I have would never underrate a woman like you." I grinned. "I'm not proud and I do what it takes to survive." I held out my hand and opened it to show her. It was ironic, when I had gone into the forest for personal gain I had returned with nothing, but when I had gone intending to help others somehow I had been rewarded.

On my palm lay, in a setting of woven leather, the thong broken from when I had torn it from his neck . . . *the diamond of Jeru!*

SECRET OF SILVER SPRINGS

<hr/>

IT WAS AN hour after sunup when Dud Shafter rode the roan gelding up to the water hole at Pistol Rock. The roan had come up the basin at a shuffling trot, but the man who waited there knew that both horse and man had come far and fast over rough trails.

The waiting man, Navarro, could understand that. The trail this rider had left behind him lay through some of the roughest country in the Southwest, a journey made no easier by the fact that several Apache bands were raiding and their exact location was anyone's guess. He glanced appraisingly at the sweat-stained, sun-faded blue shirt the red-haired man wore, noted the haggard lines of the big-boned, freckled face, and the two walnut-butted guns in their worn holsters.

As the man drew up, Navarro indicated the fire. "Coffee, señor? There is plenty."

Shafter stared down at the Mexican with hard blue eyes, and when he swung down he kept the horse between them. He stripped the saddle from the horse and rubbed it down briskly with a handful of desert grass, then walked toward the fire. He had not even for an instant turned his back on the Mexican.

"Don't mind if I do," he said at last.

Squatting, he placed his cup on a flat rock, then lifting the pot with his left hand, he poured the cup full of scalding black coffee. Replacing the pot alongside the coals, he glanced across the fire at Navarro and lifted the cup.

"Luck!" he said.

After a moment, he put the cup down and dug in his pocket for the makings.

"You make a good cup of coffee," he said.

Navarro lifted a deprecating shoulder and one eyebrow. His eyes had never left the big man's carefully moving hands. It was simply something to say; Navarro was a good cook, coffee was the least of his achievements . . . and he had other abilities as well.

The Mexican wore buckskin breeches, hand-tooled boots, and one ivory-butted gun. His felt sombrero was fastened under his chin with a rawhide thong.

The sound of another horse approaching brought the heads of both men up sharply. Navarro touched his lips with his tongue, and Dud Shafter shifted his weight to face the opening into the basin.

A buckskin horse came through the opening at a walk, and a man sat that horse with a double-barreled express shotgun across his saddle bows. The man was a Negro.

"Howdy!" Shafter said.

"Join us," Navarro added.

The Negro grinned and swung to the ground. He was

shorter than either of the others, but of such powerful build that his weight would have equaled that of Shafter, who was a big man in any company.

He wore a six-shooter in an open-toed holster, but as he dismounted and moved up to the fire, he kept his shotgun in his hand. He carried his own cup, as did the others, and when he squatted to pour the coffee, the shotgun was ready to his hand.

Navarro smiled, revealing even white teeth under the black of his mustache. These were men of his own kind. After a moment or two, he took a burlap sack off his saddle and began to cook. Slowly he assembled a meal, such a meal as the two strangers had certainly not seen in many weeks. Tortillas were heated on a flat rock, lean shredded beef was cooked with peppers and onions, frijoles that he had soaked since he had camped the previous night were split into three portions. As Navarro worked his magic he carefully watched his new companions.

"It takes money," he suggested, "to travel far. I know where there is money!"

Dud Shafter's chill blue eyes lifted in a curious, speculative glance. "It takes money. That's the truth."

"If you're travelin'"—the other man wiped off his seamed black hands—"and you know where there is money for the takin', you're a lucky man."

"One man cannot get this money," Navarro hinted. "Three men might."

Dud Shafter let the idea soak in, staring into the fire. He picked up a mesquite stick and thrust it into the coals, watching a tongue of flame lick greedily at the dry wood.

He looked around casually. "Would this money be nearby?" he asked.

"Sixty miles by this road, but by a way I and only a few others know, it is but twenty. There is an Apache path through the mountains. We could ride over this trail, make our collection, and return. We could get water and some rest here, then head for the Blues."

"You don't think others know this trail . . . others we might have to worry about?" Dud asked.

Navarro shrugged. "Who knows. But we will be careful. At the right moment we will hide our tracks. Also, in going there we will learn the path well. It is a chance that I believe in."

Dud Shafter rolled the idea over in his mind. He was not above driving off a few steers, especially if he didn't know whose they were. But this sounded like crime, straight from the shoulder, out and out theft. Not his style, but he *was* going to need money. There was trouble down his back trail and a winter with no work in his future.

"There is an express box," Navarro informed him, "on a stage. In that box are two small payrolls . . . small for payrolls, but good money for us. More than seven thousand dollars. Before the stage arrives at Lobo station, it passes through Cienaga Pass. That is the place."

After a moment Shafter nodded and then the Negro did too. He didn't really like the idea but he was willing to go along. What he did like, however, was the Mexican's food.

NAVARRO LED OFF because he knew the route. Dud Shafter and the Negro, who had said his name was Benzie, followed. Navarro led them into the cedars along the mountainside back of Pistol Rock, then crossed the hill and cut down its side into a sandy wash. Seven miles farther, he led them into a tangle of mesquite, cat-claw, and yeso. Steadily, their trail tended toward the blank face of the cliff, yet when they reached it, Navarro turned south for two miles, then entered a canyon. The canyon ended in a jumble of rocks, and beyond the tumbled pile of boulders was the cliff.

"Looks like you miscalculated," Dud said. "There ain't no way through there."

"Wait, *compadre*." Navarro chuckled. "Just wait!"

They rode on into the gathering dark, weaving a way among the boulders toward the face of the cliff.

The walls to right and left closed in, and the darkness shouldered its shadows toward their horses. Then a boulder-strewn, cedar-cloaked hillside lifted toward the sheer wall of rock, and the Mexican started up. Within only a few feet of the cliff, he turned his horse at right angles and started down a steep slope that led right up to the face. Concealed by the boulder-strewn hill was a path that slanted steeply down, then turned to a crevasse between two walls of rock. It was a trail that no man would ever suspect was there.

Between the walls, so close together their stirrups grazed the rock on either side, it was dark and cool. There was dampness in the air.

"It is like this for miles," Navarro said. "No danger of going astray."

They rode on and Dud nodded in the saddle, his horse plodding steadily forward. Finally, after nearly an hour's ride, the crevasse widened into a canyon, and they still rode on. Then the canyon narrowed to a crevasse again, and they passed by a trickle of water. When they had gone only a little way farther, Navarro halted.

Dud Shafter, startled from a half sleep, slid a gun into his hand. He glared around in the darkness.

"There is no trouble," Navarro said. "The trail is there." He pointed toward the black mouth of a cave. "We will enter the cave and each of you will go exactly seventy-seven steps from the time your horse starts onto the rock floor, it will be very dark. Then you must turn left. You will see an opening covered with vines, push them aside and ride through."

Navarro led the way and they rode into darkness. The echoes from the other horses' hooves made it hard for Dud to count and he discovered it was better to plug his ears with his fingertips and feel the footsteps of his horse than to try to follow the confusing sounds in the cave. At seventy-seven he reined over and momentarily dragged his left knee against the rock.

"Guess that Mex has got a bigger horse than mine," he grumbled.

Now the footfalls of their horses splashed in shallow water, then there was a dim light ahead and they pushed the vines aside and emerged into the evening air. A small trickle of water ran out from under the cover of vines and soaked the ground around their horses' hooves.

Navarro turned to face them. "We will stop here," Navarro said. "And I will tell you the way back in case I should be killed. You must follow the streambed in the cave and let your horse take thirty steps—no more.

"Turn your horse sharply right and ride straight ahead, and after you have been riding into darkness for a few minutes, you will see the trail down which we have come."

"Suppose I take more than thirty steps?" Shafter asked.

Navarro shrugged. "You will find yourself in a great cavern, the floor is crumbling and filled with many holes. One man I knew made that mistake, and his horse and he went through the floor. We heard him scream as he fell. He fell a long way, señor."

"I'll count the thirty steps," Shafter said dryly.

They bedded down and slept until dawn, then rolled out. Dud was the first one up, collecting greasewood and a few pieces of dead cedar for a fire. When he had the fire going he looked around and took stock of their position.

They had camped in what appeared to be a box canyon, and they were in the upper end of the canyon with a lovely green meadow of some thirty acres spread out before them. Not far away was a ruined adobe house and a pole corral.

When they had rested and eaten another of Navarro's meals, they mounted and the Mexican rode into the meadow. The ruined adobe stood among ancient trees and beside a pool, crystal clear. Dud glanced around with appreciation.

"It's a nice place," he said thoughtfully. "A right nice place!"

In a wooden beam over the adobe's door was carved a brand. "PV9" it read.

Benzie nodded, and shifted his shotgun. He carried it like part of himself, like an extension of his arm. He spoke little but never seemed to miss a trick.

LATER, THEY SWUNG down behind a clump of juniper on the crest of a low hill just off the stage road. Here the team would be slowed to a walk. It would be the best place.

They rode back into the juniper and dismounted. There was plenty of time. Benzie sat on the dead trunk of a tree and lit a smoke, staring bleakly off across the blue-misted bottomland of desert that stretched away toward purple hills. He had never stolen anything before.

Navarro stretched at full length on the sparse grass, his hat over his face. Dud Shafter idly flipped his knife into the end of the log. Shafter wondered about his Mexican and Negro companions, but asked no questions— and they volunteered no information.

Shafter swore softly and stared down the road. There was a warrant out for his arrest back along the trail. He hadn't stolen that bunch of cattle but he'd been with the men who did. He might as well stick up the stage; might as well have the pay as well as the blame. Still, this was a point, a branching road where a man turned toward the owl hoot or along a trail with honest men. Warrant or not, he was sitting in a fork of that road right now.

Keen as Dud's ears were, Benzie heard them first. He started up. "Some men are comin'," he said.

Navarro was off the ground like a cat. Dud ground his cigarette into the sand and moved to his horse's head, a hand over the nostrils. The three stood there like statues, waiting, listening.

At least four horses, Dud thought, listening to the hoofbeats. There was no noise of rigging or rattle of wheels . . . it was not the stage. The horses slowed and stopped.

"This is the best place," a voice said. "We'll draw back into the trees." Over some brush Dud glimpsed a flash of white as one of them moved; the man who had spoken was wearing a light-colored hat.

Holding his breath, every sense alert, Dud Shafter waited. Navarro looked at him, a droll, humorous glint in his eyes. The new men took the brush on the opposite side of some rocks. The air was clear, and a man's words could have been distinguished at a much greater distance but the voice echoed slightly.

"They'll be slowin' up right here." The same voice was speaking. "We make it a clean sweep. Joe, you take the driver. Pete, the messenger. Nobody must be left alive to tell who did it. Above all, get that old man. We'll make him talk!"

There was silence, and the three men on the other side of the trail stared at each other. Here was a complication. To speak aloud would be to give themselves away. Even the movement of their horses might have that result, for if a hoof struck stone, that would mean discovery, and each of them knew from what had been said that the men across the way were utterly ruthless.

Taking careful steps, Dud moved over to Navarro. Benzie leaned his head near.

"We don't want no killing on our hands," Dud whispered. "Stealing is one thing, killing another . . . especially if we ain't gonna get the money."

Navarro and Benzie both nodded.

"Looks like they be wantin' an old man for some reason."

Dud Shafter stared unhappily at his boots. The struggle within him was short and one-sided.

"You fellers can do as you're a-might to," he said at last. "I'm a going to butt in."

"We are partners, no?" Navarro shrugged. "We are

with you!" Benzie nodded. It had an odd kind of logic and none of them was about to let someone else get away with a robbery they had planned, even if it meant losing the prize themselves.

At that moment, they heard the rattle of wheels and a shout from the stage driver. The three leaped for their saddles even as the first shot sounded. Racing their horses through the brush, they heard a burst of firing. Then their own guns opened up.

Dud Shafter came out of the scrub with both guns ready. A big, bearded man loomed before him and turned sharply in his saddle to stare with rolling eyes; Shafter fired twice. The big man went out of the saddle and his horse leaped away.

Behind Dud, Benzie's shotgun coughed hoarsely, and he could hear the sharp reports from Navarro's smoothly handled pistol. There was a flash of light from the trees and a crashing of brush. In a matter of seconds, it was all over, and four men lay on the ground. Dud stared at the brush, for there had been a fifth. The man with the white hat was gone!

He swung down, and the passengers poured from the coach. The shotgun messenger walked up and thrust out his hand.

"Thanks, partners! You-all saved our bacon! That outfit came in shootin'!"

"You hurt?" Dud asked, staring at the man's pale face.

"Winged me," the messenger said.

Shafter turned, feeding shells into his guns, and saw the passengers gathering around. A tall man in a beaver hat, a flamboyantly dressed woman, a solid-looking man with a heavy gold chain, a hard hat, and muttonchop whiskers. Then an old man with a beard, and a young girl evidently his daughter.

This must be the man the robbers had mentioned. He was short with pleasant blue eyes and a glint of humor in his face.

"Some shootin', boys! Thank you."

Dud walked slowly from one dead man to the other. None of them was familiar to Dud.

The man with the muttonchop whiskers thrust out his hand.

"My name is Wendover," he said. "James T. Wendover of Wells Fargo. You men saved our shipment and I can assure you you'll be rewarded. Can you tell us where you live?"

Shafter hesitated, then with a jerk of his thumb, he indicated the box canyon where they had camped beside the ruined adobe.

"We got us a sort of a ranch back up in there," he said. "The three of us."

"Good! Now what do you call it, and what is your name?"

"My name's Shafter," Dud replied. "The ranch is the—"

"The Silver Springs Ranch," Navarro added smoothly.

At the name, the old man started and his eyes hardened as he stared from one to the other. Puzzled, Shafter noticed the girl had put her hand on her father's arm, and the grateful light was gone from her eyes.

Wendover turned away to where the other woman passenger was dressing the messenger's wound. That left Shafter and his companions standing with the old man and the girl.

She stared at him with accusing eyes. "So you're the ones!"

Shafter shook his head. "I don't know what you mean, ma'am," he said simply, "but we probably ain't. Actually, we're just sort of riding through, like."

"You told that man you owned Silver Springs!" she protested indignantly.

"No, señorita," Navarro protested. "We have to tell him something. We could very much use the reward. It is a good place to wait."

"We'd been warned to expect trouble," the old man said. "My name is Fanning, and this is my granddaughter, Beth. Silver Springs belonged to my brother, a long time ago. We were goin' to get off when we got there, but the driver wasn't exactly sure where it was. Are we there now?"

"Yeah," Dud agreed, "this is it. But you folks better know this. Them fellers we shot it out with, they were aiming to kill everybody on that stage, when we overheard 'em. What they was after was you, Mr. Fanning. They said they were going to make you talk."

"So that was it?" Fanning's jaw hardened. "Well, I'd like to find who was behind this! He's the man I want!"

"One of 'em got away," Benzie suggested. "Could be 'twas him."

Navarro and Benzie appointed themselves a burial committee for the dead men, and Dud walked back to the stage to unload the baggage belonging to Fanning and Beth. Wendover was obviously nervous, wanting to get on to the stage station at Lobo Wells.

Leading the Fannings' horses that had been tied to the back of the stage, and with the girl's bag in his hand and a couple more hung to the saddle horn, Shafter led the way back toward the ruined adobe. As he walked, he explained about the little valley, and the condition of things, but Beth was not disturbed. She walked into the ruined building, took a quick look around, and then came out.

"We can fix it up!" she said. "You'll help, won't you?"

Dud, caught flat-footed, assured her that he would.

"Good!" Beth said. "Now if you'll get on your horse and ride down to that stage station and just get us some supplies——" She opened her purse, searching for money.

He turned and started for the Wells. Yet as he rode his thoughts were only occasionally with the girl. He was thinking more of the man in the white hat, and the fact that Fanning knew something, something that would cause men to contemplate murder.

The stage station was one of four buildings at Lobo Wells. There was a rest house and eating place in the station, and the station's office and a storeroom. The other buildings were the Lobo Saloon, the freight office of Bert Callan, and the Mickley General Store. Dud swung down at the hitching rail in front of Mickley's and walked in.

Ben Mickley was in low conversation with a tall man in a fringed buckskin coat. Both men turned to look him over, seeing his big-boned freckled face and the shock of rust-red hair under his battered sombrero. As he collected his order, he was conscious of their scrutiny.

"New around here, ain't you?" Mickley suggested conversationally.

Dud grinned at the proprietor. "Not that new. I spent a moment or two out there tying my horse up," he said, and added tentatively, "going to start ranching on the Silver Springs place."

"I'm afraid not."

Shafter's eyes shifted to the man in the buckskin jacket. He was smooth-featured with a drooping mustache and dark eyes. His jaw was hard, and there was a tightness in his expression that Shafter read as well as he read the low-hung, tied-down guns. The man was bareheaded.

"I reckon yes." Shafter's voice was calm. "We moved in there, my pards and me, and we figure to stay. We're riding for Jim Fanning, who owns the place."

"Corb Fanning filed on that place, a long time ago," said the hard-jawed man. "He was killed, and it lapsed. That spring now belongs to me."

"Lapsed?"

"I filed on it, mister. It's private property now . . . my property."

Dud did not smile. He did not even feel like smiling. He turned around to face the other man, and in his dusty, trail-worn clothes, with his uncut red hair and big freckled hands, he looked like what he was—a hard-bitten man who had cut his eye teeth on a gun butt.

"Where's your hat, stranger?" he asked quietly.

"Don't you go to proddin' him! That's Bert Callan and he's no stranger to me. He runs the freight company hereabouts." Mickley warned Dud, "And I don't want any shooting in my store. You understand?"

The icy blue eyes held Callan's eyes and Shafter spoke slowly. His hand rested lightly on his gun butt.

"All right, Mickley, throw that sack of stuff over your back, and walk out the door ahead of me—alongside of this hombre. Unless this hombre wants to try some six-foot distance shootin'!"

Bert Callan stared into the cold blue eyes and decided

uncomfortably that he didn't want to try it. At a distance, yes, but six feet? Neither of them would live. It was out of the question. He shrugged and followed Ben Mickley to the door.

Dud Shafter threw the sack of groceries over his saddle bows.

"Now you two can go back inside," he said coolly.

"You-all better move off that spring and fast!" Callan's face flushed dark with anger and his hand moved toward his gun.

"You just put on that white hat, if it's yours, and come on up. You come up and tell us to move!"

He swung a leg over his horse and turned the horse into the trail. Then, at a canter, he moved out of town.

Ben Mickley stared after him, hard-eyed. "That's a mean one, Bert. You better soft-pedal it with him!"

"Mean, huh!" Callan flared. "The man's a fool! Go to shootin' in there, we'd both die!"

"That's right," Mickley said thoughtfully, "you would."

SHAFTER RODE UP to Silver Springs shortly after sundown; as he drew up to the adobe, he saw a man move in the shadows. It was Benzie, with his shotgun.

"All right?" Benzie asked. "No trouble?"

Navarro walked up as Dud explained briefly.

"There will be trouble," he ended. "They want this place. In fact they may own it."

Beth Fanning called to them.

"Come and get it before I throw it away!"

When they were eating, she looked over at Dud.

"What did you three plan on doing? Riding on when you get your money?"

He detected the worry in her voice and leaned back

on his elbow, placing his plate and coffee cup on the ground.

"Maybe we'd better stick around," he said. He looked over at Jim Fanning. "You want to tell us what this is all about?"

Fanning hesitated, chewing slowly. "Reckon you fellers have helped us a mite," he finally said. "What do you think, Beth? This is your say-so as much as mine."

The girl lifted her eyes and looked at Dud for a long moment, then at Navarro and Benzie.

"Why, tell them," she said, "I like them all, and we have to trust our friends."

Dud swallowed and looked away, and he saw Benzie's face lighten a little. The Negro looked up, waiting. It was something, Shafter thought, being trusted that way. Especially when you didn't deserve it. A little one way or the other, and they might have robbed that stage themselves.

"We've got a map," Fanning said. "My brother, Corbin, he filed on this place. He come west with six wagons, and he aimed to stay right here. He brought a sight of money along, gold coin it was. Had it hid in his own wagon, nigh to forty thousand dollars of it. It was cached here on the place, and he sent me the location in a letter."

"What happened to him?" Navarro asked softly.

"Injuns. At least they say it was Injuns. Now that these fellers are lookin' for me, I don't know. Beth and I came here to restart the place and that money was goin' to help us do it."

"Can you find it?" Dud asked. He was thinking of forty thousand dollars, and that all three of them were broke. It was a lot of money. How far could Navarro be trusted? Or Benzie? Or himself?

"Maybe. Now that I'm settin' here the directions aren't as clear as I'd like."

"You could let us help you," he said. "But maybe it would be a good idea to have us ride out of here an' you find it on your own . . . you shouldn't trust anyone you don't know."

"No," Beth interrupted. "You saved our lives. I say we should get it now and deposit it with the Wells Fargo. Then it's their worry."

Shafter nodded. "Well, that's best, I'm sure."

He scowled, remembering the man in the white hat and the man at the stage station. Too bad their glimpse of the rider who escaped had been so fleeting. He had taken no part in the fighting, and when Shafter and the others broke from the brush, he had fled at once, as if fearing to be seen.

When morning had come, Jim Fanning left the breakfast table and returned with a fold of papers. They all walked outside. Carefully he laid out the letter in a patch of sunlight.

"This here drawing," he said slowly, "don't nowhere make sense as I'd like. There's the 'dobe all right. Over yonder is the flat-faced cliff, an' here's the stream from Silver Springs. But lookee here, this says, 'gold buried under the . . . ne.' The ink is smudged, it don't make sense."

Navarro looked up sharply, his eyes meeting Shafter's across the fire. Slowly he got up and walked around the fire and knelt over the map. Dud knew what he was thinking, and what Benzie must have in mind. The cave was under a vine, or behind a vine, if you wanted it that way.

Shafter stared down at the map. In the cave then. But he didn't speak up and neither did the others.

"LOOK OUT!" HE said softly. "Watch it!"

Dud got to his feet and Jim Fanning smothered the letter in his fist. Navarro and Benzie got up, too. A tight-knit bunch of riders were walking their horses up the canyon toward them. One of the two men in the lead was Bert Callan.

Eight of them. No, there was another rider following.

Nine to four, and a girl in the way of the shooting. Dud Shafter's jaw set hard.

"Callan—he's one of them men—will want me," he said quietly. "The rest of you stay out."

"We're partners, amigo," Navarro said softly. "Your fight is my fight."

Benzie moved out toward the adobe, then halted. Jim Fanning was by the fire, and the girl close to him.

"So? Caught up with you, did we?" Callan stared hard at Shafter. "You're on my place and we're gonna clear you out. First, though, we're gonna have a talk with the old man here."

There could be no backing down. One sign of weakness and none of them had a chance. Then he recognized the ninth rider.

"You in this, too, Mickley?" Dud demanded sharply. "If you're not, ride out of here!"

"You've got gold hidden on this place," Mickley said. "Let us have it and you can all go on your way. If there's shootin', you'll all die—and so will the girl."

"And so will some of you," Dud replied stiffly. "I think we can handle it."

"No," Navarro said suddenly. "I do not wish to die!"

Shafter could scarcely believe his ears. He would have backed the Mexican to a standstill in any kind of a fight, but here he was giving up!

Before he could speak, Navarro said quickly:

"I will tell you, señors, so do not shoot! I think of the lady, of course!"

Callan snorted, but Mickley nodded eagerly.

"Of course! So where is the gold?"

Navarro reached over and took the letter from Fanning's surprised fingers before the older man could close his fist.

"Here! You see? It says the gold is under the vine."

Mickley stared at the letter over Navarro's shoulder. The other men held their guns steady. If that had been Navarro's plan—to take them by surprise and shoot—it was wasted. This bunch had their rifles over their saddle horns, ready for action. No, there was no question, much as Dud hated to admit it, Navarro had gone yellow.

"Under the vine?" Callan stared. "What vine?"

"But surely, señor," Navarro protested, "you know of the vine that covers the cave mouth? It is there, where the spring flows from the rock. Behind that hanging vine there is a cave. And I think I know where the gold is!"

"You know?" Mickley stared at him suspiciously. "Where?"

"There is a ledge, señor, with something upon it. You walk in, say forty paces on your horse, and there you are!"

Forty paces! Shafter's face stiffened, then relaxed, and he tried to keep the gleam from his eyes.

"Damn you!" Shafter burst out furiously. "You sold us out!"

"Let's go!" Mickley said eagerly. "Let's get it!"

"The box will be ver' heavy, señor," Navarro warned. He rolled a smoke with nerveless fingers. "It will take several men."

"That's right," Mickley agreed. The storekeeper bound up a piece of a canvas ground sheet around a three-foot stick to make a torch. "You"—he motioned to three of the men—"you come and help move the money. Bert, you stay and keep an eye on these folks. I don't trust 'em. Nor you," he added, turning on the Mexican. "Come with us!" He handed Navarro the stick and set a match to the bundle on the end.

Navarro's face paled, and his eyes lifted to meet Dud's. He started to speak, to voice a protest, but Navarro gave a slight, almost imperceptible shake of his head.

"Of course, señor," he said gently. "Why not?"

Mickley turned abruptly toward the cave entrance. As he turned, the bright silver on the butt of his pistol caught Dud's eye. He remembered the flash he had seen during the robbery. It was Mickley! The store owner had planned all this!

Dud Shafter stared after him, and Benzie swallowed, his eyes wide and white. Neither Fanning nor Beth understood, and they could only believe Dud looked so because of the betrayal.

"They'd better find it," Bert Callan warned. He sat his horse beside the remaining three men.

Well, Navarro's attempt to cut the odds had helped

some. It was three to four now, if the shooting started. If only Beth were out of the way!

He looked at her, trying to warn her with his eyes, but she failed to grasp his meaning, and moved closer.

He glanced around, and saw with panic that the group had disappeared behind the vine. Mentally, he counted their steps. Suddenly his hard, freckled face turned grim.

"Run, Beth!" he yelled.

Callan's face blanched, then suddenly his hands swept down for his guns and they came up spouting fire. But too slow, for Dud Shafter's gun was blasting almost before Callan's cleared the holster!

But at the same instant, there was a great crash of falling rock from within the cave, and screams of agony! Then more falling rock, and in the midst of it the roar of guns as Shafter, Benzie, and Fanning opened up on the remaining riders!

Shafter's first shot struck Callan high in the chest and rocked him in the saddle, unsettling his aim so that Callan's bullet went wild. Then Dud, firing low and fast, triggered two more slugs into the gunman. Suddenly, loose in the saddle, as though all his bones and muscles had turned to jelly, Callan rolled and fell, like a sack of wheat into the grass.

The first blast of Benzie's shotgun had blown a rider clear out of his saddle even as his hands lifted his rifle, and for the rest, that was enough. The two remaining men held their hands high.

Dud turned, thumbing shells into his gun, and started at a stumbling run toward the cave. One of his legs felt numb and he remembered a stunning shock when something had struck his knee as the shooting began. Yet as he reached the cave mouth, the vines were shoved aside and three men rushed out. Two of the would-be robbers, and behind them—Navarro!

Shafter let out a whoop of joy and held his gun on the two riders, but they had no fight left in them. They looked pale and sick.

Dud stared at the Mexican. "You're safe? I thought you'd betrayed us, then I thought you'd committed suicide!"

Navarro looked white and shaky himself, and his black eyes were large in his handsome face.

"You forget, amigo, that I knew what was to happen! At the moment we reached the thirtieth step, I stopped and, holding my torch high, pointed ahead! There was a ledge, and on it a fallen rock that in the shadows did not look unlike a chest. They rushed forward, and *poof!* They were gone! It was awful, señor! A horrifying thing which I hope never to see again!"

"Mickley? Mickley was the man who wore the white hat. When he started for the cave, I recalled the flash of silver from his gun, the same I saw on the trail!"

"*Sí,* Mickley and one other, who was close behind them. These? They were frightened and ran. It was most terrible, amigo."

They walked back to the adobe. Beth, her face stark-white, her teeth biting her lower lip, was standing beside Benzie, who held the two riders under his shotgun.

"You two"—Shafter motioned with his six-gun to the men from the cave—"line up over there with them others!"

They obeyed, avoiding the bodies of Callan and the man Benzie had killed. Dud's hard face was remorseless.

"Your boss died back in the cave," he said, "and

there's the other one." He motioned to Callan. "Now who do you hombres work for?"

A lanky man in a worn vest swallowed and said, "Shafter, I reckon we all done run out of a job! We shore have!"

"Then I'll give you one." Dud Shafter's voice was quiet. "Plant these two hombres over against the cliff and plant 'em deep. Then if I was you, I'd climb into leather and light a shuck. They tell me," he added grimly, "they are hiring hands up in the Wind River country."

Gingerly, Shafter examined his knee. It was already turning black, but evidently a chunk of rock from the foundation of the house had ricocheted against his leg, for there was no sign of a bullet.

Fanning shrugged hopelessly. "An ugly fracas," he said, "and we ain't no closer to the gold!"

Dud glanced up, pulling down his pant leg. "I don't know where it is but I'll lay a bet Navarro knows! He wouldn't have taken them into the cave unless he knew that wasn't the right place."

"*Sí.*" The Mexican nodded. Turning, he pointed to the brand chiseled into the cliff behind the adobe. "See? Corb Fanning's brand—the PV Nine—which the vaqueros, of which I was one, shortened to call the Pea Vine! Where else would a man bury his gold but under his own brand?"

THE UNEXPECTED CORPSE

SOMEHOW I HAD always known that if she got in a bad spot, she would call on me, just as I knew that I would never turn her down. Maybe it was because I had encouraged her in the old days when being an actress was only a dream she'd had.

Well, it was a dream that had matured and developed until she was there, rising to greater heights with every picture, with every play. It was never news to me when she scored a success. Somehow, there had never been any doubt in my mind.

When my phone rang, I'd just come in. A few of the boys and I had been getting around to some nightspots, and when I came in and tossed my raincoat over a chair, the telephone was ringing its heart out.

It was Ruth. It had been six months since I'd seen her, and I hadn't even known she knew my number; it wasn't in the book.

"Can you come over, Jim? I'm in trouble! Awful trouble!"

Sometimes she tended to dramatize things, but there was something in her voice that warned me she wasn't kidding.

"Sure," I told her. "Just relax. I'll be there in ten minutes."

Light rain was falling and it was quiet outside. A few late searchlights probed the empty sky, and my tires sang on the pavement. I took backstreets because for all I knew, the cops might be having another shakedown of cars, and I didn't want to be stopped. Not that it would mean anything, I wasn't carrying a gun even though I had a permit, but I wanted to avoid delay.

She opened the door quickly when I knocked. The idea that it might be someone else never seemed to enter her head. She was wearing an evening gown, but she looked so much like a frightened little girl that it seemed like old times again.

"What's the trouble?" I asked her.

"There's a . . . there's a dead man in there!" She indicated the door to what I surmised was the bedroom.

"A *dead* man?" Of all the things it might have been, this was one I'd never imagined. I put her aside and went in, careful to avoid touching anything.

The guy was lying on the bed, one leg and one arm dangling over the side. He was dead all right, deader than a mackerel.

My guess would have put him at fifty years old. He might have been a few years younger. He was slim, dapper, and wore a closely clipped gray mustache. His eyes were wide open and blue. There was an amethyst ring on his left hand. Carefully, I felt his pockets. His billfold was still full of money. I didn't count how much, after I saw it was plenty. The label of his suit said that his name was Lawrence Craine.

The name rang a bell somewhere, but I couldn't place it. Spotting a little blood on his shoulder, I saw he had been stabbed behind the collarbone. In such a stab, most of the blood flows into the lungs. That must have been the case, for there was very little blood. At a rough guess, the guy was five-ten or -eleven. He must have weighed a hundred sixty or thereabouts.

Ruth, I still called her that although she was known professionally as Sue Shannon, was sitting as I'd left her, white as death and her eyes big enough and dark enough to drown in.

"Well, tell me about it," I suggested. "Tell me how well you knew him, what he was to you, and what he was doing here."

She had always listened to me. I suspected she had been in love with me once. I know I had with her. However, it was more than that, for we were friends, we understood each other. She tried to answer my questions now, and though her voice shook a little, I could see she was trying to keep herself from getting hysterical.

"His name is Larry Craine. I don't know what he does except that he seems to have a good deal of money. I've met him several times out on the Strip or at the homes of friends. He seemed to know everyone.

"He had found out something about me, something I didn't want anyone to know. He was going to tell, if I didn't pay him. It would have made a very bad story and it was the sort that people would tell around. It would have ruined me.

"I didn't think he would do it, and told him I didn't

think so. He laughed at me, and gave me until tonight to pay him. I don't know how he got here or how he got in. I went out at eight o'clock with Roger Gentry, but we quarreled and he disappeared. After a while, Davis and Nita Claren drove me home. Then I found him."

"You haven't called the police?"

"The police?" Her eyes were wide and frightened. "Do I have to? I thought that you could hush it up."

"Listen, honey," I said dryly, "this man is *dead*! And he's been *murdered*. The police always seem to be interested in such cases."

"But not here! The body I mean, couldn't you take it someplace else? In stories they do those things."

"I know. But it wouldn't work." I picked up the phone and when I got Homicide, I asked for Reardon, praying he would be in. He was.

"Reardon? Got one for you, and a very touchy case. In the apartment of a friend of mine." I explained briefly, and she stood at my elbow, waiting.

When I hung up, I turned around. "Kid," I warned her, "you're going to have a bad time, so take it standing. The body is here, and if they find out about this blackmail, they've got a motive."

When the squad car pulled into the drive, I was standing there with my arms around her and she was crying. Over her shoulder, I was looking at the wall and thinking, and not about her. I was thinking about this guy Craine. I couldn't make myself think Ruth had done it.

However, there was a chance, even if a slim one. Ruthie, well, she was an impractical girl, and always seemed somewhat vague. But underneath was a will that would move mountains. It wasn't on the surface, but it was there.

Also, she knew a man could be killed in just that way. She knew it because I remembered telling her once when we were talking about some detective stories we'd both read.

Reardon came in and with him were Doc Spates, the medical examiner, a detective named Nick Tanner, a police photographer, and a couple of tired harness bulls.

Sue, I decided to stick to calling her Sue as everyone else would, gave him the story, looking at him out of those big, wistful eyes. Those eyes worked on nearly everyone. Apparently, they hadn't worked on Larry Craine. I doubted if they would work on Reardon, who, when it comes to murder, is a pretty cold-blooded fish.

He rolled his cigar in his cheek and listened; he also looked carefully around the room. Reardon was a good man. He would know plenty about this girl before he got through looking the place over.

When she finished, he looked at me. "Where do you figure in this, Jim? What would she be needing with a private eye?"

"That wasn't it. We knew each other back in Wisconsin long before she ever came out here. Whenever she got in trouble, she always called me."

"Whenever . . ."

He looked at me sadly, letting the implication hang. I didn't tell him any more but I knew he would find out eventually. Reardon was thorough. Slow, painstaking, but thorough.

Doc Spates came in, closing up his bag. "Dead about two hours. That's pretty rough, of course. Whoever did it, knew what he was doing. One straight, hard thrust. No stabbing around. No other cuts or bruises."

Reardon nodded, chewing his cigar. "Could a woman do it?"

Spates fussed with his bag. "Why not? It doesn't take much strength."

Sue's face was stiff and white and her fingers tightened on my arm. Suddenly I was scared. What sort of a fool's chance I was building my hopes on I don't know, but all of a sudden they went out of me like air from a pricked balloon, and there I stood. Right then I knew I was going to have to get busy, and I was going to have to work fast.

Just then Tanner came in. He looked at me and his eyes were questioning. He was holding up an ice pick.

"Doc," he said as Spates reached the door. "Could this have done it?"

"Could be." Spates shrugged. "Something long, thin, and narrow. Have to examine it further before I can tell exactly. Any blood on it?"

"A little," Tanner said. "Close against the handle. But it's been washed!"

Reardon was elaborately casual when he turned around. "You do this?" he asked her.

She shook her head. Twice she tried to speak before she could get it out. "No, I wouldn't . . . couldn't . . . kill anyone!"

To look at her the idea seemed preposterous. Reardon was half convinced, but I, knowing her as I did, knew that deep inside she had something that was hard and ready.

"Listen," I said, "let me call Davis Claren and have him come over and pick up Sue. She'll be at his place when you want her."

He looked at me thoughtfully, then nodded. After I'd

phoned and come back into the room, I saw he had slumped down on the divan and was sitting there, chewing that unlighted cigar. Sue was sitting in a chair staring at him, white and still. I could see she was near the breaking point and was barely holding herself together.

Only after she had gone off with her friends did he look up at me. "How about you? You do it?"

"Me?" I demanded. "Why would I kill the guy? I never knew him!"

"You knew her," he stated flatly. "She looks like she has a lot of trust in you. Maybe she called on you for help. Maybe she called on you *before* the guy was dead instead of after."

"Bosh." That was the only answer I had to that one.

When he finally let me go, I beat it down to my car. It was after four in the morning, and there was little I could do. It felt cold and lonely in my apartment. I stripped off my clothes and tumbled into bed.

THE TELEPHONE JOLTED me out of it. It was Taggart. I should have known it would be him. He was Sue's boss and, as executives went in Hollywood, he was all right. That meant he was basically honest but he wouldn't ever get caught making a statement that couldn't be interpreted at least three different ways. And if the winds of studio politics changed, he'd cut Sue loose like a sail in a storm.

"Sue tells me she called you," he barked. "Well, what have you got?"

"Nothing yet," I told him. "Give me time."

"There isn't any time. The D.A. thinks she did it. He's all hopped up against the Industry, anyway. I'm sending a man over to your office at eight with a thousand dollars. Consider that a retainer!" *Bang;* he hung up the phone.

It was a quarter to eight. I rolled out of bed, into the shower, into my clothes, and through a session with an electric razor so fast that it seemed like one continuous movement. And then, when I was putting the razor away, the name of Larry Craine clicked in my mind.

A week ago, or probably two, I'd been standing in front of a hotel on Vine Street talking to Joe. Joe was a cab starter who knew everybody around. With us was standing a man, a stranger to me, some mug from back East. He spoke up suddenly, and nodded across toward the Derby.

"I'll be damned, that's Larry Craine!" said the man. "What's *he* doing out here?"

"I think he lives here," Joe said.

"He didn't when I knew him!" The fellow growled.

With the thousand dollars in my pocket, I started hunting for Joe. I'd never known his last name, but I got it pretty quick when I looked at a cabbie over a five-dollar bill. It was Joe McCready and he lived out in Burbank.

There were other things to do first, and I did a lot of them on a pay phone. Meanwhile, I was thinking, and when I finally got to Joe, he hesitated only a minute, then shrugged.

"You're a pal of mine," he said, "or I'd say nothing. This lug who spotted Larry Craine follows the horses. I think he makes book, but I wouldn't know about that. He doesn't do any business around the corner."

"What do you know about Larry Craine?"

"Nothing. Doesn't drink very much, gets around a lot, and seems to know a lot of people. Mostly, he hangs around on the edge of things, spends pretty free when there's a crowd around, but tips like he never carried anything but nickels."

Joe looked up at me. "You watch yourself. This guy we were talkin' to, his name is Pete Ravallo. He plays around with some pretty fast company."

He did have Craine's address. I think Joe McCready knew half the addresses and telephone numbers in that part of town. He never talked much, but he listened a lot, and he never forgot anything. My detective agency couldn't have done the business it did without elevator boys, cab starters, newsboys, porters, and bellhops.

That was how I got into Craine's apartment. I went around there and saw Paddy. Paddy had been a doorman in that apartment house for five years. We used to talk about the fights and football games, sitting on the stoop, just the two of us.

"The police have been there," Paddy advised, "but they didn't stay long. I can get y' in, but remember, if y' get caught, it's on your own y' are!"

This Craine had done all right by himself. I could see that the minute I looked around. I took a quick gander at the desk, but not with any confidence. The cops would have headed for the desk right away, and Reardon was a smart fellow. So was Tanner, for that matter. I headed for the clothes closet.

He must have had twenty-five suits and half that many sport coats, all a bit loud for my taste. I started at one end and began going through them, not missing a pocket. Also, as I went along, I checked the labels. He had three suits from New Orleans. They were all pretty shabby and showed much wear. They were stuck back in a corner of the closet out of the way.

The others were all comparatively new, and all made

in Hollywood or Beverly Hills. At first that didn't make much of an impression, but it hit me suddenly as I was going through the fourteenth suit, or about there. Larry Craine had been short of money in New Orleans but he had been very flush in Hollywood. What happened to put his hands on a lot of money, and fast?

When I hit the last suit in line, I had netted just three ticket stubs and twenty-one cents in money. The last suit was the payoff. When I opened the coat, I saw right away that I'd jumped to a false conclusion. Here was one suit, bought ready-made, in Dallas.

In the inside coat pocket, I found an airline envelope, and in it, the receipt for one passenger from Dallas to Los Angeles via American Airlines. Also, there was a stub, the sort of thing given to you after a street photographer takes your picture. If you want the snapped picture, you can get it and more of them if you wish, if you want to pay a modest sum of money. Craine hadn't been interested.

Pocketing the two articles, I slipped out the back way and let Paddy know I was gone. He looked relieved when he saw me off.

"Nick Tanner just went up," he said.

"Thanks, Paddy," I told him.

I walked around in front and saw Reardon standing by the squad car. Putting my hands in my pockets, I strolled up to him.

"Hi," I said. "How's it going?"

His eyes were shrewd as he studied me. "Not so good for Miss Shannon," he said carefully. "That ice pick did the job, all right. Doc Spates will swear to it. We found blood close up against the handle where it wasn't washed carefully. It's the same type as his blood.

"Also," he added, "we checked on her. She left that party she was at with Gentry and the Clarens early, about three hours before it was over, which would make it along about ten-thirty. She was gone for all of thirty to forty-five minutes. In other words, she had time to leave the party, go home, kill this guy, and get back to the party."

"You don't believe that!" I exclaimed.

He shrugged and took a cigar from his pocket. "It isn't what I believe, it's what the district attorney can make the jury believe. Something you want to think about." He looked up at me from under his eyebrows as he bit off the end of the cigar. "The D.A. is ambitious. A big Hollywood murder trial would give him lots of publicity. The only thing that would make him happier would be a basement full of communists!"

"Yeah." I could see it all right, I could see him riding right to the governor's chair on a deal like that. Or into the Senate. "One thing, Reardon. If she had done it, wouldn't she have had the Clarens come in with her to help her find the body? That would be the smart stunt. And she's actress enough to carry it off."

"I know." He struck a match and lit the cigar, then grinned sardonically at me. "But she's actress enough to fool you, too!"

Was she? I wasn't so sure. I'd known her a long time. Maybe you never really know anyone. And murder is something that comes much too easily sometimes.

"Reardon," I said, "don't pinch Sue. Hold off on it until I can work on it."

He shrugged. "I can't. The D.A.'s already convinced. He wants an arrest. We haven't another lead of any kind.

We shook his apartment down, we made inquiries all over town. We don't have another suspect."

"We've been buddies a long time," I pleaded. "Give her forty-eight hours. Taggart's retained me on this case, and I think I've got something."

"Taggart has, eh?" He looked at me thoughtfully. "Don't give me a runaround, now. The district attorney thinks he has a line on it himself. It seems Craine's done some talking around town. He thinks he's got a motive, though he's not saying what it is yet."

"Two days?"

"All right. But then we're going ahead with what we've got. I'll give you until . . . let's see, this is Monday . . . you've got until Wednesday morning."

SUE WAS WAITING for me when I got there. She was a beautiful woman, even as tight and strained as she was.

"Is it true? Are they going to arrest me?"

"I hope not." I sat down abruptly. "I'd let them arrest me if I could."

"No, you won't." I looked up and her eyes were sharp and hard. "You came into this because I asked you, and I won't have that happen."

It was the first time I'd seen her show her anger, although I knew she had it. It surprised me, and I sat back and looked at her and I guess my surprise must have shown because she said, defensively, "Don't you talk that way. That's going too far!"

"Well you've got to help me. Just what did Craine want from you?"

"Money." She shrugged. "He told me he wanted ten percent of all I made from now on. He said he had been broke for the last time, that now that he had money he was always going to have money no matter what it cost."

"Did you talk to him many times?"

"Three times. He had some letters. There was nothing bad in them, but the way he read them made them sound pretty bad. It wasn't only that. He knew some stories that I don't want told, about my uncle."

I knew all about that, and could understand.

"But that wasn't all. He told me I had to give him information about other people out here. About Mr. Taggart, for instance, and some of the others. He was very pleased with himself. He obviously was sure he had a very good plan worked out."

"Does Taggart know about this?"

"No one does. You're the only one I've told. The only one I will tell."

"Did Craine ever hint about how he got this money he had?"

"Well, not exactly. He told me I needn't think I could evade the issue because he was desperate. He told me there wasn't anything he would hesitate to do. He said once, 'I've already gone as far as I can go, so you know what to expect if you try to double-cross me.' "

When she left, I offered the best reassurances I could dig out of a mind that was running pretty low on hope. Reardon was careful, and if he couldn't find anything on Larry Craine, there was small chance I could. My only angle was one that had been stirring in the back of my mind all the time.

Where did Larry Craine get his money?

He had been living in Hollywood for several months. He lived well and spent a good bit. That meant that wherever he had come into money, it had been plenty.

To cover all the bases I sent off a wire to an agency in New Orleans.

My next move was a shot in the dark. There was only one person I knew of who had known Craine before he came to Hollywood. I was going to see Pete Ravallo.

He was in a hotel on Ivar, and it didn't take me but two hours and twenty dollars to find him. I rapped on the door to his room, and he opened it a crack. His eyes studied me, and I could see he vaguely remembered my face.

"What'd you want?" he demanded. He was a big guy, and his voice was harsh.

"Conversation," I said.

He sized me up a minute, then let the door open and I walked in. He waved me to a seat and poured himself a drink. There was a gun in a shoulder holster hanging over a chair back. He didn't offer me a drink, and he didn't look very pleased.

"All right," he said. "Spill it!"

"I'm a private shamus and I'm investigating the murder of Lawrence Craine."

You could have dropped a feather. His eyes were small and dark and as he looked at me they got still smaller and still darker.

"So you come to me?" he demanded.

I shrugged. "One night down on the street, I heard you say something about knowing him in New Orleans. Maybe you could give me a line on the guy."

He studied me. Somehow, I felt sure, there was a tie-up, a tie-up that went a lot further than a casual meeting. Ravallo had been too pleased at seeing Craine. Pleased, and almost triumphant.

"I don't know anything about the guy," he said. "Only

that he used to be around the tracks down there. I knew him by sight like I knew fifty others. He used to put down a bet once in a while."

"Seen him since he's been here?" I asked carefully. Ravallo's face tightened and his eyes got mean. "Listen," he said. "Don't try to pin that job on me, see? You get to nosing in my business and you'll wind up wearing a concrete block on your feet! I don't like cops. I like private coppers a lot less, and I like you still less than that! So get up and get out!"

"Okay." I got up. "You'd better tell me what you can, because otherwise I'm going back to New Orleans . . . and Dallas!"

"Wait a minute," he said. He went over behind me to the phone and spun the dial.

"Come on over here," he said into the phone. "I've got a problem."

The hair on the back of my neck suddenly felt prickly and I turned in time to see the sap descending. I threw up an arm, catching him above the elbow. I grabbed his wrist and jerked him forward into the back of the chair, then I lunged forward, hit the carpet with my knees, and, turning, stood up.

Pete Ravallo threw the chair out of his way and came toward me; his voice was cold. "I told you, and now I'm going to show you!" He cocked his arm and swung again.

It was a bad thing for him to do. I hit his arm with my open palm and at the same time I knocked his arm over, I slugged him in the stomach with my left.

He doubled up, and I smacked him again, but the big lug could take it, and he charged me, head down. I sidestepped quickly, tripped over a suitcase, and hit the floor all in one piece. The next thing I knew I got the wind booted out of me and before I could get my hands up, he slugged me five or six times and I was helpless.

He slammed me back against the wall with one hand and then swung the blackjack. He brought it down over my skull, and as everything faded out, I heard him snarling: "Now get lost, or I'll kill you!"

When I came out of it, I was lying in a linen closet off the hall. I struggled to my feet and swayed drunkenly, trying to get my head clear and get moving. I got out in the hall and straightened my clothes. My face felt stiff and sore, and when I put my hand up to my head, I found blood was caked in my hair and on the side of my face. Then I cleaned myself up as best I could and got out.

It was after eleven, and there was a plane leaving for Oklahoma City at about twelve-thirty. When it took off, I was on it. And the next morning, Tuesday morning, I was standing, quite a bit worse for wear, in front of the *Dallas Morning News*.

When a crook comes into a lot of money, it usually makes headlines. What I had learned so far was ample assurance that what had happened had happened near here. I went to the files of the paper and got busy.

It took me some time, but when I had covered almost two months, I found what I was looking for. It was not a big item, and was well down on an inside page. If I had not been covering it with care, I would never have found the piece at all.

MURDERED MAN BELIEVED GANG VICTIM

Police today announced they had identified the body of the murdered man found in a ditch several miles

south of the city. He proved to be Giuseppe Ravallo, a notorious racketeer from Newark, N.J. Ravallo, who did two terms in the New Jersey State
Prison for larceny and assault with a deadly weapon,
was reported to have come here recently from New
Orleans where he had been implicated in a race-
fixing plot.

Ravallo was said to have come to town as the advance
man for eastern racketeers determined to move into the
area. He was reported, by several local officials whom he
approached, to be carrying a considerable amount of
money. No money was found on the body. Ravallo had
been shot three times in the back and once in the head by
a .38-caliber pistol.

So there it was. Just like that, and no wonder Pete Ravallo had wanted to keep me out of the case!

The photo coupon was still in my pocket. At the pho-
tographers shop it took me only a few minutes to get it.
When I had the picture, I took one look and headed for
the airport.

IN LOS ANGELES there was a few minutes' wait to claim
my luggage, and then I turned toward a cab. I turned,
but that was all. A man had moved up beside me. He was
small and pasty-faced, and his eyes were wide and
strange. There was nothing small about the feel of the
cannon he put in my ribs.

"Come on!" he said. "That car over there!"

There are times for bravery. There are also times when
bravery is a kind of insanity. Tonight, within limits, I
was perfectly sane. I walked along to the car and saw the
thick neck of a mug behind the wheel, and then I was

getting in and looking at Pete Ravallo. There were a lot of people I would rather have seen.

"I can't place the face," I said brightly, "but the breath smells familiar!"

"Be smart!" Ravallo said. "Go ahead and be smart while you got the chance!"

The car was rolling, and Pasty Face was still nudging me with the artillery.

"Listen, chum!" I suggested. "Move the gun. I'm not going anyplace!"

Pasty Face chuckled. "Oh, yes, you are! You got some things to learn."

We drove on, and eventually wound around in the hills along a road I finally decided was Mulholland Drive. It was a nice place to dispose of a body. I'd probably wind up as part of a real estate plot and be subdivided. In fact, I had a pretty good idea the subdividing was planned for right quick.

When the car pulled in at the edge of the dark road, I knew this was it.

"Get out!"

Ravallo let Pasty Face unload first, and then he put his foot in my back and shoved.

Maybe Pasty Face was supposed to trip me. Maybe Ravallo didn't realize we were so close to the canyon, but that shove with his foot was all I needed. I took it, ducked the guy with the gun, and plunged off into the darkness.

It wasn't a sheer drop. It was a steep slide off into the dark, brush-filled depths of a canyon whose sides were scattered with boulders. I must have run all of twenty feet in gigantic steps before I lost balance and sprawled, headfirst, into the brush.

Behind me a shot rang out, and then I heard Ravallo swear.

"After him, you idiots! Get him!"

Kicking my feet over, I fell on the downhill side of the bush and flame stabbed the night behind me, but I wasn't waiting. This was no time to stand on ceremony and I was not going to take a chance on their missing me in the darkness of that narrow canyon. I rolled over, scrambled to my feet, and lunged downhill.

Then I tripped over something and sprawled head-long. A flashlight stabbed the darkness. That was a different story, and I lay still, feeling for what I'd tripped over. It was a thick branch wedged between the sprawling roots of some brush. Carefully, I worked it loose.

Somebody was coming nearer. I lay quiet, waiting and balancing my club. Then I saw him, and he must have moved quietly for he was within two feet of my head!

He took a step and I stuck my club between his feet. He took a header and started to swear. That was all I needed, for I smacked down with that club. It hit him right over the noggin and I scrambled up his frame and wrenched the gun from his hand.

"Stan?" Ravallo called.

I balanced the gun and wet my lips. There were two of them, but I was through running.

I cocked the gun and squared my feet, breaking a small branch in the process.

He fired, but I had been moving even as I realized I'd given away my position. I hit the dirt a half-dozen feet away. My own pistol stabbed flame and he fired back. I got a mouthful of sand and backed up hurriedly. But Pete Ravallo wasn't happy. I heard him whispering hoarsely, and then heard a slight sound downhill from me.

I turned, and Ravallo's gun stabbed out of the dark and something struck me a blow on the shoulder. My gun went clattering among the stones, and I knew from Ravallo's shout that he knew what had happened.

Crouching like a trapped animal, I stared into the blackness right and left. There was no use hunting for the gun. The noise I would make would give them all they needed to shoot at, and Pete Ravallo was doing too well at shooting in the dark.

Fighting desperately for silence I backed up, then turned and worked my way cautiously back through the brush, parting it with my hands, and putting each foot down carefully so as not to scuff any stones or gravel.

I was in total darkness when I heard the sound of heavy breathing, and close by. It was a cinch this couldn't be Pete Ravallo, so it must be the thick-necked mug. I waited, and heard a slight sound. I could barely see the dim outline of a face. Putting everything I had into it, I threw my left!

Beggar's luck was with me and it smashed on flesh and he went sliding down the gravel bank behind him. Instantly, flame stabbed the night. One bullet whiffed close by, and then I began to run. I was lighter than Pete, and my arm was throbbing with agony that seemed to be eased by the movement even as pressure seems to ease an aching tooth. I lunged at that hill and, fighting with both feet and my one good hand, started to scramble back for the top.

Ravallo must have hesitated a moment or two, trying to locate his driver. I was uphill from him anyway, and by the time he started I had a lead of at least forty yards and was pulling away fast. He tried one more shot, then held his fire. A light came on in a distant house.

Tearing my lungs out gasping for air, I scrambled over the top into the road. The car was sitting there, with the motor running, but I'd no thought of getting away. He still had shells, probably an extra clip, too. I twisted into the driver's seat and threw the car into gear and pointed it down the embankment. There was one sickening moment when the car teetered, and then I half jumped, half fell out of the door.

In that wild, fleeting instant as the car plunged head-first downhill, I caught a glimpse of Pete Ravallo.

The gangster was full in the glare of the headlights, and even as I looked, he threw up his arms and screamed wildly, insanely, into the night! And then all I could hear was the crashing tumble of the car going over and over to the bottom of the canyon.

For what seemed a long time I lay there in the road, then crawled to my feet. I felt weak and sick and the world was spinning around so I had to brace myself to stand. I was like that when I heard the whine of a siren and saw a car roll up and stop. There were other sirens farther off.

Reardon was in the third car to arrive. He ran to me.

"What happened? Where's Ravallo?"

I gestured toward the canyon. "How'd you know about him?"

While several officers scrambled down into the canyon, he helped me to the car and ripped off my coat.

"Joe McCready," Reardon said. "He knew you'd gone to Dallas, and he heard the cabbies say that Ravallo was watching the airport. So, I wired Dallas to see if they knew anything about Craine or Ravallo. The paper told me that you found a story about Giuseppe Ravallo's body. So I had some boys watching Pete at this end while we tried to piece the thing together.

"They had gone for coffee and were just getting back when they saw Ravallo's car pulling away. A few minutes' checking and they found you'd come in on the plane. We thought we'd lost you until we got a report of some shooting up this way."

Between growls at the pain of my shoulder, I explained what had happened. There were still gaps to fill in, but it seemed Ravallo had been trying to find out who killed his brother.

"He either had a hunch Craine had done it for the money Giuseppe was carrying, or just happened to see him and realized he was flush. That would be all he would need to put two and two together. However he arrived at the solution, he was right."

Fishing in my coat pocket, I got out the snapshot. It was a picture of Giuseppe Ravallo, bearing a strong resemblance to Pete, sitting at a table with Larry Craine.

"Maybe Craine left New Orleans with Ravallo, and maybe he followed him. Anyway, when Craine left New Orleans he was broke, then he hit Dallas and soon had plenty of money. He bought a suit of clothes there, then came on here and started living high and fast. Ravallo was back behind him, dead."

My arm was throbbing painfully, but I had to finish the story and get the thing straightened out.

"Pete must have tailed him to Sue's apartment, maybe one of those goons down there in the canyon was with him. He probably didn't know where he was going and cared less. He saw his chance and took it. Pete seems the vendetta type. He would think first of revenge, and the money would come second. Her car evidently drove up before he had the money. Or maybe he didn't even try to get it."

Reardon nodded. "That's a place for us to start. I don't think you'll have to worry about the D.A." He grinned at me. "But when you took off to Dallas, you had me sweating!"

All the way back to town, I nursed my shoulder and was glad to get to the hospital. The painkillers put me under and I dreamed that I was dying in a dark canyon under the crushing weight of a car.

When I fought my way back to life after a long sleep, it was morning and Sue Shannon was sitting there by the bed. I looked up at her thoughtfully.

"What?" she asked.

"I thought I was dying in a dream . . . and then I woke up and thought I'd gone to heaven."

She smiled.

"I was wondering if I'd have to wait until you found another corpse before I saw you again?" I asked.

"Not if you like a good meal and know of a quiet restaurant where we can get one."

My eyes absorbed her beauty again and I thought heaven could wait, living would do for now.

THE ROUNDS DON'T MATTER

Y OU GET THAT way sometimes when you're in
shape, and you know you're winning. You can't
wait for the bell, you've got to get up and keep moving
your feet, smacking the ends of your gloves together. All
you want is to get out there and start throwing leather.

Paddy Brennan knew he was hot. He was going to
win. It felt good to weigh a couple of pounds under two
hundred, and be plenty quick. It felt good to be laying
them in there hard and fast, packed with the old dyna-
mite that made the tough boys like Moxie Bristow back
up and look him over.

Moxie was over there in the corner now, stretched out
and soaking up the minute between rounds as if it were
his last chance to lie in the warm sunlight. You wouldn't
think to look at him that Moxie had gone the distance
three times with the champ when the champ was good.
You wouldn't think that Moxie had a win over Deacon

Johnson, the big black boy from Mississippi who was mowing them down.

You wouldn't think so now, because Moxie Bristow was stretched out on his stool and breathing deep. But he knew that all his breathing wasn't going to fix that bad eye or take the puff out of those lips.

Paddy was right. He was going good tonight. He was going good every night. He was young, and he liked to fight, and he was on the way up. He liked the rough going, too. He didn't mind if he caught a few, because he didn't take many. He liked to see Caproni down there in the ringside seats with Bickerstaff. They handled Tony Ketchell, who was the number-one heavyweight now. And in the articles for tonight's fight, there was a clause that said he was to fight Ketchell on the twenty-seventh of next month if he got by Bristow.

The bell clanged, and Paddy went out fast. When he jabbed that left, it didn't miss. It didn't miss the second or the third time, and then he turned Bristow with a left and hit him on the chin with a chopping right. It made Moxie's knees buckle, but Paddy Brennan didn't pay any attention to that. Their legs always went rubbery when he socked them with that inside right cross.

Moxie dropped into a crouch and bored in, weaving and bobbing. The old boy had it, Paddy thought. He could soak them up, but he was smart, too. He knew when to ride them and when to go under and when to go inside.

Paddy had a flat nose and high cheekbones, but not so flat or so high that he wasn't good-looking. Maybe it was his curly hair, maybe it was the twinkle in his eyes, maybe it was the vitality, but he had something. He had something that made him like to fight, too.

He moved in fast now, hooking with both hands. Bristow tried a left, and Paddy went inside with three hard ones and saw a thin trickle of blood start from over Moxie's good eye.

Moxie was watching him. He knew it was coming. Paddy walked in, throwing them high and hard, then hooked a left to the wind that turned Moxie's face gray. He had Moxie spotted for the right then, and it went down the groove and smacked against Bristow's chin with a sickening thud. Moxie sagged, then toppled over on his face.

PADDY TROTTED TO his corner, and when he looked down he could see Caproni and Bickerstaff. He was glad they were there, because he had wanted them to see it. He wished Dicer Garry were there, too. Dicer had been Paddy's best friend, and he might have guessed more of what was in the wind than anyone else.

Brennan leaned over the ropes, and Caproni looked up, his face sour.

"Now Ketchell, eh?" Paddy said. "I'm going to take your boy, Vino."

"Yeah?" Caproni said. His eyes were cold. "Sure, sure . . . we'll see."

Paddy chuckled, trotting across the ring to help Moxie to his corner. He looked down at Bristow, squeezing the other fighter's shoulder.

"Swell fight, mister. You sure take 'em."

Moxie grinned.

"Yeah? You dish 'em out, too!" Paddy squeezed Moxie's arm again and started away, but Moxie held his wrist, pulling him close. "You watch it, look out for Vino. You got it, Irish. You got what it takes. But look out."

Sammy came out of Brennan's corner. "Can it, Mox. Let's go, Paddy." He held out Paddy's robe. Sammy's face looked haggard under the lights, and his eyes shifted nervously. Sammy was afraid of Vino.

Paddy trotted across the ring and took the robe over his shoulders. He felt good. He vaulted the ropes and ducked down to the dressing rooms under the ring. Sammy helped him off with his shoes.

"Nice fight, Paddy. You get Ketchell now." But Sammy didn't look happy. "You don't want to rib Vino like that," he said. "He ain't a nice guy."

Paddy didn't say anything. He knew all about Vino Caproni, but he was remembering Dicer Garry. Dice had been good, but he hadn't got by Ketchell. Maybe Dicer could have whipped Ketchell. Maybe he couldn't. But he fought them on the up and up, and that wasn't the way Caproni or Bickerstaff liked to play.

Dicer and Paddy had worked it out between them three years ago.

"Give me first crack at it, Paddy?" Dicer suggested. "We've been pals ever since we worked on the construction crew together. You've licked me three times, and you know and I know you can do it again."

"So what?" Brennan said.

"So . . ." Garry mused. "You let me get the first crack at the champ. You let me take the big fights first. You come along after. That way maybe I can be champ before you get there. You can have a fight for the belt anytime. You'll beat me eventually if I'm still there. We've been pals too long. We know what's up."

And Garry had almost made it. He knocked out Joe Devine and Bat Turner, got a decision over Racko and a technical kayo over Morrison, all in a few months. Then they matched him with Andy Fuller, who was right up there with the best, and Dicer nearly killed him. So he was matched with Ketchell.

Caproni and Bickerstaff had worked a few years on Ketchell. He was in the big money, and he had been taken along carefully. He was good. But could he beat Dicer?

Paddy Brennan peeled the bandages and tape from his fists and remembered that last note he had from Garry.

> *They tried to proposition me. I turned them down. This Vino ain't no good. He got tough with me and I hit him. I broke his nose.*
>
>

Dicer

SERGEANT KELLY O'BRIEN stopped in, smiling broadly. The sergeant was father to Clara O'Brien and Clara and Paddy were engaged. You could see the resemblance to Clara. O'Brien had been a handsome man in his day.

"'Twas a grand job, son. A grand job. You've never looked better!"

"Yeah," Paddy said, looking up. "Now I get Ketchell, then the champ."

Brennan picked up his soap and stepped into the shower, put his soap in the niche in the wall and turned on the water. With the water running over him, he reached for the soap. All the time he was thinking of Garry.

If it hadn't been for that truck crashing into Dicer's car, he might be fighting his best pal for the title now, and a tough row it would have been. If it hadn't been for that truck crash, Tony Ketchell might have been out of the picture before this. Dicer Garry would have whipped Ketchell or come close to it. Vino Caproni had known that, and so had Bickerstaff.

The worst of it was, he might never have guessed about that truck if he hadn't seen the green paint on Bickerstaff's shoe sole. He'd been out to see Dicer's car, and seen the green paint that had rubbed off the truck onto the wreck. And it was almost fresh paint. Then later that day, he had talked with Bickerstaff.

The gambler was sitting with one ankle on the other knee, and there was green paint on the sole of his shoe, a little on the edge.

"That was tough about Dicer," Bickerstaff said. "Was his car smashed up pretty bad?"

"Yeah," Paddy told him, and suddenly something went over him that left him outwardly casual, but inwardly alert, and deadly. "Yeah, you seen it?"

"Me?" Bickerstaff shook his head. "Not me, I never go around wrecking yards. Crashes give me the creeps."

IT WAS A little thing, but Paddy Brennan went to O'Brien, who had been a friend of Garry's, too.

"Maybe it don't mean a thing," Paddy said, "or again maybe it does. But when you figure that Ketchell's had a buildup that must have cost seventy grand, you get the idea. Ketchell's good, and maybe he would have beat Dicer, but then again maybe he wouldn't. It was a chance, and guys like Vino don't take any chances."

O'Brien nodded thoughtfully.

"I've wondered about that. But it all looked so good. You know how Dicer used to drive—anything less than sixty was loafing. And he hit the truck, that was obvious enough. Of course, it would have been a simple matter to have had the truck waiting and swing it in the way. Garry drove out that road to his camp every morning.

"If you are right, Paddy, it was an almost foolproof

job. The driver, Mike Cortina, he'd never had an accident before; he'd been driving for three years for that same firm. He was delivering that load of brick out that road, so he had a reason to be there. They had a witness to the crash, you know."

WHEN HE HAD finished his shower, he dressed slowly. The sergeant had gone on ahead with Clara, and he would meet them at a café later. Sammy loitered around, looking nervous and cracking his knuckles.

"Look, Paddy," he said suddenly, "I don't want to speak out of turn or nothing, but honest, you got me scared. Why don't you play along with Vino? You got what it takes, Paddy, an' gosh—"

Paddy stopped buttoning his shirt. "What is it? What d'you know?" he asked, staring at Sammy.

"I don't know a damn thing, Brennan. Honest, I—"

"Do you know Cortina?" Paddy asked, deliberately.

Sammy sank back on the bench, his face gray.

"*Shut up!*" he whispered hoarsely. "Don't go stickin' your neck out, Paddy, *please!*"

Paddy stood over Sammy, he stared at the smaller man, his eyes burning.

"You been a good man, Sammy," he said thickly. "I like you. But if you know anything, you better give. Come on, *give!*"

"Farnum," Sammy sighed. "One of the witnesses— he runs a junkyard in Jersey. He used to handle hot heaps for the Brooklyn mob."

Brennan finished dressing. Then he turned to Sammy, who sat gray-faced and fearful.

"You go home and forget it, Sam. I'll handle this!"

———

SOMEHOW THE DAYS got away from him, in the gym, and on the road, getting ready for Ketchell.

"It's got to be good, Clara," he told her. "I got to win this one. It's got to be a clean win. No decision, nothing they can get their paws into."

He liked the Irish in her eyes, the way she smiled. She was a small, pretty girl with black hair and blue eyes and just a dash of freckles over her nose. Paddy held her with his hands on her shoulders, looking into her eyes.

"After this is over, we can spend all the time we want together. Until then I've got work to do."

"Be careful, Paddy," she begged him. "I'm afraid. Daddy's been talking to someone about that man—the one with the yellow eyes."

"Vino?"

"Yes, that's the one. A friend told Daddy he used to work a liquor concession for Capone when he was young. And now he is in with some bunch of criminals who have a hot car business over in Brooklyn."

"Brooklyn?" Paddy's eyes narrowed. Car thieves in Brooklyn . . . ?

Paddy Brennan went back to the hotel and started for the elevator. The room clerk stopped him.

"Two men came in to see you, Mr. Brennan. They were here twice. They wouldn't leave their names."

"Two men?" Paddy looked out the door. "One of them short and fat, the other dark with light eyes?"

"That's right. The dark one did the talking."

If Vino was looking for him, it meant a proposition on the Ketchell fight. He picked up the phone.

"If anybody calls, I'm not in, okay?"

Let them wait. Let them wait until the last night when

they couldn't wait any longer, when they would have to come out with it. Then— He dialed the phone.

TWO NIGHTS LATER Paddy Brennan sat on his bed in the hotel and looked across at the wiry man with the thin blond hair.

"You found him, did you?" he asked.

The man wet his lips.

"Yeah, he quit his job drivin' the truck six months after the accident. He's been carrying a lot of do-re-mi since then. I trailed him over to Jersey last night, drunk. He's sleeping it off at a junkyard right now."

Paddy got up. He took out a roll of bills and peeled off a couple.

"That's good," he said. "You stand by, okay? Then you go tell O'Brien about six o'clock, get me? Don't tell him where I am, or anything. Just tell him what I told you and don't miss. There's going to be a payoff soon. You do what I tell you, and you'll get paid a bonus."

At about nine-thirty tonight he would be going into the ring with Tony Ketchell, and the winner would get a chance at the title. In the meantime, there were things to do—the things Dicer Garry would have done if it had been Paddy Brennan whose broken, bloody body had been lifted from the wreckage of his car. They were things that had to be done now while there was still time.

THE JUNKYARD WAS on the edge of town. A light glowed in the office shack. Behind it was the piled-up mass of the junked cars, a long, low warehouse, and the huge bulk of the press. It was here the Brooklyn mob turned hot cars into parts, rebuilt cars, or scrap. Farnum, the convenient witness, ran the place. He had testified that

Dicer Garry had hit the truck doing eighty miles an hour, that the driver hadn't had a chance to get out of the way.

Paddy Brennan's face was grim when he stopped by the dirty window and peered in. Cortina—he remembered the man from the inquest—was sitting in a chair tipped back against the wall. He had a bottle in his hand and a gun in a shoulder holster.

Farnum was there, too, a slender, gray-haired man who looked kindly and tired until you saw his eyes. There were two others there—a slender man with a weasel face and a big guy with heavy shoulders and a bulging jaw.

Paddy swung the door open, and stepped in. He carried a heavy, hard-sided case in his hand. Farnum got up suddenly, his chair tipped over.

Cortina's face tightened. "Speak of the devil! Muggs, this is Paddy Brennan, the guy who fights Ketchell tonight. He won't be the same afterward, so you'd better take a good look."

Muggs laughed, and he leaned forward aggressively. Farnum looked shocked and apprehensive. He was sitting close to Cortina, and Paddy's eyes covered them.

"What's the suitcase for? You skipping out on Ketchell?"

"Dicer Garry was a friend of mine," Paddy said quietly. He set the case down carefully on the floor.

The man with the weasel face got up suddenly.

"I'm not in this," he said. "I want out."

"You sit down," Brennan told him, pointing at the corner. "Stay out if you want but keep still."

Muggs was a big man who carried himself with a swagger, even sitting down.

"How about you?" Brennan asked. "Are you in on this, or are you going to be nice?"

Muggs got up. He was as tall as Brennan and twenty pounds heavier.

"You boxers are supposed to be good. What happens when you can't use that fancy stuff with a lot of fancy rules?"

"Something like this," Brennan said, and hit him. His right fist in a skintight glove struck with a solid crack, and Muggs was falling when the left hook hit him in the wind. It knocked him into his chair, which splintered and went to the floor with a crash.

Cortina tilted his bottle back and took another drink. He was powerful, a shorter man than Brennan, but heavier.

"Nice goin'," Cortina said. "Muggs has been askin' for that."

"You're next," Brennan said. "Garry was a pal of mine. It's going to look mighty funny when the D.A. starts wondering why the principal witness and the driver of the death car turn out to be friends and turn out to be running with a mob that backs Caproni and Bickerstaff."

"Smart pug, aren't you?" Cortina said, putting his bottle down carefully. "Well, I hate to disappoint Ketchell and the fans, but—"

His hand streaked for the gun, had it half out before Paddy kicked the legs out from under the chair. It came out, but Cortina's head smacked up against the wall, the gun sliding from his hand.

Farnum broke for the door, and Brennan caught him with one hand and hurled him back against the desk so violently that he fell to the floor. Then Brennan picked up the gun and pocketed it.

"Get up, Cortina," he said quietly. "I see you've got to learn."

The trucker made a long dive for Brennan's legs, but

Paddy jerked his knee up in the Italian's face, smashing his nose. Then Brennan grabbed him by the collar, jerking him erect, and slammed him back against the wall. Before he could rebound, Paddy stepped in and hooked both hands to the body. The Italian's jaw dropped and he slumped to the floor.

Farnum was getting up. He wasn't a strong man, and the violence of that shove had nearly broken him. Brennan pushed him into a chair.

"You've got a chance to talk," he said. "I've only got a few minutes, and then I'm going to keep that date with Ketchell. You either talk, or I'm going to beat you both until you'll never feel or look the same again."

Brennan turned to Muggs, still sitting on the floor.

"You had enough, friend? Or do you take some more of that dish?"

"You busted my ribs," said Muggs.

Paddy Brennan remembered the broken body of the Dicer. He stepped up to Cortina and pulled him to his feet. He hit him a raking left hook that ripped hide from his face, then two rights to his body, then jerked the heel of his hand up along Cortina's face.

"That isn't nice," Paddy said. "I don't like to play this way, but then you aren't nice boys."

He stepped back.

"Think you can take that, Farnum?" He pulled the junkyard operator to his feet. "What do you say? Talk or take a beating."

"Shut up, Farnum," Cortina muttered, "or I'll kill you!" Paddy hit Cortina between the eyes, and the man fell hard. Paddy walked over, and setting the case flat on the table, he popped the latches.

TEN MINUTES LATER he came out and got into his car. With him he had Farnum and Cortina. The Italian's face was raw and bloody, but Farnum was scarcely more than frightened, although one eye was growing black, and his lips were puffed. Paddy put the case in the trunk of his rented car.

SAMMY WAS PACING up and down the arena corridor when he came in.

"Paddy!" He rushed over, his face worried. "What happened?"

"Nothing," Brennan said quietly. He carried the heavy case to the door of the shower room and set it inside. He turned back to Sammy. "Let's get dressed."

He was bandaging his hands when Vino came in with Bickerstaff. Vino's sallow face cracked into a brief smile, and he gave Brennan a limp hand.

"Just dropped in. How about a little talk?"

"Sure," Paddy said. "Sure enough, I'll talk. Take a powder, Sammy."

Sammy hesitated. Then he turned and went out, closing the door softly behind him.

Bickerstaff sat down astride a chair, leaning on the back of it. He wore a cheap blue serge suit, and his black shoes were high-topped, but showed white socks above them. His pink, florid face looked hard now, and his small blue eyes were mean.

"Get on with it," Brennan said, drawing the bandage across his knuckles again and smacking his fist into his palm. "What's up?"

"You got plenty, kid," Vino said. "You sure made a hit beating Bristow that way. There is a big crowd out here tonight."

"You're telling me?" Brennan said. "So what?"

"We spent a lot of dough on Ketchell," Vino said carefully. "He's good, plenty good. Maybe he can beat you."

"Maybe."

"It's like this, Paddy," Vino said, striving to be genial. "We ain't in this racket for our health. Suppose you beat Ketchell. Who will you fight next? The champ? Maybe. If not there ain't a good shot in sight. Then, we lose a lot of gold. We paid off to get him where he is."

"What's on your mind?" Brennan demanded. "Get to the point." He cut a band of tape into eight narrow strips.

"Suppose you lose?" Vino suggested. "Suppose you take one in the sixth. It ain't too late to lay some bets. Then we give you a return fight, see? We all make dough. Anyway," he added, "you should tie up with us. Ketchell won't last. You will. You need a smart manager."

"Yeah?" Brennan asked. "How smart? An' where does Sammy get off?"

"Look," Bickerstaff suggested. "I got a couple of youngsters, a middle and a welter. Let Sammy take care of them. You need somebody smart, Brennan. You got color, you got a punch, you can make some real gold in there."

"What gives you the idea I think you're smart?" Paddy asked. He was putting the strips between his fingers and sticking them down. "I haven't seen any champions you boys handled. Ketchell wouldn't be in the spot he's in now if Dicer hadn't been killed."

Vino took his cigarette from his mouth very carefully. He held it in his fingers, the burning end toward him, and looked up like gangsters do in the movies.

"Maybe he would, maybe not," he said noncommittally.

"I'd like to have had another crack at Garry," Brennan said. "I wanted that guy."

Bickerstaff's face was frozen.

"I thought you two were pals," he said.

"Us?" Brennan shrugged, sliding from the rubbing table to his feet, beginning to move his arms around. "We were once. When things got serious, when he started thinking about the title . . . well, you know how those things are, the friendship didn't last."

Vino stood very still.

"Yeah?" he said.

Bickerstaff spoke up. "What about this fight? You ain't got but a few minutes."

"I'm not going to play," Brennan said. "What would I get? I can beat Ketchell. What can you guys do for me that I can't do for myself?"

"We can take care of you," Bickerstaff said. "Ketchell hasn't lost any fights since we had him."

"You got a break," Brennan said. "Just like I did when Garry got killed." He shook his head. "You know, I heard about you guys, I heard you were smart. I thought maybe when Garry got it that you guys pulled the strings. I figured you were wise, that you stood by your fighters, that you saw they won, or they lost for good money. But when I got down there, it was only an accident. So I say nuts to you."

"We can be tough," Bickerstaff said, his eyes hard.

"Don't make me laugh," Brennan told him, jabbing with his left. "What good would it do you to get tough with me after Ketchell's finished? That wouldn't be smart. I'm looking for a manager, but I want somebody smart."

Vino's eyes were cold. "Just what is this, Brennan? You're stalling."

"Sure." Paddy stopped and hitched up his tights. "Sure, I'm stalling. You said you weren't in this racket for your health. Well, I'm not either. I'm going where the dough lays. I can't see how I'm going to make out with you guys. So I'm going out there and cop a Sunday on Ketchell's chin."

The door opened, and Sammy stuck his head in.

"Better get set, Brennan. It's time to go."

When the door closed, Bickerstaff looked at Vino, then back at Brennan.

"Listen," he said. "What if we showed you how smart you would be to tie up?"

Brennan chuckled. "You look like tinhorns to me. What if some of the big mobs wanted in?"

Vino snapped his cigarette into the shower.

"I am the big mob," he said flatly.

"Yeah? You and every dago kid down on the corner."

Vino's eyes hardened, he straightened, but Bickerstaff cut in. "Get smart, kid. We take care of our boys. Look at Ketchell."

"An accident," Brennan said. "A car accident saved him."

"There's accidents, and *accidents*," Vino said, softly.

"Tryin' to kid me?" Brennan pulled his robe around his shoulders. "I saw that car and there was a witness."

"Only dumb guys make it plain," Bickerstaff said. "We know our stuff."

"Well, that would be a joke on Garry, the rat," Brennan said. "He thought he was the smart one."

"You get in there with Ketchell," Vino said. "You take one in the sixth. Make it look like an accident. Then we'll bill you with him again for a big gate, and you win.

We'll see you get the title if you sign with us. And we'll take care of you."

"Listen, Vino," Brennan said. "It sounds good, but don't give me this 'accident' malarkey. You got lucky and so you're acting like a big shot. If you're real lucky maybe I'll run into a truck while I'm climbing into the ring!"

"Don't be stupid, you punk!" Vino stepped close. "I fixed Garry. He wouldn't play, see?" He paused, staring at Brennan. "I don't like boys that don't play. So I had that truck there; I had witnesses there. I even had a guy ready if the truck didn't finish it. Now you do as you're told or we'll finish you!"

Bickerstaff's face was strained. "Vino," he said, "what if he drops a dime on us?"

"Yeah?" Vino sneered. "If I even thought he'd dime us out, I'd cook him. One sign that he ain't going to play ball, and he gets it."

"I don't rat," Brennan said quietly. "I don't have to rat. All right, I'll play ball. I'll play it the way you never saw it played before."

THE LIGHTS WERE bright over the ring. Paddy Brennan felt good, getting away from Vino and Bickerstaff. He rubbed his feet in the resin, and the old feeling began to come over him. He trotted to his corner, where Sammy was waiting.

"What's up, kid? You goin' to tell me? Is it a flop?"

Brennan rubbed his feet on the canvas, dancing a little.

"In the sixth," he said. "They want me out in the sixth. They want to give you a welter and a middle and take me for themselves."

Sammy looked up, and Brennan realized how small he was.

"Oh?" he said. "So they want that, do they?"

"Keep your chin up, Sammy," Brennan said. "Let's get this one in the books. Then we'll talk."

When the bell clanged, Ketchell came out fast. He looked fit, and he moved right. He'd come up the easy way, but he'd had the best schooling there was. Paddy had a feeling this wasn't going to be easy. Ketchell's left licked out and touched his eye. Paddy worked around Ketchell, then feinted, but Tony backed off, smiling.

Brennan walked in steadily, feinted, feinted again, and then stabbed a quick left to the face and a right to the chin. The punches shook Ketchell and made him wary. His left jabbed again, and then again.

He circled, went in punching. He shot a left to the head, and bored in, punching for the body, then to the head, then took a driving right that bounced off his chin. It set him back on his heels for a second, and another one flashed down the groove, but he rolled his head and whipped a right to the body that made Ketchell back up.

When the round ended, they were sparring in the center of the ring, and Paddy Brennan went to his corner, feeling good. The bell came, but not soon enough. He leaped to close quarters and started slugging. He felt punches battering and pounding at him, but he kept walking in, hitting with both hands. Once Tony staggered, but he stepped away in time before Brennan could hit him again.

Then a solid right smashed Paddy on the head, and a left made the cut stream blood. Momentarily blinded, a right smashed on his chin and he felt himself falling, and then a flurry of blows came from everywhere, and he fought desperately against them. When he realized what was happening again, the referee was saying nine, and then the bell was ringing. He staggered to his corner and flopped on the stool. Sammy was working over him.

"Watch it, kid," Sammy said, gasping. "Take nine every time you're down."

"Once was enough," Paddy said. "I'm not going down again."

"*Once?*" Sammy's voice was very amazed. "What do you mean—*once?*" He paused, staring at Brennan intently. "What round is this?" he demanded.

"End of the second," Brennan said. "What's the matter? You punchy?"

"*You* are," Sammy said. "This is the fifth coming up. You've been down four times."

Then the bell rang again, and Paddy went out. Ketchell was coming in fast and confident. A raking left snapped at his face, and Paddy rolled his head. Suddenly, something inside him went cold and vicious. Knock him down four times? Why, the—

His right thudded home on Ketchell's ribs with a smash like a base hit, then he hunched his shoulders together and started putting them in there with both hands. Ketchell backed up.

Suddenly Paddy Brennan felt fine again. His head was singing, his mouth was swollen, but he hooked high and low, battering Ketchell back with a rocking barrage of blows. A right snapped out of somewhere, and he barely slipped it, feeling the punch take his shoulder just below his ear.

Then, suddenly, Ketchell was on his knees with his nose broken, and blood bathing his chest and shoulders. The bell sounded wildly through the cheering, roaring crowd.

It was the sixth.

When he stood up, he could see Vino down there. Vino's eyes were on him, cold and wary. Paddy Brennan remembered Dicer.

He walked out fast, and Ketchell came in, but he could see by Ketchell's eyes what he was expecting. Paddy feinted and slid into a clinch, punching with one hand free.

"They make it easy for you, don't they?" he said. "Even murder?"

Brennan broke and saw Ketchell's face was set and cold. There was a killer in him. Well, he'd need it. Paddy walked in, hooking low and hard, smashing them to the head, slipping short left hooks and rights and all the while watching for that wide left hook of Ketchell's that would set him up for the inside right cross. Through the blur, he saw Ketchell's face, and he let his right down a little where Ketchell wanted it and saw the left hook start.

His own right snapped, and he felt his glove thud home. Then his left hooked hard but there was nothing in front of him and he moved back. He could see Tony Ketchell on the floor, and hear someone shouting in the crowd. He could see Bickerstaff on his feet, his face white, and behind him, Vino, his face twisted, lips away from the teeth. Then the referee jerked his arm up, and he knew he had won the fight.

CLARA CAME RUNNING to meet him in the dressing room. She had been crying, and she cried out when she saw his face.

"Oh, your poor eye!" She put up her hand to touch it, and then he grabbed her and swung her away . . . Vino was standing in the door with a gun in his hand.

"You're a real smart kid, huh? Back up, sister. Lover

boy and I are walking to my car. You'll be lucky if you get him back."

Brennan lunged with his right in the groove and saw the white blast of a gun and felt the heat on his face. Then his right landed, and Vino went down.

All of a sudden, Clara had him again, and the room was full of people. Sergeant O'Brien was picking Vino up, and Vino was all bloody, and his face twisted in hate.

"Get offa me, copper!" he snarled. "You haven't got anything on me I can't get fixed—"

"You're under arrest for murder," O'Brien said to Vino. "You and Bickerstaff and Cortina. And when this hits the papers the boys in Brooklyn won't fix you up, they're going to drop you like a hot potato."

Vino's face turned a pasty white.

"You got nothing but this pug's say-so," he declared.

"Oh, yes, we have," O'Brien said. "We've got Farnum's statement, and Cortina's. But we don't need them. We were in the next room when you talked to Brennan. We had a wire recorder microphone hung on the shower partition. It was Paddy's idea."

When they had gone, Brennan sat down slowly on the table.

He pulled Clara toward him. "They're all big money fights from now on, Clara. There'll be time now . . . time for us."

"But we'll fix that eye first," she said. "I don't intend to have my man dripping blood all over everything."

She hesitated.

"I can't stand seeing you hurt, but, Paddy—I guess it's the Irish in me—oh, Paddy, it was a grand, grand fight, that's what it was!"

TIME OF TERROR

_____

W HEN I LOOKED up from the menu, I was staring into the eyes of a man who had been dead for three years.

Only he was not dead now. He was alive, sitting on the other side of the horseshoe coffee counter, just half a room away, and he was staring at me.

Three years ago I had identified a charred body found in a wrecked car as this man. The car had been his. The remains of the suit he wore were a suit I recognized. The charred driver's license in his wallet was that of Richard Marmer. The size, the weight, the facial contours, the structure of the burned body, all were those of the man I knew. I was called upon to identify the body because I had been his insurance agent, and I had also known him socially.

On the basis of my identification, the company had paid the supposed widow one million two hundred twenty thousand dollars. Yet the man across the room was Richard Marmer, and he was not dead.

Who else could know of my mistake? His wife? Was *she* still alive? Was I the only person alive who could testify that the man across the room was a murderer? For he must be responsible for the man whose body was found. The logic of that was inevitable.

He was getting up from his place, picking up his check. He was coming around the counter. He sat down beside me. My flesh crawled.

"Hello, Dryden. Recognized me, didn't you?"

My mouth was dry and I could not find words. What could one say at such a time? I must be careful . . . careful.

He went on. "It's been a long time, but I had to come back. Now that you've seen me I guess I'll have to tell you."

"Tell me what?"

"That you're in it, too. Right up to your neck."

"I don't know what you're talking about."

"Have some more coffee, we have a lot to talk about. I took care of all this years ago . . . just in case." He ordered coffee for both of us and when the waitress had gone, he said quietly, "After the insurance was paid to my wife, one hundred thousand dollars was deposited to an account under your name at a bank in Reno."

"That's ridiculous."

"It's true. You took your vacation at June Lake that year, and you fished a little at Tahoe." Marmer was pleased with his shrewdness . . . and he had been shrewd. "I knew you went there to fish, and I knew when your vacation was so I timed it all very carefully. The bank officials in Reno will be prepared to swear you deposited that money. I forged your signature very carefully. After all"—he smiled—"I practiced it for almost a year."

They would believe I had been bribed, that I had been in on it.

He could have done it, there was no doubt of that. He had imitated me over the phone more than once; he had fooled friends of mine. It had seemed merely a peculiar quirk of humor until now!

"It wouldn't stand up," I objected, but without hope, "not to a careful investigation."

"Possibly. Only it must first be questioned, and so far there is no reason to believe that it will ever be doubted."

There *was* a reason; I was determined to get in touch with the police, as soon as I could get out of here, and take my chances.

"You see," he continued, "you would be implicated at once. And of course, you would be implicated in the murder, too."

The skin on my neck was cold. My fingers felt stiff. When I tried to swallow my throat was dry.

"If murder is ever suspected, they will suspect you, too. I even"—he smiled—"left a letter in which I said that you were involved . . . and that letter will get to the district attorney. I have been very thorough, Dryden! Very thorough!"

"Where's your wife?" I asked him.

He chuckled and it had a greasy, throaty, awful sound. "She made trouble." He turned a bit and something metallic bumped against the counter. I looked down. The butt of a flat automatic protruded from the edge of his coat. When I looked back up, he smiled.

"It's all true, Dryden. Come out to the car, I'll prove it to you."

My thoughts fluttered wildly at the bars of the cage he was building around me. And yet, I doubted that it was really a cage at all. He had killed an innocent man, now it seemed he had killed his wife, what was there to keep him from killing me, too? He had nothing to lose, nothing at all. What he had told me of the involved plot to implicate me was probably a lie. Somehow I couldn't imagine a man who would kill someone in order to cash in on his life insurance, and then kill his wife, giving up one hundred thousand dollars on the off chance that it would keep me quiet. Marmer just wanted to get me out to the car. He wanted to get me out to the car so he could kill me.

What was left for me? What was the way out? There had been an officer in the army who told us there was always a way out, that there was always an answer . . . one had only to think.

Fear.

That was my salvation, my weapon, the one thing with which I could fight! Suddenly, I knew. My only weapon lay before me, the weapon of my mind. I must think slowly, carefully, clearly. I must be an actor.

Here beside me was a man who had killed, a man with a gun who certainly wanted to kill me. My only weapon was my own mind and the fear that lay ingrained deep in the convolutions of his brain. Though he was behaving calmly he must be a frightened, worried man. I would frighten him more. What was the old saying about the guilty fleeing when no man pursued? I must talk to him . . . I must lie, cheat, anything to keep myself alive. There was an old Arabic quotation that I had always liked: "Lie to a liar, for lies are his coin; steal from a thief, for that is easy; lay a trap for the trickster and catch him at first attempt, but beware of an honest man."

His fear was my weapon, so I must spin around this man a web of illusion and fear, a web so strong that he would have no escape . . .

"All of you fellows are the same"—I picked up my coffee, smiling a little—"you plan so carefully and then overlook the obvious. I always liked you, Marmer," that was a lie, for I never had, "and I'm glad to see you now."

"Glad?" He stared at me.

"What I mean," I made my voice dry and a little tired, "should be obvious. I'll admit I was startled when I saw you here, but I was not worried because this could be an opportunity for both of us. You can save your life and I can regain my reputation with the company."

"What the hell are you talking about?" He stared at me. He was skeptical, but he was not sure. That was my weapon . . . he could not be sure.

For what mind is free of doubt? In what mind lies no fear? How great then must be the fear of a man who has murdered twice over? The world is his enemy, all eyes are watching him. All ears are listening, all whispers are about him.

When could he be sure that somebody else, some clerk, some filling station attendant, somebody who had known him . . . when could he be sure he was not seen?

A criminal has two qualities in excess of other men, optimism and egotism. He believes things will turn out right for him and he believes he is smarter, shrewder . . . or at least he believes that on the surface . . . beneath lies a morass of doubt, a deep sink of insecurity and fear.

"Marmer," I spoke carefully and in a not unfriendly tone, "you've been living in a fool's paradise. Not one instant since you committed your crime have you been free. Your wife got your insurance money so you believed your crime had been successful."

Behind the counter was a box of tea bags, it was partly behind a plastic tray of spoons but I could see CONSTANT COM . . . written on the box.

"You forgot," I continued, "about Constant."

"What?"

"Bob Constant was an FBI man, one of their crack operators. He quit the government and accepted a better-paying job as head of the investigation setup in our insurance company.

"He'd been in the business a long time and such men develop a feeling for *wrongness,* for something out of place. So he had a hunch about your supposed death."

Oh, I had his attention now! He was staring at me, his eyes dilated. And then as I talked I actually remembered something that had bothered me. I seemed to see again a bunch of keys lying on a policeman's desk . . . his keys. Something about those keys had worried me, but at the time I could find nothing wrong. How blind I had been! Now, at last, I could see them again and I knew what had been wrong!

"He checked all your things, and when he came to your keys, he checked each one. Your house key was not among them."

He drew a quick, shocked breath. Then he said, "So what?" But he did not look at me, and his fingers fidgeted at his napkin.

"Why should a man's house key not be in his pocket? He was puzzled about that. It was not logical, he said. I objected that your wife could let you in, but he would not accept that. You should still have a key.

"Suppose, he asked me, that the dead man is not the insured man? Suppose the dead man was murdered and substituted, and then at the last minute the murderer remembered the key . . . perhaps his wife was away from home . . . then he would take that key from the ring, never suspecting it would be noticed.

"So he began to investigate, the money had been paid, but that was not the end. Your wife had left town, several months, at least. But probably you didn't trust her with all that money. She had said she was going to live with her sister . . . only she didn't. He knew that within a few hours. Then where had she gone?

"You see, Marmer? Bob Constant (I was beginning to admire my invention) was suspicious, so he started the wheels moving. All over the United States a description went out, a description of you and of your wife. New people in a community were quietly looked over, your relatives were checked. Your sister-in-law had been getting letters from your wife, and then they stopped. Your sister-in-law was worried.

"More wheels started turning," I said quietly, "they are looking for you now in a thousand cities. For over a year, we have known you were alive. For over two years evidence has been accumulating. They don't tell me much about it. I'm only a small cog in a big wheel."

"You're lying!" His voice was louder, there was an underlying strain there.

"We dug up the body," I continued quietly, ". . . doctors keep records of fractures, you know, and we wanted to check this body for a broken bone that had healed.

"Did you ever watch a big police system work? It doesn't look like much, and no particular individual seems to do very much, yet when all their efforts mesh on one case the results are prodigious. And you . . . you are on the wrong end of it.

"No information is safe. Baggage men, hotel people, telephone operators, all are anxious to help the police if only to be known as cooperative in case they want to fix a parking ticket."

I was talking for my life, talking because I knew this man was willing to kill me, and that he could do it now and there would be small chance that I could protect myself in any way. Suppose I grabbed him suddenly, and throttled him? Suppose I killed him? I couldn't do that. I couldn't do it because I didn't know if I could and because of the fear that he hadn't been lying, that he had, in fact, set me up.

Never had life been so beautiful as then! All the books I wanted to read, the food I wanted to taste, the hours I wanted to spend at many things, all of them seemed vastly greater and more beautiful than ever before.

Fear . . . it was my only weapon . . . if I was lucky he might let me go or, more realistically, if I got away he might choose to go into hiding rather than pursue me. I also realized I might have another weapon . . . hope.

"They can't miss, Marmer, you're not safe and you never have been. Did you ever see a man die in a gas chamber? I have. You hear that it is very quick and very easy. You can believe that if you like. And what is quick? The word is relative.

"Did you ever think how that could be, Marmer? To live, even for an instant, without hope? But in those months on death row, waiting, there is no hope."

"Shut up."

He said it flatly, yet there was a ring of underlying terror in it, too. Who was to say what responsive chords I might have touched? "Have it your own way," I said, then I moved to close the deal. "You can beat the rap if you're smart."

"What?" He stared at me, his interest captured in spite of himself. "What do you mean?"

"Look," I was dry, patient. "Do you think that I want to see you dead? Come on, man, we've been friends! The insurance company could be your ally in this. Suppose you went to them now . . . Suppose you went up there and confessed, and then offered to return what money you have left? You needn't even return it all." I was only thinking of winning my safety now. I was in there, trying. "But some is better than none. They would help you make a deal . . . extenuating circumstances. Who knows what a good lawyer could do? We've only been collecting evidence on you, that you weren't dead. We've nothing on the dead man in the car; we've nothing on your wife. They would be glad to get some of their money back and would cut a deal to help you out. You could beat the death penalty."

He sat very still and said nothing. He was crumpling the paper napkin in his fingers. I dared not speak. The wrong move or the wrong word . . . at least, he was worried, he was thinking.

"No!" He spoke so sharply that people looked up. He noticed it and lowered his voice. "Come on! We're getting out of here! Make one wrong move or say one word and I'll let you have it!"

He said no more about showing me the deposit from Reno. Had I thrown away my chance at life by pushing him too hard? Had I forced him to kill me? We got up.

Maybe I could have done something. Perhaps I could have reached for him, but there were a dozen innocent people in that café; within gun range. I wanted no one else injured or killed even though I wanted to save myself.

We paid our checks and stepped out into the cool night air . . . a little mist was drifting in over the building. It would be damp and foggy along the coast roads.

We walked to his car, and he was a bare step behind me. "Get behind the wheel," he said, "and drive carefully. Don't get us stopped. If you do, I'll kill you."

When we were moving, I spoke to him quietly. "What are you going to do, Rich? I always liked you. Even when you pulled this job, I still couldn't feel you were all wrong. Somewhere along the line you didn't get a decent break, something went wrong somewhere.

"That's why I've tried to help you tonight, because I was thinking of you."

"And not because you were afraid to die?" he sneered.

"Give me a chance to help you . . . I'd rather die than go through what you have ahead, always ducking, dodging, worrying, knowing they were always there, closing in around you, stifling you.

"And now, of course, there will be this. Those people in the café saw us leave together. They'll have a good description of you."

"They never saw me before!"

"I know . . . but they have seen me many times. I've always eaten in there by myself, so naturally the first time I sat with somebody else they would be curious and would notice you."

Traffic was growing less. He was guiding me by motions, and he was taking me out toward Palos Verdes and the cliffs along the sea. The fog rolled in, blanketing the road in spots. It was gray and thick.

"The gas isn't like this fog, Marmer," I said, "you don't see it."

"Shut up!" He slugged me backhanded with the gun. It wasn't hard, he didn't want to upset my driving.

"It isn't too late . . . yet. You can always go with me to the company."

"You stupid fool, I'm not going to turn myself in."

"You should, because it's only a matter of days now, or hours."

The gun barrel jarred against my ribs and peeled hide. "Shut up!" His voice lifted. "Shut up or I'll kill you now!"

Bitterly, I stared at the thickening fog. All my talking had been useless. I was through. I might fight now, but with that gun in my ribs I'd small chance.

Suddenly I saw a filling station. Two cars were parked there and people were laughing and talking. I was not going to die! I was . . . I casually put the car in neutral, aimed for an empty phone booth beside the road, and jerking up on the door handle, lunged from the car. The gun went off, its bullet burning my ribs, the muzzle blast tearing at my clothes. I went over and over on the pavement, the surface of the road tearing my shoulder, my knees, my hands. There was a crash of metal, the sound of breaking glass, and then silence. I rolled over, turning toward the wreck. The people at the gas station stared, frozen.

Then the car door popped open and after a moment a figure moved, trying to get out of the car, trying to escape. The hand clutching the gun banged on the roof as Marmer tried to lever himself up. The dark form took one step and cried out, his left leg collapsed under him, and he fell to the ground. He rolled on his side, the gun moved in the darkness. There was a shot.

My hands were shaking and my lips trembled. I picked myself up off the road and staggered toward the car.

Richard Marmer's head was back and there was blood on the gravel. He must have put the gun in his mouth and pulled the trigger a moment after he discovered that his leg was broken . . . a moment after he had finally realized he was trapped.

SLOWLY, MY LEGS shaking, I turned and started down the road toward the filling station.

I was alive . . . alive . . .

The fog drifted like a cool, caressing hand across my cheek. Somebody dropped a tire iron and people were moving toward me.

WHAT IS LOUIS L'AMOUR'S
LOST TREASURES?

LOUIS L'AMOUR'S LOST TREASURES is a project created to release some of the author's more unconventional manuscripts from the family archives.

Currently included in the series are *Louis L'Amour's Lost Treasures: Volume 1,* published in the fall of 2017, and *Volume 2,* which will be published in the fall of 2019. These books contain both finished and unfinished short stories, unfinished novels, literary and motion picture treatments, notes, and outlines. They are a wide selection of the many works Louis was never able to publish during his lifetime.

In 2018 we will release *No Traveller Returns,* L'Amour's never-before-seen first novel, which was written between 1938 and 1942. In the future, there may be a selection of even more L'Amour titles.

Additionally, many notes and alternate drafts to Louis's well-known and previously published novels and short stories will now be included as "bonus feature" postscripts within the books that they relate to. For example, the Lost Treasures postscript to *Last of the Breed* will contain early notes on the story, the short story that was discovered to be a missing piece of the novel, the history of the novel's inspiration and creation, and information about unproduced motion picture and comic book versions.

An even more complete description of the Lost Treasures project, along with a number of examples of what is in the books, can be found at louislamourslosttreasures .com. The website also contains a good deal of exclusive material, such as pieces of unknown stories that were too short or too incomplete to include in the Lost Treasures books, plus personal photos, scans of original documents, and notes.

All of the works that contain Lost Treasures project materials will display the Louis L'Amour's Lost Treasures banner and logo.

LOUIS L'AMOUR'S LOST TREASURES

POSTSCRIPT

By Beau L'Amour

O*ff the Mangrove Coast* is one of my favorite collections of Louis L'Amour stories. This has a lot to do with the number of references to my father's actual life that it contains, some of which are more obvious than others. For example, the Oregon locations Louis featured in "Fighters Should Be Hungry"—Portland, St. Johns, and Astoria—were all places with which he was familiar. Louis lived in Portland, worked in St. Johns, and spent a good deal of time in Astoria as a young man. I am also pretty sure that Bickerstaff, one of the tough guys in "The Rounds Don't Matter," was named after a man in the garment business who may have taken advantage of my father and a number of other people in Klamath Falls, Oregon . . . though it must be said that the fault might also have been that of Mr. Bickerstaff's supplier.

In "The Unexpected Corpse" we meet Sue Shannon, a Hollywood starlet who was almost without a doubt inspired by Ann Steely, an actress friend of my father's better known as Cathy O'Donnell. Like Sue, Ann seems to have had an unhappy childhood (though the part about the unmentioned "trouble" with her uncle is almost certainly fictionalized) and dreamed of a life in the theater. Like Jim, the narrator of the story, Dad encouraged her and provided unsparing advice about the dedication required to make her dreams a reality. Though Ann and Louis corresponded somewhat flirtatiously while he was overseas during WWII and she was living in Oklahoma, they saw each other only a few times once Dad moved to Hollywood. I have little doubt, however, given the tone of their letters and Ann's somewhat dramatic approach to life, that if she had ever gotten in trouble she would have called on him, just as Sue calls on Jim.

Looking carefully at "The Cross and the Candle," I believe that the café my father describes in the opening paragraphs is a quainter and quieter version of La Vie Parisienne, the Paris nightclub owned by the celebrated singer and actress Suzy Solidor.

Here are a couple pieces extracted from letters Louis wrote to his parents from France during the waning days of the war:

```
There seems some evidence that
part of the family [the L'Amour
family] either were connected with
Surcouf, the cordair [corsair] and
great Breton hero, or were with him
on his ships. So, I'm going down
tomorrow evening to see Suzy
Solidor, a great grand daughter of
his who owns the Chez Suzy, a night
club on the Rue St. Anne, near the
```

Louvre . . . It seems she was a few
years ago one of the great beauties
of Europe; that she was also a
famous model; that she is still
striking and attractive . . . I
dropped by the night club last night
but it was full to the doors and not
a place anywhere, but I told the
doorkeeper I was a writer, and came
of an old Breton family . . . So I
have an appointment with Suzy
tomorrow night at ten.

And . . .

The place has over a hundred
portraits of her done by all the
famous artists of the past thirty
years. She is about fifty, or
perhaps a few years younger, and
still something of a woman.

Many of these portraits were indeed painted by significant artists like Picasso, Braque, and Tamara de Lempicka. It is interesting, given the subject of Louis's story, that Suzy herself was convicted of being a collaborator. I am unaware of the exact charges but I suspect this was more related to the popularity of her club with Nazi officers than to her having possibly betrayed beautiful resistance fighters or secret societies of crusaders.

Out of all these stories the one that is the most personal and true to Louis's life is "It's Your Move." Though it wasn't published in the 1980 collection *Yondering,* I consider it part of that same continuum. These stories were Dad's reminiscences of the men (and women) who, as Robert Service put it, "don't fit in," the disenfranchised wanderers of the 1920s and '30s: hobos, itinerant laborers, refugees, sailors, and soldiers of fortune.

The *Yondering* series is incomplete, but it set out to present this world and these people in a selection of short stories set in three different cities; San Pedro, California, in the 1920s ("Old Doc Yak," "It's Your Move," "And Proudly Die," "Survival," and "Show Me the Way to Go Home"); Shanghai, China, in the 1930s ("The Admiral," "Shanghai, Not Without Gestures," and "The Man Who Stole Shakespeare"); and Paris in the 1940s ("The Cross and the Candle" and "A Friend of the General"). Other stories, like "Death Westbound" and "Thicker Than Blood," and Louis's first novel, *No Traveller Returns,* told the tales of the ships and trains, the treks and voyages, that connected the world in the era between the great wars of the twentieth century.

A good deal of the action in "It's Your Move" takes place at the Seamen's Church Institute in San Pedro. Many men "on the beach" (out of work) used the Institute as their meeting place, living room, clubhouse, or office. Sometimes, when he could spare the change, Dad would shower and sleep there. Here he is describing it in a recorded interview:

. . . the Seamen's Institute was a place like a YMCA but for sailors. The Seamen's Institute, which was very well conducted, they had beds which you could get for fifty cents a night. They had showers and

```
whatnot and they also had a library
there and a big room where there
were a lot of checker tables and we
had some of the finest checker
players, I think, there ever was
anywhere would come into that room.
```

The character of Sleeth, whom Louis, in the same interview, indicates was based on a real person, also shows up in *Louis L'Amour's Lost Treasures: Volume 1*. In *Samsara*, a mysteriously personal set of story fragments dealing with reincarnation, Sleeth recognizes the young hero as a man he has known in a past life and provides him with the connections to continue his enlightenment once he arrives in the Far East. Sleeth also tells the protagonist of a hidden archive, the stored memories of those reborn, going back to the dawn of time.

This archive is located in western China, and it is just possible that another fragment, also in *Lost Treasures: Volume 1*, titled "Journey to Aksu," might have been planned as a continuation of that unfinished novel. One draft out of many briefly connected the two. In *Samsara*, Sleeth provides the hero, a young man who shares a good deal of my father's history, with connections in Shanghai, while "Journey to Aksu" deals with a mercenary soldier who discovers a city in China's Xinjiang region that contains some sort of ancient and mysterious secret. A fascinating series of connections, and all stemming from a character who may have been a real person!

"Off the Mangrove Coast" is another title that has a connection to Dad's semiautobiographical *Yondering* series. In the summer of 1939 Louis related a similar tale as if it were true to columnist Roger Devlin of the *Tulsa Tribune*. In his column, Devlin wrote:

Louis condensed four thrilling weeks of treasure hunting into a few agonizingly casual sentences. Happened up in the Malay States, he recalled. Some native ruler had fled a revolution a few years before, loading all his gold and jewels on a river boat. Hurricane came up, ship sank.

"It was believed to be several million dollars of treasure in the ship's strong room," Louis said. "A bunch of [us] obtained a boat and with four weeks' supply of food aboard, we set out to be wealthy.

"We charted the currents of the river, figuring just where the ship might have drifted. That took time. But finally, in diving outfits, we found a sunken vessel, and we were fairly certain it was the right one.

"The only trouble was that it was half drifted over with sand, and it took us a long time to clear that off. Then we found the ship was made of teak, just about the hardest wood going, and even harder after its long immersion. Took a long time to break through the side of the vessel. By then, too, we were

running short of food. Had to live
on the few fish we could catch.

"At last we were just about ready
to break into the strong room. We
felt we already had the treasure in
our hands, when--" He paused . . .

"When another hurricane came up.
We managed to live through it, but
by the time it quieted down the
treasure ship was completely buried
in the sand. Far's I know she's
still there."

Now, the jury is out on whether I really believe all
that. Louis himself noted that there were some mistakes
in Devlin's retelling of the story. But while Dad did spend
some time—even longer than four weeks—in the Feder-
ated Malay States and Netherlands East Indies (today's
Malaysia and Indonesia), and did sail past Darvel Bay,
the location for the wreck in "Off the Mangrove Coast,"
it is highly unlikely he was able to take time off for treasure hunting.

But regardless of its potentially fictional aspects and
whatever inconsistencies may have been added by the reporter, this tale does form a sort of "first draft" for the
short story "Off the Mangrove Coast."

In the entire Louis L'Amour catalog, there is probably
no story that has existed in so many variations as "The
Diamond of Jeru." It has been both a short story and a
novella, a USA Network movie, and a three-hour dramatized audio production. The existence of all these versions seems even more extraordinary when one considers
that the story itself was almost never published at all!

I confess, most of these incarnations are my fault. "The Diamond of Jeru" was a relatively crude pulp story, which as fate would have it, just kept turning into a solution I could use to solve one problem after another. From an initial dislike, my fondness for it has grown exponentially. It's now a bit sad to think that the following history of its evolution will probably be my final opportunity to explore its many aspects.

In the summer of 1951, Louis L'Amour pounded out the short story eventually titled "The Diamond of Jeru." It ran twenty pages, written, no doubt, in just a couple of days. Given its style, I suspect that it was intended for the men's adventure magazines—publications like *Real Adventure* or *MALE,* which were the death rattle of the grand old prewar adventure pulps. These magazines featured frantic "Scorpions Pierced My Flesh!" headlines and even more lurid cover art.

With their emphasis on "real life" adventure, it might seem that this genre was right up Louis's alley, but in reality he was never very comfortable with it. However, the traditional pulp magazines were dying like flies, and book publishers had yet to take a liking to his material, so he really couldn't rule out anything that paid an honest dollar.

Dad made only one attempt to sell "The Diamond of Jeru," sending it in June 1951 to a New York agent who later became notorious for his haphazard business practices. The agent did not place it with a magazine; in fact, he may never have taken it from its envelope. My father's copy went into a pile that later went into a box . . . a box that was filled with unpublished stories and was left in the back of a closet, to be discovered forty years later in the months following his death. Most of those stories were eventually published in the 1990s, but "The Diamond of Jeru" almost didn't make the cut.

Though "Jeru" was always slated to be included in this collection, partway through the process I removed it, feeling that it was not really good enough. Then I got a call from the editor I was working with; the page count for *Off the Mangrove Coast* was coming up short. I considered sticking the original version of the story back in. But even that wasn't a solution—it was only around twenty pages and we needed several times that many.

The answer to all our problems was for me to rewrite it, reworking the narrative into an eighty-page novella. I didn't dislike everything about "Jeru" by a long shot: Borneo, the basic configuration of the characters, and the journey up a mysterious river into the heart of the jungle all had classic appeal. I just wasn't quite sure how all the elements would come together or if I could elevate the story to match the rest of my father's work.

The version of "The Diamond of Jeru" that you have read earlier in this volume is very much a combination of my dad's talents and my own. Although I had previously adapted his work into screenplays, dramatized audios, and things of that sort, this was the first time I had really ever written a story *with* him, so to speak. I was in my late thirties, and he had been gone for ten years, but the result of that process made me feel closer to him than ever. In a very minor way, I got a brief chance to *be* him.

Here is his original 1951 version:

When Lacklan brought his wife to Marudi, he was looking for diamonds, but when we learned he intended to

take her up river with him, we
decided he was a fool.

The northeast jungle of Borneo was
no place for such a girl as Helen
seemed to be, although as it turned
out he was lucky to have brought her
along.

Helen Lacklan was one of those
lush and gorgeous blondes who take a
tan so beautifully, and whose bodies
are so magnificent that one never
suspects them of brains. Moreover,
she had the extraordinary faculty of
always seeming perfectly neat and
perfectly cool. In the sultry heat
of the equator that isn't merely an
achievement, it's a miracle.

Lacklan was a tall man, slightly
stooped, his face betraying his
arrogance and impatience. From the
first I could see he was fiercely
jealous of her, but I could not see
that she gave him any occasion for
it. Never have I seen a man so
positive of his basic rightness on
every question.

As I've said, he came to Borneo
looking for diamonds. Now they find
diamonds around Bandak, around
Kusan, and near Matapura, to name
only a few places. They also find
some rare colors in the Sarawak
River. Most so-called "fancy" stones

are found in Borneo, for diamonds
come in a variety of colors,
including black.

Naturally, they sent him to me.
I'd been in the East Indies almost a
year and was ready to get out, but
it was money I needed. And Lacklan
had money.

Moreover, I wanted one more try up
river myself. Diamonds had become a
specialty of mine and that was why
they sent him to me. Since coming to
Marudi, I had collected every iota
of information on diamonds in that
section of Borneo, and some of the
facts began to add up very curiously
to say the least.

Marudi was the principal town of
the district, which means little.
They do a bit of trade in beeswax,
rattans, gutta-percha, rubber,
camphor, edible bird's nests and
some products of the mines, of which
there were a variety. Gold, silver,
cinnabar, iron, and even coal. A few
coastal steamers come up the river
but sometimes a full month would go
by and there would be none at all.

My place was a deserted bungalow
which I'd adopted and repaired. When
Lacklan and his wife appeared, I was
seated on the veranda idly reading
from Norman Douglas' *South Wind.*

When they turned in the path, I got to my feet and walked to the door. "Come in," I invited, "it isn't often I have visitors."

When they came up on the porch, I noticed at once that Helen's eyes went at once to the book I had been reading. She glanced up quickly, and smiled. "It's rather wonderful, isn't it?"

My immediate reaction was surprise. It was my impression that a girl with her rather emphatic physical equipment would have time for little else. "It's an old friend," I said, smiling.

Lacklan looked from one to the other of us puzzled and irritated. "You're Kardec?" he demanded. "I'm John Lacklan."

"That's right. Mike Kardec. And it's nice to have you come over. This," I asked, turning to her, "is Mrs. Lacklan?"

Lacklan wasted no time. "I understand you're the authority on diamonds?"

"Well," I hesitated over that one, "maybe. Will you sit down? I'll order a drink."

Raj was already at my elbow. He was a Sea Dyak, not over sixteen, but his mind was as quick and intelligent as anyone I've ever encountered.

"Scotch," Helen said, "with soda . . . about half." Raj nodded brightly and glanced at Lacklan, who waved a careless hand. "The same," he said.

When Raj returned with our drinks, he handed them around and Helen sat there sipping hers and watching me. From time to time, she glanced at her husband and, although she said nothing, I had an idea that she missed nothing.

"You've been up the Baram, above Long Sali?"

"Yes." I saw no reason for explaining just how far I had gone. Marudi was a rough sixty miles from the mouth and Long Sali was a village a hundred and fifteen miles further up river. Actually, I had crossed the island to Tarukan once, and had been down the backbone of mountains that divided Sarawak from Borneo proper for more than sixty miles.

"Are there diamonds up there? Gem stones?"

"There are," I agreed, "but they are scattered and hard to find. Most of the stones are alluvial and are washed out of creeks back up the river. Nobody has ever located their source."

"Good! Can you take us three?"

"Us?" I was surprised. "Your wife, too?"

"She goes where I go."

"You know your business best," I said carefully, "but that's no country for a woman. It's jungle, it's miserably hot, and there are natives up there who have never seen a white man, let alone a white woman. Some of them can't be trusted."

"We'll be armed." His manner was brusque and I could see his mind was made up. Perhaps they had already discussed the matter, but from all appearances, it would not have mattered to him what she thought about going. Nor would he have considered worrying about her. "You speak the language?" he asked.

"I speak market place Malay," I said, "and a scattering of Dyak. Also," I added dryly, "I know that country."

"Will you go?" he demanded.

"Not to take Mrs. Lacklan," I said, and then looked over at her. "I don't want to offend you, Mrs. Lacklan, but it is a very rough

country, bad enough for men alone,
and with a woman along . . ."

"I'd as soon stay here, John," she
suggested quietly, "and I think
Mr. Kardec is right. I might make
trouble for you."

"Nonsense!" he replied irritably.
"I want you to go."

She turned to me. "Won't you
reconsider then? I'd promise not to
be any trouble."

"All right," I shrugged it off,
"but remember, I'm not promising you
any diamonds. Nobody can do that.
You've one chance in a thousand of
finding a stone of gem quality."

When he had settled the terms,
they went to the door and Helen
hesitated there. "Thank you," she
said graciously. "I enjoyed the
drink."

It is only once in a lifetime that
a man sees such a woman, and I
confess I looked after them with
envy for him. It made my throat dry
out and my blood throb in my pulses
just to look at her, and it was that
as much as anything else that made
me hesitate. A man needed all his
attention on such a trip as
this . . . and no man could remain
other than completely aware of such
a woman when she was near him.

Nothing moves fast in the tropics, yet despite that I had lined up the boats, boatmen and equipment within two days, and they were to join me for a last evening before we went up river. Yet as they walked up the path, I knew something had gone wrong.

"Kardec?" Then he saw me. "We've made other arrangements. I'll pay what expense you've incurred."

"Other arrangements?" I was puzzled. "You've decided not to go?"

"We'll be going, but with someone else. How much do I owe you?"

Frankly, it made me angry. The deal had been all set, and now . . . I stated my price and he paid me. Helen merely stood there saying nothing, yet it seemed to be her face was showing some resentment or anger that I had not seen there before.

"Mind telling me how you're going?"

"Not at all. But it doesn't seem to matter, does it?" His very arrogance and coolness angered me, and also to have all my excellent planning go for nothing.

"It matters a great deal," I told him. "There's no other white man available, and if you go back in there with a native, you're a fool!"

"You're calling me a fool?" He turned on me sharply, his eyes ugly. For a minute I thought he was going to swing on me and I'd have welcomed it. Until I'd come to the Far East, I'd been a fair to middling light-heavy. I'd have liked nothing so much as to see him lose a few teeth.

"Look," I said, restraining my own anger, "within the past four years several different groups have gone up country from this coast, and only two have come back, excepting myself. Those two had white guides."

"So what?" The words were a sneer. He didn't like me and he would have liked taking a poke at me. I knew that.

"Didn't this native show you a diamond? A big stone? Something about twenty carats?"

They were surprised, both of them. "And what if he did?"

"You tried to buy it and he wouldn't sell. Am I right?"

"And if you are?"

"And if I am right this was the same fellow who guided the parties from Marudi before, also from Kuching, from Sibu and Saratok. None of them ever came back."

"You're implying that he had them killed? For what reasons? For the diamonds they found?"

"Diamonds mean nothing to them. I believe he used the one stone he has to lure them up river so he can murder them for their possessions."

"Nonsense!"

"He was an old man, wasn't he? With a face like a dried prune?"

Their expressions cleared. "No," Lacklan was triumphant. "He was a youngster. No older than your house boy."

So they had switched, that was all. The trick was the same. And they were not the first natives to do that. It had been done by the Piutes in Colorado, with gold nuggets for bait.

"Have it your own way, Lacklan. It wouldn't matter if you were going alone, but you're taking your wife along."

His face flamed and his eyes grew ugly. "My wife is my own concern," he said, "and none of your affair."

"You're right, of course, only I'd do a lot of thinking before I'd let bullheadedness risk my wife's life. Risk your own all you like."

"Nonsense!" Lacklan scoffed.

"You're merely sore because you lost the business."

So they walked away and I could see Helen talking with him as they went up the road toward town. Whatever she said, I heard him answer angrily. Yet her words must have had some influence because that night I was talking to Vandover.

"Say," he said, smiling at me, "what was this story you told the Lacklans about some native luring white men into the jungle? They had it all garbled. Didn't sound like you, at all."

There were four of us there on the veranda of the resident officer's bungalow. "Van," I said, "I believe you'll all agree that I've devoted a lot of time to tracing diamond stories?"

"No doubt about it. But this yarn is a bit thick, isn't it?"

"Remember Carter? That was two years before my time, but he came down from Hong Kong on a vacation. He met some native down on the coast who had a big diamond and wouldn't sell it. The native agreed to show him where there were more. He went up river and was never heard of again.

"A few months later, the same

thing happened to Trondly at Kuching. There were two who went up country from Sibu and Igan, and another from Bintulu. All had the same story to tell before they went up river."

"You think it was the same old native? The same diamond?"

"What else? A native finds a gem stone and sells it, he spends the little he gets, and that's the end of it. This way, that stone represents a permanent income. Rifles, ammo, blankets, trinkets, food, clothing, tools and trade goods . . . and every few months a new supply."

"Fantastic idea." Vandover rubbed his long jaw. "Sounds like something that old blighter of a Jeru might cook up."

"It could be," Fairchild agreed. "You'd better call Kuching on it. Sounds to me like a police matter."

My Scotch tasted good. Turning the glass in my fingers, I looked over at Fairchild. "Using your outboard? Fact is, I'm thinking about following them up river. That fat head can fry in his own juice for all of me, but I'd not like to see Helen Lacklan trapped because of him."

"Use it," Fairchild assented. "If Rector wasn't due in tomorrow I'd go with you."

By daylight the native huts and banana and rubber plantations were behind me. The strong brown stream was muddy and there were occasional logs, but this outboard was a good one and we were making better time than Lacklan would be making. They had started several hours before me and were making good time. I did not attempt to overtake them because I neither wanted them to think me butting in nor did I want old Jeru to know I was following.

My belt gun was a .45 Colt automatic with four extra clips, and I was carrying a Mannlicher big game rifle, a beautiful weapon. It gave me a comforting feeling to have the guns there as I watched the boat push its way up the Baram. The river trended slightly to the south-southeast and then took a sharp bend east, flowing down from among a lot of eight thousand foot peaks. Mostly jungle, yet there were places where stretches of table land waved with grass. This was wild country, rarely visited, and there were small herds of wild elephants, and a good many buffalo.

Only Raj accompanied me. Although a Sea Dyak of the coast, he spoke a number of the dialects and had been with me on my earlier trips. He knew old Jeru well and liked him none at all. From a blotto, the hollowed out tree trunk that is the native boat, he learned from three natives that the boy guiding the group was Jeru's nephew and that all the boatmen were from his village.

The river narrowed and grew increasingly swift. We were well into the Kapuas Mountains, the rugged chain that is the spine of Borneo and terminates in the thirteen thousand foot dome of Kina Balu. The air was clear and the heat less oppressive at the increased altitude.

It was Raj who sighted the boats, concealed under overhanging brush on the riverbank. It was almost at the base of a huge taban tree. Concealing our own boat, we started toward Jeru's village.

Nobody needed to tell me what we were walking toward. We were miles from any possible aid, in an area where it would be extremely difficult to prove any crimes against the natives. We faced a situation from which we must extract

ourselves by our own abilities . . .
or die.

At the same time, old Jeru was
cunning. He had been careful to
cover his actions, careful to avoid
coming too often to the same port to
recruit his prospective victims,
careful to see that no attention was
directed to himself. It had been my
own curiosity about the origin of
the various diamonds reported that
had drawn my attention to him . . .
but of this he was unaware.

John Lacklan and his wife stood in
the center of the clean-swept
village compound. Around them
clustered the villagers, their faces
hard with greed and evil with
murderous eagerness. Jeru's nephew
had disappeared and they stood
alone. Even as we reached the edge
of the compound, we saw several
stalwart fellows push their way to
the front rank of the natives.

"Which one of you will show us to
the stream where the diamonds were
found?" Lacklan asked.

There was no reply, no sound but a
faint shuffling of feet on the hard
ground, only silence and watching
eyes. Helen said something to
Lacklan, but he shook his head. For

the first time, he seemed to be
aware of his danger.

"I'll pay well," Lacklan
persisted, and for him his voice was
surprisingly mild. "Who wants to
show me that stream?"

Still no voice lifted, and then
suddenly a young boy darted from the
crowd and jerked the rifle from
Lacklan's hand. He was totally
unprepared for the action, his
attention centered on the warriors,
and he lost balance and almost fell,
yet he grabbed wildly at the rifle.
Yet even as his hand shot out, a big
native bumped into him and knocked
him off balance to the ground. He
fell hard, and all laughed.

Helen Lackland stood very still,
poised, erect, waiting. She had no
idea what to do and, obviously, she
was frightened, yet I never admired
her more than in that moment. And
then the natives started to crowd
forward.

Stepping from the jungle, I
shouted.

A dropped bomb could have startled
them no more. With shrill cries of
astonishment and alarm, they turned
around to face us. With Raj carrying
my rifle at port arms (how I wished
it was a shotgun!), I walked to the

center of the crowd and took my stand beside Helen Lacklan.

Lacklan was getting to his feet. His face was gray and his eyes glittered. Blood trickled from a cut on his cheekbone. "You, is it?" He glared at me. "Did you put them up to this?"

"John!" Helen was shocked. "What are you saying? They've come to help us!"

"Have they?" Lacklan stared at me, eyes narrow with dislike. "I prefer to wait and see."

Ignoring him, I turned to her. "Mrs. Lacklan," I spoke quietly, "we were afraid of this and followed you. We told them at Marudi, but there is no chance of help. We shall have to get out of this on our own."

"Give me that gun," Lackland said angrily, "I'll show you how to get out of here!"

"If you'll look," I said grimly, "you'll see at least ten guns among the natives. At this range, we wouldn't have a chance."

Jeru had come from his hut and his staring eyes were cold as those of a snake. I knew that my arrival must present a problem to even his savage and primitive kind. Never before had he been followed? Were the white men growing suspicious?

All around me was the evidence that my suspicions had been correct. The rifles, several hatchets, a brass lantern or two, articles of clothing . . . the village was crammed with loot. Was I the only white man? Or had others come? Were others still coming?

"Jeru," I said, using all the authority I could muster, "return Tuan Lacklan's rifle. We go now to hunt for diamonds."

He made no move, just stood there looking at me out of that dried up prune of a face, yet if we could just make the boats . . .

"Look!" Lacklan grabbed Helen's arm excitedly. "Look at the size of that uncut diamond hanging on Jeru's neck!"

"That's not a diamond," I said, never taking my eyes from Jeru, "it's quartz, or something."

"Spirit rock!" Raj whispered to me. "That sekali kuat spirit."

"What does he say?" Lacklan demanded.

"He says that rock has a very strong spirit. This is a new one on me."

"I think I know." Helen stared

curiously at the stone. "It looks like chalcedony. It's probably an enhydro."

Lacklan looked at Helen as if he had never seen her before. "What's an enhydro? I never heard the word. What does it mean?"

The natives were edging nearer. Never in my life had the feel of a Colt in my holster been so good. Yet no matter how fast I shot I'd be lucky to get more than two or three of them before they closed in . . . and then we wouldn't have much time.

Like that . . . it was no way for a man to die, no way at all. This was a situation where mere nerve and a gun wouldn't help. They were too close, there were too many of them. They were altogether too close.

"There's water inside such stones," Helen was speaking quickly. "When the stone is moved, the water often moves. Primitive people often believe a spirit is imprisoned in the rock."

My .45 slid into my hand. Lacklan was staring at the natives, his jaw muscles working. "Jeru!" I yelled. "The rifle!" My gun was trained on his chest. "Return the rifle and call off your people or I shoot the Orang Batu!"

That stopped them. Most of them knew some Malay, and they would certainly know what I meant by the Man of the Rock.

"No good." Jeru stared at me sullenly. "You maybe kill me. Rock dead. The Man of the Rock is gone."

Lacklan was looking longingly at my pistol. I could see the fear and impatience riding him.

Helen looked at Jeru's crystal, but she spoke to me. "Would it help," she suggested, "if you could put the spirit back in the rock? It can be done."

If there was fear in that girl it did not show. If she was trembling it was not in her voice. Here was a woman to walk beside a man, not behind him . . . and certainly not one who would always be fighting to get ahead of him.

It was a gamble, but what else had we. "Jeru," I spoke contemptuously, "the Man of the Rock has left you because of your wickedness." I spoke in Malay, but I knew that he and at least some of the tribe would comprehend me. "You are evil. You have murdered and robbed from your friends the white men who came in peace. You have enriched some of your tribe by theft, but the spirit

of your tribe has gone away. You are
alone now. Sickness and death will
come upon your village unless the
spirit returns. Many sons will die.
The strong men of the village will
die. The game will go from the
forests and the fish from the river.
There will be hunger and evil in
your huts, and there will be evil
and death in your hearts."

Malay is a rolling and beautiful
language when spoken well. Their
eyes were upon me, struggling to
follow. I knew enough of the words
were known to them to give them at
least the sense of what I spoke.

"You lie!" He said it without
strength, sullenly, resentfully,
fearing in his heart that what I
said was true. There was murmuring
among the people.

"I do not lie! The spirit of the
rock is friendly to the white man
and to the white woman. We can bring
him back to your village if your
hearts are right. If he does not
return, your village will die and
the ants will pick over your bones
and the people of Jeru will be no
more."

Whatever it meant, I was gaining
time. In the back of my brain, there
was a vague recollection that

certain quartz crystals contain water or liquid carbon dioxide, and sometimes these are seen as floating bubbles with the rock. Once that water is gone, however . . .

They stared at me, dark superstition stirring within them. Jeru was old and wise, yet superstitious as the rest of them. To these people each rock, each tree, each mountain held a spirit. Yet the spirit of this rock which Jeru wore from his neck was one where the spirit could be seen. It was there, they knew it was there. How long it had been in the village, no man could guess, but now the spirit was gone.

"Only we who are close to the spirit can induce him to return." Their eyes were upon me, haunted, staring.

Out of the side of my mouth I said, low-voiced, "Lady, you'd better be right! What's the gag? How's it done?"

She, too, whispered. "I'll need a kettle or pot, one with a lid. The stronger the better. And a hot fire."

Among the objects in the village was a large iron pot with a lid that I had already seen. Suddenly, I

stepped forward. "Now!" I said, and
knew if this didn't work I was going
to kill old Jeru, at least. "Bring
the rifle to me! You!" I pointed at
one big Dyak. "Bring that pot! You,
you, and you! Build a fire! Gather
stones to place under the pot.
Quick!"

They moved almost without
thinking, and I turned swiftly on
Jeru. "I have no anger for Jeru nor
for his people. I shall induce the
Man of the Rock to return, but he
will stay with you only so long as
you do not do evil to the white men
who are your friends. The things you
have stolen, all must be returned to
Tuan Vandover to free you of evil!"

Other villagers had turned now and
were helping to build high the fire.
They were excited as children. This
was magic, and magic they longed to
see. "Get the rock, Mike," Helen
told me, "and put it in the pot
about two-thirds full of water. Put
the lid on and weight it down with
rocks, then boil that water and
hope!"

"If steam or pressure splits that
stone," I said, "we'd better be the
first to know!"

"I've seen it done with a pressure

cooker," she said. "My dad was a mineralogist."

Then the water was boiling and the lid of the kettle weighted down. I stepped back and faced the flames. "Now don't laugh," I said. "They need something to impress 'em!"

With my hands outstretched toward the flames, I repeated Hamlet's soliloquy in solemn tones, really hamming it up, but good.

In all this time there had been no word from John Lacklan. He stood back at one side, glowering. Maybe I wrong the guy, but I doubt if he even thought of the time we'd gained, of the fact that we might pull them out of the hole. All he was thinking about was that I had been right about Jeru and the diamond and that it was his wife and I who were doing something about it. What was cooking in that narrow skull of his I couldn't guess. I only hoped he'd save it until we were out of here.

"What if this doesn't work?" he sneered.

"You better pray that it does," I replied shortly.

He started at Helen. "You never told me you knew anything about stones!"

"You never gave me a chance, John," she said quietly, and then she lifted her eyes to his. "I was really in love with you, John, but you made it harder and harder to stay that way. You never let me help you, John. You always knew. You always had to be right. Even as a little boy, if you couldn't pitch you wouldn't play."

We watched the flames around the kettle. How much steam would build up inside? How much pressure? How much would it take? I knew nothing of such things. Nor was there, I expect, any general rule. The problem of each stone might be original and different.

Slowly, as the time passed, the natives began to gather around. "Raj," I whispered, "if anything goes wrong, it's every man for himself."

"Yes, Tuan." He looked at me briefly. "If all not well they be very angry. They think much of Orang Batu. Him all right, you be very big man."

There was no use delaying. It was now or never. Some time had passed, and now all waited. Slowly, with a long stick, I moved the fire away, then pushed the rocks from the top of the kettle and pushed off the lid. Instantly, steam billowed up, a great gust of it, and muttering some audible words, using two sticks as tongs, I fished in the kettle for the rock, then lifted it out.

Helen moved close beside me. The steam cleared . . . she gave a little gasp.

My mouth was dry. Turning slowly, with infinite care, I looked over the faces that stared at me. They ringed around us, their eyes wide, expectant. Old Jeru was in the front rank, and now he stepped forward. "How is it with the Orang Batu?" he asked.

Helen said nothing and some native shifted his callused feet on the hard earth. The only good thing was the feel of that Colt in my hand. Helen was looking at the rock again.

"Mike!" Her voice was excited. "Look!"

But I had seen . . . There was one tall, intelligent looking man of some forty years in the group. He had fine features and a strong body. I had noticed there was no friendliness visible between this man and Jeru.

"The Man of the Rock has come back to you," I said, "and he will stay

and bring prosperity to your village
as long as there is no evil among
you."

Jeru took a hesitant step forward,
hand outstretched to receive back
the fortune of the village, but
taking the crystal, I stepped past
him and placed it in the hand of the
tall man of whom I had noticed much.
"You," I said, "will be the keeper
of the Orang Batu. Jeru brought only
evil to your village. You will keep
this and you will speak with the
words of the Orang Batu!"

Sure it was politics! But there
was concentrated evil in the face of
the old devil Jeru, and no man with
such a face could be liked . . .
The tall man, however, was
different . . . Besides, in case of
a fight it is always wise to have
the young and strong on your side.

Jeru? He stepped back like I'd
slapped him, actually seeming to
shrivel. The new chief was no dope.
He stepped out and accepted the rock
and looked at it, and when he moved
it there stirred under the thin
surfaces of the rock a small shadow
shaped like a man. The natives
crowded around to look, and like
Carl Sandburg's "Fog," we departed
on cat feet.

Oh, yes! I did linger . . . just a moment longer.

So that was the story we told the [word missing], and it was the story we talked about, Fairchild, Vandover and I, in the later hours. "What a man couldn't do," Fairchild said, "with a woman like that!"

"What you could do, Fairchild. Or Kardec. Not Lacklan."

"What do you mean?"

Vandover stoked his pipe. "He's all ego, yet she saved his life, pulled him out of the mess he got them into. He'll never forgive her."

Then I remembered what he had said when we got into the boat. "I supposed you two are satisfied," he'd said, "being the whole show."

The next time I saw her it was morning. She came down the path of the bungalow alone. "We're flying out," she said. "I've come to say goodbye."

"I take back what I said, that this country isn't for a woman like you."

She smiled at me, a little forlornly, I thought. "No, Mike, you were right." Her eyes met mine. "I lost a husband here, Mike."

"Hadn't you lost him before?" I asked gently.

She hesitated, looking out over the garden. "Maybe. Or he lost me, or something."

"Sorry," I said, but I lied in my teeth, and she knew it.

"You made the trip for nothing," she said. "It wasn't fair."

"No," I told her, "not for nothing."

She looked at me, hesitated, then said quietly, "Mike, I'd never suggest such a thing to John, but you . . . you're a bigger man. John would never accept anything from me, not even . . . partnership. But Mike, I . . . I'm a wealthy woman, Mike, and I heard you were guiding us just for passage money. Would you let me pay it to you now? You earned it, you know."

She was a very beautiful girl. A very wonderful girl. A very desirable girl. "It won't be necessary."

"You're not just proud? You could pay me back if you liked?"

"No, it isn't being proud. Remember, when I hung back a bit at the village?"

"Yes, of course." She was puzzled.

My hand came from my pocket. "Never under rate a man who has lived as I have, Helen. Just as a

```
man who has lived as I have would
never under rate a woman as lovely
as you." I smiled. "In this sort of
life, well, one always . . ." I
opened my hand.
   On my palm lay an easy twenty-five
carats . . . the diamond of Jeru!
   THE END
```

Whenever I work on one of these old stories, I initially focus on trying to make it a representation of the best of my father's talent, to the point of considering what had happened in his life up to the date it was written and doing research into what he had been writing and reading at the time. After that, however, I try also to fulfill the *story,* to listen to what *it* wanted to become as an entity separate from my father. Once he began writing, Dad would always try to follow where a story would lead him. I do not necessarily have the same unconscious ability and my sensitivities are somewhat different, but I try in my own way to deliver a similar result.

One of my first problems when it came to revising "The Diamond of Jeru" was that I knew almost nothing about Borneo and had little time before the book's deadline to do research. As luck would have it, an acquaintance recommended several wonderful books. *Stranger in the Forest* by Eric Hansen is the account of the author's journey from one side of the island and back, on foot, mostly alone. It is filled with wonderful detail and absolutely saved my bacon over and over. Together with Redmond O'Hanlon's *Into the Heart of Borneo* and a classic from my father's library, *World Within* by Tom

Harrisson, I had the backbone of a library on the world's third-largest island.

So I was off and running. I started expanding the narrative, creating a similar but more nuanced plot, using the same basic characters but trying to make them more complex and human. My editor kept calling: "Where's the book? Deadlines! Deadlines!" I knew where I was going but not necessarily all the things that were going to happen along the way. "They're still going upriver," I'd tell him. "You have to give me more time!" Finally, it was finished and the manuscript was shipped off to New York. My experience with diamonds, the tribes of Sarawak, Jeru, Mike Kardec, and John and Helen Lacklan was over . . . or so I thought.

A year or so after the collection *Off the Mangrove Coast* was published, I got a call from Michael Joyce. Mike is a good friend of mine and we had briefly worked together in the film business a decade earlier. I believe that the first production he worked on was *Star Wars* (the original 1977 film) and his last credit, before retirement in 2004, was the pilot for the Sci-Fi Channel's reboot of *Battlestar Galactica*. He was a veteran line producer who had the capacity to make any type of film.

Mike was returning from a location scout in North Africa for a potential USA Network movie. During the long flight he'd had a discussion with one of their executives about the fact that they were considering doing a classic adventure piece.

As soon as he landed he called me to ask if I had something of Dad's that might be appropriate, and of course I had a number of different alternatives. After several days of discussion about the likely locations and what the budget of the film might be, we decided to show them "The Diamond of Jeru."

In my experience it's virtually impossible to sell a project to any studio or network unless there is some sort of preexisting demand. Because, in this case, we had that on our side we were able to make a sale in short order.

The contracts for the underlying rights (the story itself) were finished by early December, a time when the entire film business starts to shut down for the holidays. Mike had arranged to bring me on as a producer (an offer so generous it still astounds me), but the more I considered the story the more I realized that I wanted to write the screenplay as well.

That was vastly easier said than done. Studios and networks are very particular about whom they hire as writers, usually choosing from an extremely exclusive though ever-changing list. While I had scripts to show and I'd been hired a few times in the past (on films that ultimately did not get produced), I knew it was very unlikely that I could submit myself (always seen as grossly self-serving) and actually be hired to write the screenplay. If I was going to pull this off, I would have to write the entire script on spec and then hope for divine intervention, too!

Though not quite divine intervention, there were two things in my favor. One was that the holidays were approaching and nobody was going to be looking for a writer until they all came back to work in the second week of January. The other was that there were contract negotiations with both the writers' and screen actors' unions scheduled for early summer. All film production would need to wrap prior to a potential strike in case the negotiations failed. That meant that the network would want to get the production started as quickly as possible . . . or would have to wait until the new contracts were signed.

Waiting in the film business is a death sentence; in this case waiting would likely mean the film would never get made and the money spent to option it would have been wasted. Therefore, if there was a chance to finish the production before the negotiations started, the network was going to be very motivated to take advantage of it. Hollywood myth is full of fanciful examples, but *this* is what an actual "break-in" opportunity looks like.

I started writing. My job was to adapt the novella that I had written from my father's short story. The way I think about it, it is deadly for a writer doing an adaptation to feel too beholden to the underlying material . . . even if you were one of the original authors. It is always important to activate a new layer of creativity and discover new qualities in the work so that it remains fresh and continues to evolve.

When working on the novella, the rules I'd made for myself about deviating from Dad's style had restricted my approach to the story. The original short story and the novella were written in first person: a story told by Kardec from his interior perspective and in the past tense. Movies are, by their nature, mostly present tense, and they are told from an exterior perspective. Audience members are shown what the characters do; they are not told how they feel or what they think. Those things are indicated by the context.

Since I was again expanding the story to fill the USA Network's eighty-nine-minute time requirement, that meant, first and foremost, that I had the opportunity to deal with John and Helen Lacklan in a close and personal way, rather than just as characters only seen through Kardec's eyes. What exactly were the Lacklans' marital problems? Why did they come, of all places, to Borneo? I also wanted to portray more of the life of Borneo natives, dealing with them in a more complex manner than just Mike Kardec's friend Raj and Jeru, the villain. Then there were a similar set of questions about Kardec and what he was doing in Sarawak. What the heck was his backstory?

I had only a few weeks to write the script, so I had to burn the candle at both ends. Often I was writing out rough drafts of scenes while I was supervising the edit of the dramatized audio production of *Son of a Wanted Man*. Late at night I would polish and refine those drafts before I finally went to bed. Over the holidays I drove to Colorado, stopping occasionally to type up my various ideas and mental notes. I wrote on the road, in our cabin, and in a hotel room in Santa Fe, creating an adventure in the tropical rain forest while surrounded by the Rocky Mountain winter. Returning to Los Angeles, I had just enough time to do yet another draft before the network resumed work for the new year.

My gamble paid off: Suddenly I was both writer and executive producer. Then again, that's not nearly as impressive as it sounds. The script, of course, became the property of the network, and from that point on it was my job to turn it into whatever they wanted it to be. Producers are rarely as influential as most of them would like others to believe. When the creative executives at the network say "Frog," you jump. You do exactly what the bosses say, when they say it. Within days there were a great many notes for revisions, some of which I found helpful and some that made me want to tear out my hair and caused me to wonder if I could ever create something that would satisfy both myself and the studio—feelings that most screenwriters know all too well.

But it didn't matter—we were off and running.

By early February we were in Australia, where the Queensland coast would double for the Borneo rain forest. The next few weeks were a whirlwind of location scouting, local casting, and more rewrites—some by myself, some by the director, and even more of them by anyone with the political clout to insist on a change . . . typical for a movie production, but confusing and disheartening for a first-time screenwriter.

One of the exciting aspects of doing "The Diamond of Jeru" in northern Australia was that we ended up making a lot of things ourselves; costumes, props, and buildings were all constructed from scratch. Previously, I had worked only around Los Angeles, where a phone call to a rental house was all it took to make the most exotic items show up within hours. This was definitely like Hollywood in its early years.

All films are an exercise in compromise: what you want balanced against what you need. The last-minute rewriting and restaging of scenes that have only existed in your mind is part of both the excitement and the disappointment. One big advantage to having worked on a number of other films was that I was well aware that we were not there to shoot the script; we were there to make a movie. The work is a constant process of change and adaptation, and often what had seemed easy back in L.A., or on paper, became impossible under actual circumstances.

Not having the budget to travel to a large enough

river or to shoot a particular stunt required a significant change to the opening. Having only two days to shoot Jeru's fight with Kardec meant rewriting and recasting the Dyak as a much larger, younger man. We did not have enough time to shoot the details of the fight that would demonstrate that, even as an older guy, Jeru was very good at fighting with a parang, the Indonesian version of a machete. You confront a problem and make an adjustment. No plan of battle ever survives contact with the enemy.

For this writer, one of the wonderful aspects of making the film was the way parts of 1950s Sarawak came to life. Locations that I had half imagined, and props and costumes that I had never thought of, all took on a sense of concrete reality, if only for the few days that we were working on a certain scene. After the construction crew had gone home I could sit quietly in Kardec's bungalow, walk the streets of Marudi (re-created in a nineteenth-century railroad carriage factory), or relax on the verandah of the District Officer's Residence (the old parliament building now surrounded by the campus of the Queensland University of Technology).

I had a chance to live in a tropical rain forest, deal with mosquitoes so thick you could hardly breathe without getting a mouthful, and trust that the crocodiles wouldn't attack until they became used to your presence (at least that's what we were told!). Though it seemed too late in the process to really take advantage of it, these details helped to make the fictional time and place of the story real to me . . . or at least to bolster my imaginary version of it all.

In the years that followed I discovered I was feeling nostalgic for my re-creation of 1950s Marudi, a place that had never really existed. My father loved to travel back to the locations he had written about in his books, and I was just beginning to discover why.

By midsummer, we were nearly finished editing the film and I was moving on to other projects. I had rewritten the original short story and then written and produced the movie; it seemed like I was finally finished with "The Diamond of Jeru."

After wrapping up the *Son of a Wanted Man* audio, a process nearly as complicated as making a film, I visited a Random House sales conference in Fort Myers, Florida. One afternoon the executive in charge of the audio division asked me if I had any plans to follow up with another long-form dramatized audio. I was happily surprised, because *Son of a Wanted Man* had taken a long time to produce and, given its cast of over twenty actors, it had been fairly expensive. I wasn't the least bit sure that they'd ever want to do another!

Thinking about the situation, I decided that after being involved in fifty or so Western audio dramas, I really wanted to try something completely different. Whatever it was, however, it had to be something that had its own distinct soundscape, and something that existed in a very particular and identifiable time and place.

Several different stories were considered, but none of them had the right mixture of characters, and the amount of time it would have taken to get a completely new script together was too great. I especially wanted to have an interesting leading lady. Since I had already written the movie script for "The Diamond of Jeru," I figured that could become the foundation for an audio play just as easily as the unproduced movie script to *Son of a*

Wanted Man had become the basis of that audio production. Sarawak of the 1950s would surely have its own wonderfully exotic environment, the sense of the time period conveyed by the dialogue would be as distinct as in a Western, and the sound of mid-twentieth-century technology seemed to be rapidly becoming as out of date as that of the nineteenth! In many ways, the script was perfect.

While the film script for "The Diamond of Jeru" was a tight eighty-nine minutes, the finished Random House audio was required to run around twice as long. That difference would allow a lot more room to expand the story yet again and I could play with several themes and aspects of the plot that would add greater breadth and depth to the characters. Also, all the experiences I'd had working on the film became fodder for new details and scenes, ideas I never would have had prior to going to Australia and re-creating Sarawak. Eventually, I got in touch with USA Network and we came to an agreement that would let me use the film's script as the basis for an audio dramatization.

As I started lengthening the script, it was amazing how different aspects of the story came to life in completely new ways. While the film had expanded to cover John and Helen's side of the story, the audio was able to give more time to the world of the Borneo natives. I found ways to wrap the history of Sarawak into the plot, creating more of a backstory for Jeru and allowing Raj to become significantly more than a sidekick for Mike Kardec. Without the expense of sets or locations to worry about, the audio could also "go places" and "do things" that would never be possible in a reasonably budgeted movie. As wonderful a place to shoot as Australia was, it didn't have vast cave networks or thirteen-thousand-foot mountains. The beautiful thing about an audio drama is that making something sound right is an awful lot cheaper than making it look right!

In the end, the audio play ended up being just as much an adaptation of the film script as the film script had been an adaptation of the novella, and as the novella had been an adaptation of Dad's original short story. Each was a completely separate beast, and with every telling the story both gained and lost various qualities. I'd be hard pressed to say which one I like the best; each is its own example of its medium and moment in history.

Production of "The Diamond of Jeru" audio commenced in October 2007, using the core crew from the *Son of a Wanted Man* audio: myself as writer and director, Paul O'Dell as producer and editor, Phil Shenale as composer, and Howard Gale and Ken Goerres as engineers and audio consultants.

One of the most demanding aspects of producing "The Diamond of Jeru" audio was the casting. We had characters who were American, Malaysian, British, Australian, Indian, Chinese, and Korean. When we first advertised on the various casting websites we got over two thousand responses, and we had to whittle those down to a number we could actually manage. As it was, we took about six weeks to audition some four hundred actors. The process was exhausting and a bit like being in the hotel business: You had to always be "on," efficient, hyperalert, and hospitable.

While we spent just over a week in the studio recording the actors' voices, the entire production period—which included cutting the dialogue, creating and editing the sound effects, refining the scenes, composing and editing the music, and then mixing it all down—took around 450 working days. Because of our other responsibilities, like producing the graphic novel of *Law of the Desert Born*, we ended up working on an extremely drawn-out schedule. Regardless, it was a very fun and creative time and I'm quite proud of all we were able to accomplish. Anyone interested can go to thediamondofjeruaudio.com for a great deal more information, photos, and videos.

In hindsight, if there is anything I regret about the production of the audio it is that I didn't get things off to as clean and clear a start as I did with the film or novella adaptations. Dad was always good about getting into the meat of a story right away, and you can see that his original short story did that very efficiently. As the versions I worked on added complexity and detail from novella to film to audio, they took longer and longer to get going. Looking back on the audio script, I actually believe that immediacy and complexity could *both* have been achieved. But, as Dad well knew, there comes a moment when you have to just move on and tell the next story, and more than enough ink has been spilled on "The Diamond of Jeru"!

Beau L'Amour
October 2018

ABOUT LOUIS L'AMOUR

*"I think of myself in the oral tradition—
as a troubadour, a village tale-teller, the man
in the shadows of the campfire. That's the way
I'd like to be remembered—as a storyteller.
A good storyteller."*

IT IS DOUBTFUL that any author could be as at home in the world re-created in his novels as Louis Dearborn L'Amour. Not only could he physically fill the boots of the rugged characters he wrote about, but he literally "walked the land my characters walk." His personal experiences as well as his lifelong devotion to historical research combined to give Mr. L'Amour the unique knowledge and understanding of people, events, and the challenge of the American frontier that became the hallmarks of his popularity.

As a boy growing up in Jamestown, North Dakota, he absorbed all he could about his family's frontier heritage, including the story of his great-grandfather who was scalped by Sioux warriors.

Spurred by an eager curiosity and desire to broaden his horizons, Mr. L'Amour left home at the age of fifteen and enjoyed a wide variety of jobs including seaman, lumberjack, elephant handler, skinner of dead cattle, miner, and an officer in the transportation corps during World War II. He was a voracious reader and collector of books. His personal library contained 17,000 volumes.

Mr. L'Amour "wanted to write almost from the time I could talk." After developing a widespread following for his many frontier and adventure stories written for fiction magazines, Mr. L'Amour published his first full-length novel, *Hondo*, in the United States in 1953. Every one of his more than 120 books is in print; there are nearly 300 million copies of his books in print worldwide, making him one of the bestselling authors in modern literary history. His books have been translated into twenty languages, and more than forty-five of his novels and stories have been made into feature films and television movies.

His hardcover bestsellers include *The Lonesome Gods*, *The Walking Drum* (his twelfth-century historical novel), *Jubal Sackett*, *Last of the Breed*, and *The Haunted Mesa*. His memoir, *Education of a Wandering Man*, was a leading bestseller in 1989. Audio dramatizations and adaptations of many L'Amour stories are available from Random House Audio Publishing.

The recipient of many great honors and awards, in 1983 Mr. L'Amour became the first novelist ever to be awarded the Congressional Gold Medal by the United States Congress in honor of his life's work. In 1984 he was also awarded the Medal of Freedom by President Reagan.

Louis L'Amour died on June 10, 1988.